Praise for *The Midwives' Escape*

"The biblical story of the Exodus leaves a great deal to the imagination. Maggie Anton has helped fill in some of the narrative gaps with her fictionalized rendition of this epic story. Particularly helpful is her use of female characters to humanize the events, struggles, doubts, and triumphs of the mixed multitude that left Egypt for a new life."

—Dr. Victor H. Matthews, Professor Emeritus of Religious Studies, Missouri State University, and author of *Manners and Customs in the Bible*

"This imaginative retelling of the Exodus story weaves the fabric of women's lives—as well as the lives of those from other traditions who joined the Hebrews on their quest—into the foundational narrative of our people. Readers can see a fuller, more inclusive picture of what might have happened during those times."

—Rabbi Beth Lieberman, literary editor and revising translator of *The JPS Tanakh*

"An entertaining and engrossing novel portraying the Exodus from Egypt, wandering in the wilderness of Sinai, and entry into the land of Israel told through the unusual viewpoint of two women—both midwives and members of the non-Israelite mixed multitude. Anton weaves the biblical story with traditional interpretation and contemporary insight and sensitivity."

—Rabbi Pamela Barmash, Professor of Hebrew Bible and Biblical Hebrew, Washington University in St. Louis

"Leave it to the masterful Maggie Anton to make the past come alive. Through her eyes, the old and familiar become challenging, offering us new and deeper insights into what it means to be human. This book is a gem!"

—Dr. Rabbi Bradley Shavit Artson, Vice President, American Jewish University, and Dean and Professor of Philosophy, Ziegler School of Rabbinic Studies

"An insightful and inventive novel that tells the story of the Exodus from a new perspective. There is a wealth of detail about everyday problems not discussed in the biblical narrative. Read it and you will never think about the Exodus the same way again."

—Kenneth Seeskin, Professor Emeritus of Jewish Civilization, Northwestern University

"*The Midwives' Escape* is a page turner that retells the Exodus and desert wanderings through the eyes of women. In an unexpected twist, the two main characters are part of the mixed multitude who leave with the Israelites. Weaving together biblical, Jewish, and archaeological sources, this narrative surprises and delights at every turn."

—Kristine Henriksen Garroway, Professor of
Hebrew Bible, Hebrew Union College

Praise for *The Choice*

"Maggie Anton utilizes the characters' authentic voices to address social justice while still entertaining the reader with an engaging romance."

—Jackie Ben-Efraim, Special Collections
Librarian, American Jewish University

"Maggie Anton presents a tale of characters inspired by Chaim Potok's novels, imagining their future struggles and triumphs. Using her unique blend of historical fiction, Jewish history, and Talmudic text, she provides a glimpse at American Jewish life in the 1950s and allows us to share in the lives of powerful yet familiar characters. Thank you, Maggie, for letting us know what happened next!"

—Rabbi Marla J. Feldman, Executive Director,
Women of Reform Judaism

"Anton gives evocative voice to the generation of our mothers, whose questions and bold solutions, especially about the most intimate of subjects, laid the foundation for the contemporary transformation of women's status in Jewish learning and law."

—Rabbi Susan Grossman, Senior Rabbi, Beth Shalom Congregation,
Columbia, Maryland, and co-editor of *Daughters of the King*

"*The Choice* is a marvelous piece of Midrash (early rabbinic interpretation of a classical text) or, as it's called today, fan fiction. Anton aptly illuminates the Talmudic dictum 'Better to dwell in tandem than to sit abandoned.'"

—Rabbi Burt Visotzky, Professor of Midrash and
Interreligious Studies, Jewish Theological Seminary, and author
of *A Delightful Compendium of Consolation* and *Sage Tales*

"*The Choice* takes us into the Jewish world of love and learning and the love of learning. One can only be grateful for such an intriguing and engaging work. Maggie Anton's combination of history, imagination, and feminist reading of classical Jewish texts is impressive."

—Rabbi Laura Geller, Rabbi Emerita, Temple Emanuel of Beverly Hills, and coauthor (with Richard Siegel) of *Getting Good at Getting Older*

Praise for the Rav Hisda's Daughter Series

"Anton, the author of the acclaimed Rashi's Daughters trilogy, has penned her best book to date. Complex discussions of Jewish law and tradition as well as detailed description of the culture and customs of the times enhance truly wonderful storytelling. This absorbing novel should be on everyone's historical fiction reading list."

—*Library Journal* (starred review)—also chosen by *Library Journal* as "Best Historical Fiction of 2012"

"Another excellent historical novel from Maggie Anton. . . . As always, Anton's book is a good introduction to traditional Jewish learning, and perhaps, like Anton, readers will be motivated to discover the sources for themselves. . . . Those readers who enjoyed the Rashi's Daughters series will find this first book of Anton's next series pleasurable and educational—be sure to check out the extra resources available online."

—Rachel Sara Rosenthal, *Jewish Book Council*—also selected as a Fiction Finalist, 2012 National Jewish Book Awards

"A lushly detailed look into a fascinatingly unknown time and culture—a tale of Talmud, sorcery, and a most engaging heroine!"

—Diana Gabaldon, author of the bestselling Outlander series

"I was enthralled by Maggie Anton's *Rav Hisda's Daughter* from the start. Anton deftly weaves a novel full of characters in whom the reader finds herself invested, even those who are less likeable. The scope of time and geography is breathtaking. . . . Anton excels at the creativity inherent in historical fiction . . . such a mesmerizing tale."

—Adina Gerver, *JOFA (Jewish Orthodox Feminist Alliance) Journal*

"*Rav Hisda's Daughter* joins the annals of great historical fiction beside Jewish examples such as Anita Diamant's *The Red Tent: A Novel*. . . . Expect authentic period depth and delights when reading a work of historical fiction by Maggie Anton."

—Rabbi Goldie Milgram, *Philadelphia Jewish Voice*

Praise for the Rashi's Daughters Series

"With only scraps of information about Rashi's daughters, Anton has brought these three women to life. A stunning achievement. You will not be able to put this book down, and you may even find yourself rushing off to study Talmud. So curl up in your favorite chair and savor every moment."

—Judith Hauptman, Professor of Talmud and Rabbinic Culture, Jewish Theological Seminary, and author of *Rereading the Rabbis*

"Thanks to Anton, we have a wealth of images now, focusing on the world of 11th Century France as seen through the eyes of Joheved, Miriam and Rachel, Rashi's daughters . . . letting us see how life was lived, how religion was practiced, how religious law and superstition were inextricably entwined in the lives of people, how politics affected people's lives. Her books are as laden with knowledge as any scholarly tome, but the richly woven fictional plots, based on what Anton could find out or deduce, make reading the stories like eating an ice cream sundae—rich, delicious, and with enough substance to satisfy."

—*Atlanta Jewish Times*

"Building on the allegation that, because he had no sons, Rashi studied with his daughters, Anton imagines a community of learned and loving women. They each married intellectually gifted men and, in concert with their husbands, enriched and perpetuated their father's work. Anton's writing is fluid and her research and knowledge of text, history and ritual impressive. Each sister emerges as a unique, vividly portrayed individual."

—Gloria Goldreich, *Hadassah Magazine*

"This carefully researched work of fiction by Maggie Anton provides a rare glimpse into the little-known medieval Jewish world in which Rashi lived and worked."

—Naomi Ragen, author of *An Unorthodox Match* and *The Ghost of Hannah Mendes*

THE
MIDWIVES'
ESCAPE

Also by Maggie Anton

Rashi's Daughters, Book I: Joheved (2005)
2006 IBPA Benjamin Franklin Gold Award Winner
in the First Fiction category

Rashi's Daughters, Book II: Miriam (2007)

Rashi's Daughter, Secret Scholar (2008)
for YA readers

Rashi's Daughters, Book III: Rachel (2009)

Rav Hisda's Daughter, Book I: Apprentice (2012)
2012 National Jewish Book Award Fiction Finalist

Enchantress: A Novel of Rav Hisda's Daughter (2014)

*Fifty Shades of Talmud: What the First Rabbis Had to Say
about You-Know-What* (2016)
2017 IBPA Benjamin Franklin Gold Award Winner
in the Religion category

The Choice (2022)

THE
MIDWIVES' ESCAPE

From

Egypt

to

Jericho

MAGGIE ANTON

Copyright © 2025 by Margaret Parkhurst

All rights reserved. No part of this publication may be reproduced, distributed, or transmitted in any form or by any means, including photocopying, recording, or other electronic or mechanical methods, without prior written permission of the publisher, except in the case of brief quotations embedded in critical reviews and certain other noncommercial uses permitted by copyright law. For permission requests, write to the publisher, addressed Attention: Permissions Coordinator at the address below.

Banot Press
www.banotpress.com

ORDERING INFORMATION
Quantity sales: Special discounts are available on quantity purchases by corporations, associations, and others. For details, please contact the "Special Sales Department" at the above address.
Orders by US trade bookstores and wholesalers. Please contact BCH: (800) 431-1579 or visit www.bookch.com for details.

Cataloging-in-Publication Data

Names: Anton, Maggie, author.
Title: The midwives' escape : from Egypt to Jericho / Maggie Anton.
Description: Los Angeles, CA: Banot Press, 2025.
Identifiers: LCCN: 2024923722 | ISBN: 978-0-9763050-8-8
    Subjects: LCSH Exodus, The—Fiction. | Jews—History—To 1200 B.C.—
    Fiction. | Women—Egypt—History—Fiction. | Midwives—Fiction. |
    Historical fiction. | BISAC FICTION / Historical | FICTION / Jewish |
    FICTION / Women
    Classification: LCC PS3601.N57 M53 2025 | DDC 813.6—dc23

Illustrator: David Parkhurst

Printed in the United States of America
30 29 28 27 26 25   10 9 8 7 6 5 4 3 2 1

PREFACE

JUST OVER TWENTY-FIVE years ago, in December 1998, my family, including my husband and our two college-age children, were on winter vacation in Palm Springs, California. There wasn't a whole lot to do in the evenings except play games and see movies. Tired of the former, we decided to watch a new animated DreamWorks film, *The Prince of Egypt*. As a child, I'd seen *The Ten Commandments* many times on television and was curious how this new version would compare. My family was Jewishly well-educated, all four of us with a bar or bat mitzvah, and every year we hosted Passover Seders and attended a friend's.

To my surprise, the movie affected me profoundly, some scenes moving me to tears. I was particularly stirred by one where, as a horde of Israelites passes some Egyptian guards and taskmasters, these men throw down their weapons and uniforms to join the Exodus. I knew from Torah study that a "mixed multitude" of non-Israelites had fled Egypt with the Israelites and was impressed that *The Prince of Egypt* had accurately represented that. But I was frustrated that the movie ended just like *The Ten Commandments*, with Moses coming down Mount Sinai carrying the stone tablets.

That scene was just the beginning of forty years until the Israelites, and the mixed multitude, entered the Promised Land of Canaan. I was filled with questions: Who were the mixed multitude? Why did they leave Egypt? Where did all these people spend the "missing" forty years in the desert? What did they, both men and women, do? What skills did they have? How did they survive?

v

To attempt to answer these and other questions, I joined the Biblical Archaeology Society (BAS), a nonprofit, nondenominational organization dedicated to disseminating information about history and archaeology in the Bible lands. It does this through a print quarterly magazine, *Biblical Archaeology Review*, an award-winning website, and tours and seminars. BAS serves as an important authority and invaluable source of reliable information, providing its members access to almost fifty years of articles, both print and online, that present the latest scholarship.

I was surprised, and then intrigued, by the debates and arguments among scholars over whether the Israelite exodus from Egypt actually happened as the Bible says. If yes, what is the evidence? If no, how did the story originate? But millions of religious people believe it happened, and millions of Jews, including my family, observe Passover. I even spent several weeks in Israel, following in the Israelites' footsteps as, under Joshua's leadership, they "conquered" Canaan.

At first I was doing all this research to satisfy my personal curiosity, but eventually, as with *Rashi's Daughters*, I learned so much that I felt compelled to share my newfound knowledge. Thus my eighth historical novel, *The Midwives' Escape: From Egypt to Jericho*, was born. I wasn't too concerned about historical accuracy since even experts didn't agree on what happened when or where. After all, I would be writing fiction. But instead of writing it from an Israelite's point of view, I chose two Egyptian women as my main characters.

Why? Because at the beginning of the Book of Joshua, we learn that neither Israelite males nor those of the mixed multitude had been circumcised during the forty years since leaving Egypt. Before attacking Jericho, however, Joshua insists on all males being circumcised—which for all intents and purposes converts them and their family members into Israelites. I wanted my protagonists to be converts.

If you want more information about my sources, you can find my bibliography on the novel's website, https://midwivesescape.com/, on the Resources page.

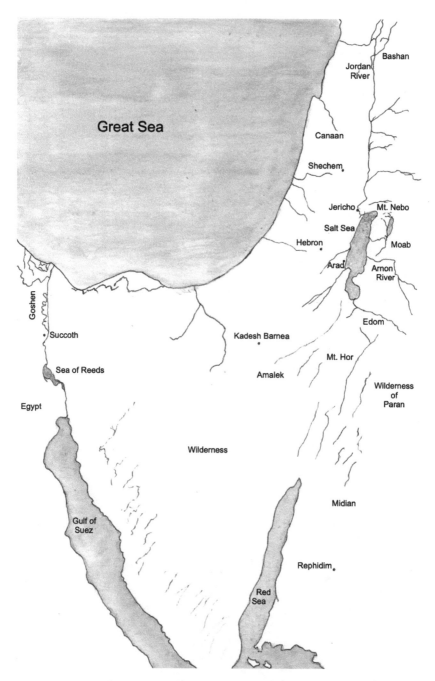
Egypt and Canaan in the late Bronze Age (1550–1200 BCE)

CHAPTER ONE

ASENET

For that night I will go through the land of Egypt and strike down every firstborn in the land of Egypt.

—Exodus 12:12

I WOKE TO THE SOUNDS of someone moving stealthily in the room. Light footsteps, soft but muffled breathing. Both getting nearer. I rolled onto my side and reached out for my husband, but he was not in our bed. I was annoyed but not panicked, for he often stayed out late drinking in the spring when the weather was temperate. I took a deep breath, but the usual sweet scent of plumeria blossoms was tainted with something foul.

I sat up and looked around. The full moon sent shafts of light through the open windows and I saw not my husband but his brother Maratti. "What are you doing here in the middle of the night?" My voice rose with alarm. "Why aren't you at the palace?"

Maratti squatted down beside me and whispered, "Shush. We don't want to wake the others." His voice shook and he swallowed several times.

Before he could say more, I grabbed his arm. "What is wrong?"

Tenth-plague cloud—hand of death—over a pyramid

He took a deep breath. "Something terrible has happened. Just after midnight, the guards around me began to collapse. At first I thought they were falling asleep or had been taken ill. But when I examined the nearest one, I realized he was dead."

"Dead . . . ?" I gulped. "Are you sure?" My horror was so great I could barely speak.

He gently put his hand over my mouth. "I don't know, but please stay quiet until I finish. Almost immediately I heard screams from the survivors in my regiment, and we could hear cries from the city below." He looked down at the floor and was silent for a long moment. "People—apparently only firstborns—are dying all over the city."

I pushed his hand away. "No. I don't believe you. It's impossible."

"It may sound impossible, but it is happening." He slammed his fist against the floor. "Survivors are panicking, so I ordered my troops with families to go home and guard against looters. The rest should remain at the palace."

It took only a moment to realize the implication of his words. "Where is my son?" I started to weep when I saw that both my husband and son were missing.

He put his arm around my shoulder and replied in a soft voice, "My brother was likely struck down at the local tavern. Your boy was already dead when I got here."

"I still can't believe it. What happened to his body?" I accused him.

"Asenet, I couldn't leave his body here for you and your daughter to find in the morning." He choked on the words. "I used one of your father's wheelbarrows to move him to the marshes and buried him."

"This is a nightmare." I sniffed back tears. "But what would kill only firstborns?"

Maratti sighed. "They say the Hebrews' god is punishing Pharaoh for not letting them go to make sacrifices in the wilderness."

"So this is one more of Moses's curses? Like the locusts and frogs?" I was angry now. "What did we ever do to him?"

"Asenet." His voice hardened. "This is nothing like the locusts and frogs. This time your son, and a great many Egyptians' sons, including the Pharaoh's, are dead."

I sobbed silently. "What happens now?"

"I think Pharaoh will relent and let the Hebrews leave. But I also think he will change his mind once they are gone."

"So you think the Hebrews, and anyone who wants to go with them, need to leave as soon as possible and get as far away as possible."

"There are now many Egyptian households that stand desolate. Their masters and mistresses are dead, and their slaves have fled. At dawn the looting will begin." Maratti stood up. "Hittites were conscripted into Pharaoh's army long ago. Now that Egypt is laid low, it is time to collect back wages."

"What?"

"Was I paid for guarding the palace? Was my brother paid for overseeing the Hebrew slaves?"

I scowled. Both men were well fed by Pharaoh and had their choice of slave women for their pleasure. Maratti may not have used them, but my husband boasted of it.

"Think of your most recent midwife clients, the wealthy ones," Maratti whispered. "How many of them paid you in full?"

I remembered how angry I felt when morning came and I realized the gold ring I'd been promised was only copper. When I grimaced and remained silent, he said, "I thought so. Now, while the moon is full and many people are too frightened to go out, you must visit the homes of these cheaters."

"So many people will be looting, it will be chaos," I protested.

He gave me a stern look. "You know where they keep their valuables. If everyone there is dead, then take what they owe you."

"Come with me."

He shook his head. "I must stay here to protect your home and your family."

I almost said *what remains of my family*, but Maratti was right. Father was too old to fight off looters, and my daughter, Shifra, was on the cusp of womanhood. I didn't want to think what evil men might do to her.

Wrapped in my dark cloak, my emptied midwife's satchel over my shoulder, I stayed in the shadows as I headed for my most recent clients' mansion. How many times had I been woken in the night to grab my satchel and attend a birth? Hundreds at least, maybe over a thousand. It almost felt like that—almost.

I couldn't think about what had happened, was maybe still happening, in all these houses. I thought back to my midwife training, to the excitement and the trepidation, the joys and the sorrows—thankfully more of the former than the latter. My grandmother had been my mentor, teaching me and my older sister with expertise and patience.

Most births were routine, culminating in a healthy baby and delighted parents, but as my experience increased, the most satisfying deliveries were the most difficult. The jubilation I felt when I was able to save a mother's or baby's life, or both, was the ultimate triumph. My reputation grew and as I began training my daughter, I came to enjoy being a teacher in addition to a practitioner.

But not tonight. The baby boy and his parents were all firstborns. Many of the household slaves probably were too. There would be no joy in this house, only sorrow. I had passed no one in the streets and though I'd heard cries and moans from inside some lamplit residences, the one I watched was dark and silent. I walked purposefully through the garden to the side entrance and let myself in, waiting as my eyes adjusted to the pale moonlight. Someone who wasn't familiar with the house wouldn't know where things were in the dark.

I hurriedly climbed to the bedrooms, avoiding slaves' bodies fallen on the stairs. I shuddered as I recalled the many mothers who had died in childbirth, screaming in agony. But these people seemed to have died painlessly. Clearly any survivors had fled, but hopefully they had not completely plundered the house. I breathed more easily when I reached the mistress's room; her body lay motionless in her bed, her newborn quiet and still in her arms. They seemed to have died in their sleep.

I remembered why I was there and shook my head to clear my mind. I had seen a jewelry case in the painted cabinet near the bed. The case was there, and I stuffed it into my satchel. There was still room, so I helped myself to the mistress's finest linen tunics. I left her cosmetics on the dressing table and crept downstairs. I thought of Maratti, captain of the palace guards. Mercenaries didn't earn a salary for their services; they were paid their share of the plunder when they defeated an enemy. But there hadn't been such a war recently.

Instead of leaving immediately, I detoured into the dining room. I had eaten there while waiting for that baby to be born and had no trouble groping my way to the storage chests. First I took the jeweled goblets. Then, my hands shaking, I filled my satchel with every gold and silver plate, cutlery item, and serving piece that would fit inside. But it was poor compensation for losing my son.

I was almost home when I heard a young child crying in the street. I started to circle to the next street when I heard a familiar adolescent voice telling the child to be quiet; it sounded like Father's apprentice. I waited for the wispy clouds to clear and tiptoed closer until I could see a young boy sitting in the street, our apprentice kneeling beside him. The younger child, whose tight curls were cut short to form a cap on his round head were identical to the older boy's, had to be his little brother. I couldn't leave them outside in tears, not on a night like tonight. Not when their mother was likely dead.

I ran to them and, finger on my lips, rushed them into my house. I attempted to calm them as I tried to recall what I knew about their family.

THE MIDWIVES' ESCAPE

7

I knew their mother was a widow who raised goats for their wool and cheese. Her husband and his brother had been fishermen until they'd both been killed when hippopotamuses overturned their boat. Only their fishing nets were salvaged. That's when she'd asked—more like begged—Father to apprentice the older one as a wainwright, who might one day be as skilled in the making and repairing of wagons and wheelbarrows as Father himself. Years earlier I'd thought that my son would follow in Father's trade, but to my dismay, he preferred the power and perquisites of a slave overseer.

I put my satchel in its usual cabinet and fastened the door. Then I turned to the boys, who were shaking with fright and probably grief as well. They looked so piteous that I hugged each one in turn. Then I spoke without thinking.

"Don't worry. You will live with us now. But first we must hurry back to bury your mother." Surely there would still be some valuables we could return with after that task was done. Thieves wouldn't enter an unfamiliar dark house until dawn.

I shouldn't have worried. The two buck goats rushed to attack me, but the boys quickly calmed them so we could dig a shallow grave in the goat pen's soft sand. Outside I counted six does, four obviously pregnant, and two kids. There was also a donkey, a good-sized wagon, and a wheelbarrow. I had no idea where anything inside was kept, but the boys did. Between the three of us, we covered the wagon floor with woven rugs, wall hangings, and bedding, after which it took all our strength to lift the heavy full-sized loom on top.

Next the boys brought out the cheesemaking pans and pots, some empty and some heavy with fermenting milk, and we carefully arranged them in the wheelbarrow, surrounded by large spoons and other utensils. We wedged everything in tightly with cheesecloth and skeins of yarn. Finally we used most of the rope to tie the fishing nets onto the donkey. I wasn't sure how we'd use them, but they were too valuable to leave behind. The boys tied the bucks to the front of the wagon and the does to the back, and then the elder startled me by running back into the house.

"We don't need any of your mother's knives, Eshkar," I shouted when I recognized what he was carrying. "I have more than enough at home."

Eshkar handed me a long butcher's knife. "These are for protection . . . just in case." These were the first words he'd spoken to me tonight.

CHAPTER TWO

ASENET

Moreover, a mixed multitude went up with them.

—Exodus 12:38

THUS ARMED, WE STARTED the long trek back to our house. The little boy, nodding with drowsiness, held on to the fishnets as he rode the donkey. Ashamed that I didn't know, or didn't remember, his name, I asked Eshkar in a whisper what his brother was called.

"Gitlam," he whispered back. "It's a Lagash name."

At first, pushing the wheelbarrow was only moderately difficult. But as I tired, it seemed to grow heavier and heavier. Yet Eshkar and I refused to abandon any of the contents. The donkey and bucks matched the wheelbarrow's pace, so our progress slowed until the sky began to lighten, when we both realized the danger we'd face if we weren't home by sunrise. I forced the wheelbarrow to keep moving while keeping my gaze down to avoid any impediments in our way.

Suddenly a man's arms encircled my waist and stopped my progress. Too weak to fight, I slumped down against his chest. "Don't give up, Asenet," Maratti whispered. "We're almost there."

I didn't have the strength to ask how he'd found us. I was just thankful that he had. Secure in his arms, I let my eyes close and my mind

9

wander back to the first time I saw him. I was about thirteen years old, and it was only a few months after I'd become a woman. I was grinding wheat into flour when I heard Father speaking with some men in the courtyard. Words like "payment," "transfer," and "how long" made me think they were bargaining over the price of a new wagon, so I didn't pay much attention to the details.

Until I heard the words "Hittite" and "wedding."

As stealthily as I could, I tiptoed to where there was a small hole in the wall between our kitchen and courtyard and peeked out. There were four men walking around so I couldn't see them all at once. Two of them, Father and another older man, were smiling and holding wine cups. Two younger men, maybe just a few years apart in age, had their backs to me. But eventually one turned sufficiently that I could see he was the man I now knew as Maratti. Before I could see the other man's face, Mother grabbed my arm and pulled me away.

The scolding she gave me later, along with a confirmation that Father and the men were indeed arranging for my marriage, was enough to keep me from sleeping well that night. However it was memories of Maratti's handsome Hittite visage that prevented me from sleeping well for months. Eventually Father came to me and revealed that I was now betrothed to a Hittite, who would move to our home. My older sister, Pua, had moved out to marry a Hebrew woodcutter who provided lumber for Father's wagons as her bride price. My two older brothers had died young, and Father wanted some grandchildren in his house. I thought marrying a Hittite and continuing to live in my natal home was better than going away to marry a Hebrew, but it wasn't like either of us had a choice.

Preparations took months. My mother and I spent most of that time weaving and sewing new clothes for me, including a long white linen veil that prevented anyone from seeing my face; but it also prevented me from seeing much of anything through it. My groom sent gold jewelry, including an intricate headpiece to hold my veil in place.

Finally it was my wedding day. I was too nervous to eat much, yet I couldn't wait to be alone together with my handsome new husband. He was even more eager than I was because he picked me up, swung me over his shoulder, and carried me into our room, which was lit only by a small oil lamp. Men outside were joking and singing lewd songs, but my veil muffled the noise. He put me down and immediately began to undress me. He was in such a hurry that he practically ripped my veil to get to my dress. I stood there with my back to him as he pulled off his clothes. Then he blew out the lamp and lowered me, naked and shivering with anxiety, to our bedding.

Thus began the worst night of my life.

He crouched down, shifted his body over mine, and wedged his leg between my knees. Next he grabbed my hips and lifted them; then he drew back and thrust his prong fully into my virginal passage. I screamed in agony, but he merely chuckled and pulled my hips closer before drawing back again. I closed my eyes and prepared for even more searing pain, but just as he entered again, I fainted.

In the morning, I woke to his leering face above mine. I braced myself for the pain sure to come at any moment, but that wasn't the worst thing. For the face of the man soon snoring next to me wasn't the handsome one I'd anticipated but that of an older, crueler man.

I had married his brother. And there was nothing to be done about it.

A year later, when I gave birth to my son, I learned that married women endured worse pain than losing their virginity. But the pain of childbirth was worth it. Sitting on a pile of cushions, nursing my baby, and looking down into his eyes until they slowly closed was a previously unimagined delight. I had a new status in the household and my husband doted on me, at least for a while. Everyone knew that the longer a boy nursed, the more likely he was to survive childhood, and most women knew that as long as they were nursing, they wouldn't get pregnant again.

I nursed that boy for four years. Another was born when the first was five, but he survived only a year. It was after another two years, and two miscarriages, that I gave birth to Shifra.

I jerked awake and found myself curled up in the wagon, which was rolling along more swiftly since Maratti added his ample strength to Eshkar's. The sky was brighter but the sun hadn't yet risen. I jumped out of the wagon and, ashamed of my sloth, helped little Gitlam with the wheelbarrow. We passed others on the road, but we kept our distance.

Ravens and crows were circling overhead when we arrived home. Father welcomed each of us with a lengthy embrace and sent us off to bed. It was dark inside, but not so dark that I couldn't see the tears in his eyes. I had no idea what was going to happen, but Father clearly was unhappy about it. I didn't feel happy about it either.

Crows and ravens flying over an Egyptian house

CHAPTER THREE

SHIFRA

That very day GOD freed the Israelites from the land of Egypt, troop by troop.

—Exodus 12:51

I COULD HEAR GRANDFATHER and Uncle Maratti urgently whispering, but I couldn't make out most words—only "Pua," "Hebrews' god," and my name, "Shifra." I would have liked to sleep longer, but there was a terrible smell. Like something rotten, only worse. So I got up and went outside to the latrine.

Uncle Maratti was waiting when I came back inside. "Hurry and get dressed. You and your grandfather must get to your aunt Pua's right away. You'll have your morning meal there."

Before I could protest, Grandfather gently stroked my hair and reassured me, "Don't worry about the stink. The air will be better in Pua's neighborhood."

I didn't have a chance to ask why Mother was still in bed or who was that little boy crying in the kitchen before Uncle Maratti rushed me and Grandfather out onto the street. The odor was even more fetid outside, and I began to cough while trying to ask what was going on.

THE MIDWIVES' ESCAPE   15

"Tie your headscarf over your nose and mouth; you'll breathe easier," Grandfather said, having done the same with his turban. "Now I can tell you what happened last night."

His grim tone invited no questions, so I was afraid to ask any.

"Last night, the Hebrew god sent a tenth plague against us, worse than all the ones before. It struck at midnight, killing every firstborn within moments." He pulled me close. "Including, I'm sorry to say, your father and brother. We can be thankful that at least they didn't suffer."

I gasped and blinked back tears, then I hugged Grandfather tighter. "But what became of them?" I couldn't bring myself to say "their bodies."

"Maratti buried them in the marshes right away, but some families didn't discover the deaths until dawn and other families were struck down entirely."

As if to demonstrate this disaster, we passed houses where bodies had been thrown carelessly in the street. Even worse, despite Grandfather's best efforts to prevent us from encountering them, jackals and ravens were feasting on the corpses. I could hear the excited caws and see more birds circling what was surely carrion below. Not having eaten since yesterday, I had little to vomit out, but I still gagged.

"Eshkar's mother died during the night, and your mother heard him and his little brother crying outside our house," he continued. "She went back with them to bury her, then they returned with the family's goats and donkey, as well as some other valuables. The boys have no other home, and it's not uncommon for apprentices to live with their master." He sighed and shook his head. "We took pity on them, so they will live with us now."

"Where will they sleep?" I wasn't at all comfortable with the idea of sharing a bedroom with two boys, even if one was half my age.

My brother had annoyed me to no end, and he didn't even sleep with me. I never knew when I would find thorns or bugs in my bedding, or even a snake. He pulled on my braids, hard, and once tied them to a chair so I fell back down when I stood up. Once he snuck into my room when I was sleeping and painted a mustache and beard on me with ashes from the hearth; for an entire day he and Father snickered when they saw me until Mother returned from delivering a baby and washed my face.

"They'll sleep in my workshop, of course."

When I was younger, Grandfather had tried to teach the wainwright trade to my brother. My brother was big and strong, like Father, so he could carry the lumber, saw the boards, and hammer in the bronze nails. But he didn't care about quality and was often negligent in his work, which infuriated Grandfather. I tried to stay out of my brother's way at that time; all their yelling frightened me. I was content to milk the goats and help Mother make cheese and bread. Even better was when she had me accompany her to help birth a new baby. But I was happiest once Father began taking my brother to work with him. The boy was a natural bully; he needed no training to boss slaves around and beat them instead of me.

That's when Grandfather brought Eshkar in as his apprentice. Eshkar was not as big as my brother, but he was tough and wiry. Nobody bullied him, and he became my protector. It wasn't long before Eshkar took over the work that my brother had neglected.

My feelings at what happened today—horror, fear, shame at my lack of grief over my father's and brother's deaths—were so jumbled that all I could do was nod glumly. So that's where the donkey and all those extra goats had come from and why Eshkar and Gitlam were at our house so early. I noticed that the stench had lessened and realized we were approaching the Hebrew Quarter, where Aunt Pua and her Hebrew husband lived. I saw no crows or ravens overhead, but Aunt Pua was older than my mother, so her body might already be buried. When we came to her street, my heart beat faster as I saw that all the doorposts were painted red, only to pound more strongly as we

Blood on a Hebrew's doorposts

approached her house and I realized that it was blood on the lintel and doorposts, not paint.

Suddenly the door opened and Aunt Pua flew out to embrace us, first her father and then me. "I am so glad to see you. How are you doing?" She hugged me even tighter. "I was so frightened for your family. It must have been awful for you."

"Asenet's husband and son are already in the ground," Grandfather told her. Then he saw her small son in the doorway and lowered his voice. "How is it that my grandson Rephaiah is still alive?"

She motioned us to come inside where her husband, Shaul, was waiting. The savory smell of fried eggs and onions made my mouth water, but I was surprised there wasn't any bread on the table. "Come sit down," she said. "I'm sure you're famished."

While Grandfather and I ate, Shaul explained. "The word came from Moses that Israelite families must slaughter a yearling kid without blemish yesterday at twilight, then use some hyssop to smear its blood on the doorposts and lintels of our houses. After that we were to eat it roasted and not go outside until morning." He shuddered, then continued in a low, strained voice. "That night would bring the tenth and final plague, a punishment to all the gods of Egypt. That night Elohim sent the Angel of Death through the land of Egypt and struck down every firstborn, both human and beast. But the blood on our houses would be a sign not to strike our inhabitants."

The plagues of frogs or locusts weren't too bad. The frogs were funny, hopping all around. And the locusts tasted nice and crunchy, once we roasted them properly. But the hailstorm and days of darkness were so scary I thought I'd never been so frightened. Yet those were nothing compared to the death that struck during the night.

I'd never thought much about death before. Though Mother tried to shoo me out of a birthing room if she expected a mother or baby to die in the process, I'd seen it happen on occasion. But those people were strangers. Now it was my father and brother who'd died. Grandfather had taught me about the three afterlife ideologies: belief in an underworld, eternal life, and rebirth of the soul.

Upon dying, a person was presented to Osiris, god of the afterlife and resurrection, lord of the dead and underworld. There the deceased faced judgment by a tribunal of forty-two divine judges, who weighed the heart against a feather of the goddess Ma'at. If a person lived in conformance with the precepts of Ma'at, who represented truth and right living, the heart balanced with her feather and the deceased was worthy to live forever in paradise with Osiris. If found guilty, the deceased was thrown to the soul-eating demon Ammit and subjected to terrifying punishment before being annihilated.

I wasn't sure I understood all this, never mind whether I believed it. I may not have liked my father, and I certainly hadn't liked my brother, but were they so bad that their hearts wouldn't balance with Ma'at's feather? Sadly, I doubted they'd led lives of sufficient truth and righteousness.

But the Hebrews didn't believe in Osiris, or any of the other Egyptian gods. Their god was certainly more powerful; however, I knew nothing of that god's rules.

Yet.

CHAPTER FOUR

SHIFRA

So Elohim led the people round about, by way of the wilderness at the Sea of Reeds. Now the Israelites went up armed out of the land of Egypt.

—Exodus 13:18

MY THOUGHTS WERE interrupted by loud voices calling out from the street. Suddenly there was such a banging at the door that I nearly jumped onto Grandfather's lap. But Uncle Shaul calmly walked to open the door and then embraced the disheveled man standing there. "What news, Ziza?"

"Good news, Cousin." Ziza pummeled Shaul's shoulder. "Word has come that Pharaoh summoned Moses and Aaron and told them that the Hebrews should swiftly depart and begone, along with their flocks and herds." Then he stood back and shook his head in apparent disbelief. "Already people are in the streets, carrying their possessions on their backs, heading east out of the city."

"You should continue alerting everyone." Shaul gently pushed his cousin Ziza out the door, then turned to us, frozen at the table. "Pua, we must quickly pack the wagon with supplies. Shifra and your grandfather should go home, help Asenet fill their wagon and

THE MIDWIVES' ESCAPE   21

wheelbarrows as well, then tie up their goats and meet us in back as soon as you can."

Before Grandfather could say anything, Pua pleaded with him, tears running down her cheeks. "Please, Father, no arguments. You and Asenet's family must leave with us. Nothing is left for anyone here."

Shaul shook his head, but he looked more gratified than sad. "Israel's GOD has defeated Egypt and all its gods."

Grandfather didn't argue. We hastily finished our food and went to the door, where I was astonished to see the street filled with people, men pulling wagons and pushing wheelbarrows, children riding goats and donkeys, all moving together as one, like a river.

Pua caught hold of my sleeve. "Tell your mother to get any payment for midwife services owed in grain. Who knows when we'll be able to harvest or buy any."

I held tight to Grandfather's hand as we pushed our way through the crowd going the opposite direction. When we reached our home, the streets were nearly empty and the stink had lessened. Mother and Maratti had apparently heard the news; Eshkar and Gitlam were already loading items into our wagon and wheelbarrow. When I told Mother what Aunt Pua had advised, she immediately emptied our midwife baskets, took hold of my arm, and hurried us outside. Weighed down by sadness and exhaustion, I followed meekly as we visited one client's house after another until our baskets were so heavy with grain that I could barely carry mine. Mother was no fool, for she sifted each bag of grain into one of ours to ensure they contained no rocks to falsely increase the weight. Most of our clients were honest, but not all, and they glared at us from faces twisted with hatred as they refilled their bags while we watched.

We returned safely, where Uncle Maratti was wearing his uniform, a leather kilt with a sword belted at his waist. "I must get back to the palace to recruit as many of my comrades as will leave Egypt. The more join us, the stronger we will be, and the fewer will be left with Pharaoh when he comes to attack us." He stood straight and tall, his voice strong and confident. "Stay well back from the others so we can catch up with you."

"Considering all the many things loaded in our wagons and wheelbarrows," Grandfather said, "we will surely be toward the end of the line."

"You seem sure that Pharaoh will not let the Hebrews go," Mother said.

Maratti's eyes narrowed. "Each time Pharaoh told Moses that the Hebrews were free to leave, it was only to make Moses lift a plague. Then Pharaoh changed his mind as soon as Moses complied. Why should it be different now?"

Mother sighed in acquiescence. "I hope you will be careful."

Maratti gave us a small salute and left us to finish packing.

It didn't take long. There wasn't time for our dough to rise, so Mother and I left it in the kneading bowls, then wrapped them in our cloaks to keep the dough moist. If it didn't rise by tomorrow, we'd bake it as flatbread.

Shaul and Pua were waiting in the alley behind their house, their son Rephaiah already astride the donkey hitched to their wagon. We stopped where the alley met the main road, giving them space to pull in front of us. "Why do you call your people Israelites?" I asked them. "Mother, Maratti, and everyone else calls them Hebrews."

Pua indicated that Shaul should answer. "A man named Israel is our ancestor. He came to Egypt many years ago when there was a famine in our homeland, Canaan."

"So that's the Promised Land where Moses is leading you?"

He smiled and nodded. "Hebrew is the language Israelites speak."

THE MIDWIVES' ESCAPE 23

While we waited, those on foot carrying packs and waterskins passed us.

I'd never seen so many people in one place. Grandfather pointed out the distinctive features of each nation: Hebrews with wavy dark hair, their men with pointed beards; Egyptian men with shaved heads, and women, including me and Mother, with dark hair, either worn straight or plaited; Akkadian men from the east wore long dark curled beards, their hair circled into a bun in the back, while the women's tresses hung to their shoulders; Hittites, whose skin was olive colored, were clean-shaven and wore their long straight dark hair tied back like a horse's tail. Eshkar and Gitlam were among the few Lagash I saw, and they stood out with their bronze skin and tight curls cut short on their round heads. I was surprised, and impressed, by how many other Egyptians were leaving.

Eventually the only people walking at the back were either herding goats or accompanying wagons. I worried about why Uncle Maratti hadn't joined us. Had he been captured and accused of deserting Pharaoh's guards? Had he been imprisoned, or worse? We were approaching the city gates, which I was surprised to see were wide open and unguarded. We had just passed through when Maratti and ten other men dressed and armed like him jumped out and took up positions alongside us. Only now Maratti and his troops also wore bronze armor and helmets, and they used spears as walking sticks. They had their own wheelbarrows, laden with shields and more weapons.

Relief washed over me. All these weapons, surely taken from Pharaoh's armory, would defend us rather than attack us.

If that wasn't impressive enough, they were followed by six women warriors whose skin was so dark it was almost black and whose hair was either cut short or piled on top of their heads. Each one carried a large bow over one shoulder and a quiver of arrows over the other. I couldn't

24   SHIFRA

stop staring at them. While all the other women, including me, Mother, and Aunt Pua, were dressed in simple white linen tunics or shifts, the Nubians wore colorful halters to contain their breasts and bronze kilts to protect their nether regions. They looked beautiful and magnificent.

Eshkar also couldn't stop staring at them, but his open-mouthed awe was tinged with a hungry expression that made me angry.

"Those are Nubian archers," Grandfather explained, his voice full of admiration. "They come from the south, the headwaters of the Nile. Their people mine gold and tin to trade with Egypt. With their tin, which our smiths mix with copper, we can smelt bronze. Bronze makes the finest weapons, stronger than tin or copper by itself."

"I heard that Nubians cut off their breasts to shoot arrows better," Eshkar whispered, clearly not interested in making weapons.

"Don't be ridiculous." I rolled my eyes at Eshkar's ignorance. "Why would they need to wear halters if they didn't have breasts?"

Eshkar looked down at the ground in embarrassment and didn't answer.

We walked for three days through the sandy desert, stopping only for midday meals. There were no trees except palms to shade us, only a variety of thorny shrubs and an occasional aromatic herb. We camped the first night on a high place called Succoth. From there I was amazed to see the enormous crowd of people ahead of us also fleeing Egypt. I was too tired to watch them for long, so tired, in fact, that I lay down in my bedroll and gazed at the rising full moon until I fell asleep.

The next morning I was awakened by a buzz of conversation. Everyone was talking at once as they pointed and stared in wonder at the giant shimmering cloud hovering above us. It looked like a rainbow had, instead of spreading in an arc across the sky, merged into an enormous orb. The jabbering only increased when the cloud began to move. At first I was frightened of its strange appearance. But when I heard

Succoth desert with palm trees

that we were to follow it, that Elohim, the Hebrew's god, had sent it to guide and protect us on our journey, my fear was replaced by curiosity. Where were we headed? How did Elohim direct the cloud where to go? How would the cloud protect us?

Soon I could see a large body of water in the distance, but to my disappointment, we encamped at the edge of the wilderness instead of heading there. I had been looking forward to a bath.

By this time we'd caught up with Shaul's cousins. It was almost pleasant to share our evening meals and set up our beds next to Aunt Pua's Hebrew relatives. As the sun set, the cloud dissolved, to be replaced by an enormous pillar of fire. There were shouts and cries of fear, and I confess that the sight of fire twisting like a tornado terrified me, unlike the benevolent cloud. Yet there was nothing I could do but curl up in my bedroll, close my eyes, and attempt to sleep.

I nearly screamed when I felt someone tugging on my blanket. But then I heard Gitlam's quiet voice near my ear. "Shifra, I'm scared." It sounded like he was fighting back tears. "Can I sleep near you?"

"I'm scared too," I whispered back to him. The poor little boy; he couldn't have been more than six. And it was less than a week since his mother died. "Where's your brother?"

"He's with your grandfather, but I don't know where." He began to cry. "We got separated and now it's nighttime."

"Did you bring any covers with you?"

"Just one."

I moved over and patted where I'd been. "Come lie here next to me. I'll put your blanket over both of us." Gitlam was a sweet child, nothing like my nasty brother. Not that I would dare tell anyone how thankful I felt that my brother, and our equally callous father, had died in the plague. Having them replaced in my family by Gitlam and Eshkar was as if Elohim had answered my prayers.

CHAPTER FIVE

ASENET

*Then Moses held out his arm over the sea and GOD drove back the
sea with a strong east wind all that night, and turned the sea into dry
ground . . . and the Israelites went into the sea on dry ground.*

—Exodus 14:21–22

"I DON'T WANT TO leave Egypt, Father." My tone was probably too
petulant to address him, but I was confident that Shifra and I could
support ourselves with our midwifery skills.

"How dare you speak to me, your father, with such disrespect?"

"I do respect you, but no matter how difficult it might be to stay
behind, it would be better than spending years trudging through a desert wilderness to reach the Hebrew's promised land." My voice rose as
I continued. "We're not Hebrews. We don't worship their god. They
probably won't even let us come with them."

Father's expression softened. "I can understand you not wanting to
leave your husband's and son's bodies behind, but I won't be separated
from Pua's family."

I understood that my sister had given my father a grandson, while
I became barren after Shifra was born. In addition I was unlikely to

acquire a new husband at my age, especially since I was already raising another man's child. I admit that I neither mourned nor missed my late husband, and I even had mixed feelings about my son, who had been growing up to mirror his father's worst habits.

"And now we're going to somehow cross the Sea of Reeds," I protested. "But I don't know how to swim. I've never even bathed in the Nile." I'd heard too many stories of crocodiles and hippos attacking people.

Grandfather must have recognized my panic. "You heard Maratti explain that the usual trade route to Canaan goes along the Great Sea past a series of Egyptian forts where this many escaped slaves would surely be killed or captured and returned to Egypt." He gave me a gentle hug. "There is no safer way to go."

Maratti walked up and interrupted us. "Don't worry, Asenet. Moses will have the Akkadians, who know the way, show us how to safely cross the marshlands in large numbers." He leaned down and said softly, "Come with me. Please don't stay behind."

My spirits had risen at the confidence in his voice, but Maratti's entreaty made me feel happier and more wanted than I could remember ever feeling. I was too overwhelmed to speak, so I looked into his eyes and nodded.

His eyes lit up, and then he continued his explanation. "The wheelbarrows and wagons will go first, well spread out, along with the donkeys and goats. Together they will crush the reeds down to form a mesh solid enough to walk on. To cross the fastest, we will walk in groups, not single file."

"We begin at dawn," Grandfather declared firmly, either ignoring or not noticing my interaction with Maratti. "The tide will be high, but the sea is shallow here. So as the tide goes out, the water will remain shallow while we cross."

Thus my family were among the first to step into the water, even before the sun rose, just behind our Akkadian guides. I grew anxious as the waves rose above my waist, but the water was warm and tranquil, and I calmed when I saw the wheelbarrows and wagons floating. Now it would take little effort to guide them along next to us as we walked. Soon the donkey and goats were swimming beside us. I worried they might swim away, but I was reassured when I saw Eshkar and Gitlam swimming over to herd them back. Of course the boys could swim; their father and uncle had been fishermen. I told myself that the Akkadians in front weren't worried, so I should focus on finding a secure foothold on the reeds below.

But my anxiety returned when I looked up to see Eshkar splashing Shifra, and she him, under the guise of teaching her to swim. I wanted to keep an eye on her, but I had to concentrate on staying upright and following those ahead of me. All I could do was keep my spying to a minimum, but my worries and frustration increased when I saw Eshkar holding her body afloat as Shifra practiced paddling with her arms and kicking her feet. Right then I could see his hands, but I couldn't watch them every moment, though she did seem to be enjoying the lesson.

To make matters worse, Father walked alongside me. "Spying on them won't achieve anything, Asenet." He gave me a knowing smile. "Except making you lose your balance."

"But she's still a child," I protested.

"Not for much longer."

I didn't answer him. I couldn't help but notice how mature Shifra's body looked under her wet shift, and I suspected that Eshkar had noticed as well—which was why I was troubled.

"I think they would make a good match," Father continued. "As my apprentice, he is likely to take over my wainwright business, and then Shifra could continue to live with us after the wedding."

I scowled at him. Father was in his midforties and I didn't like recalling that he would soon be too old to work. I liked even less being reminded that a bride leaves home and goes to live with her husband's family when they marry. "You want me to encourage them?"

30 ASENET

He shook his head. "Just don't discourage them."

Before I could reply, I finally did lose my footing. But Father caught my arm before I could slip beneath the waves. I kept my mouth closed, and as we continued on together I became distracted by the sight of an elderly woman with long white hair riding a donkey ahead of us. Carrying the woman's weight, the donkey was too heavy to swim and struggled to keep its head above water. I made my way to her and helped her dismount, after which the donkey easily began swimming. The woman, taller than me, took hold of the donkey's lead with one hand and walked alongside him. To my surprise, she reached out with her other hand, grabbed one of mine, and pulled me toward her. Then, our arms intertwined, we trudged together along the muddy ocean floor.

Everyone was in the water when Eshkar stopped and, his eyes wide with fear, pointed up at the cliffs behind us. To my horror, there was the Egyptian army—Pharaoh's chariots, horses, riders, and warriors— arrayed before our frightened eyes, their armor gleaming in the sun.

I wanted to run, to cry, to scream my fear, but I didn't do any of those things. I pushed forward in the water with all my strength.

"Was it for want of graves in Egypt that you brought us to die in the wilderness?" a man yelled at Moses.

The shrieks of terror multiplied. "What have you done to us, taking us out of Egypt?" I whispered, my throat too constricted to cry out.

Yet Moses's voice was firm. "Don't be afraid! Witness the deliverance that GOD will work for you. For the Egyptians whom you see today you will never see again!" Staff held high, he stretched his arm over the sea.

I gasped with amazement as a strong east wind suddenly blew in, driving back the water, its spray sparkling in the sunset. At the same time, it was now the Egyptians who shrieked in terror as the pillar of fire appeared and began moving back and forth in front of them,

Pillar of fire at the Sea of Reeds

32 ASENET

forcing them to remain on the cliff. All night we had the wind at our back, encouraging us to keep moving forward as we trudged through the split waters, until at dawn the tide was so low that we crossed on crushed reeds over solid ground. But just then the pillar of fire vanished and the usual daytime cloud appeared and shimmered above the shore ahead of us, glittering in the sunrise.

We had just witnessed another of Elohim's miracles.

At first the Egyptians were paralyzed. Then they abruptly burst out in pursuit. Into the sea they raced, all of Pharaoh's horses, chariots, and riders. Our previous exhaustion was replaced with panic. Even the slowest broke into a run, including the old woman, who raced to catch up with her swimming donkey. The tide began coming in, which floated the wagons again and enabled us to move faster. I restrained myself from looking back at our stragglers and the Egyptians because my footing tended to slip when I did. By this time Shifra, Eshkar, and Gitlam were at the front with Maratti and the goats, far ahead of me and Father.

I was thankful I no longer had to worry about Shifra's drowning or getting left behind, when all around us blue lotus buds began rising from the dark water, lifting and opening at the surface to reveal bright yellow centers set in a circle of sky-blue petals. I breathed in the lovely scent they released at dawn. I marveled at Elohim's message, for the essential role of this fragrant flower in Egyptian religion was its intimate association with the rising sun, creation, and rebirth. Its sensual fragrance was also renowned for its properties of attraction, enhancing lovemaking, and reducing anxiety. I could not deny that my anxiety was decreasing.

The water level continued to rise for hours, but I wasn't worried—not when I smelled the blue lotus flowers. The old woman and I concentrated only on putting one foot in front of the other until I lost my grip on my basket of midwife supplies and could only watch in dismay as it began floating away. I couldn't reach it in time, no matter how swiftly I moved. Defeated, I began to cry. But someone unexpectedly grabbed my shoulder, and I opened my eyes to see the mystery woman holding my basket out to me. As I grabbed it, she let go of me, clambered onto her donkey, and made for the shore.

I was suddenly aware that I was walking uphill and even more surprised when I looked up and there was Maratti, only a short distance away, hurriedly sloshing toward me. There were wagons now on the beach where goats greedily chomped on reeds nearby. Already men were cutting down reeds for women sitting on the sand to weave into sleeping mats. Between my relief and exhaustion, I almost fainted, but Maratti caught me and helped me toward our wagon.

I'm sure I could have made it there under my own power, but under the influence of the blue lotus, I couldn't resist the opportunity to be in his arms again. I clung to him and whispered, "I was so frightened of drowning, of my family drowning, but now we're all safe."

He turned so I looked over his shoulder. "Now the Egyptians are drowning instead."

My exhaustion changed to elation. The east wind had turned, and the high tide engulfed the Egyptians on foot, as well as their chariots and riders. The chariots, decorated with bronze, were too heavy to float, just as the Egyptians in their metal armor were too heavy to swim. By the time the last of our people had staggered out of the water, the sea had returned to its normal state, and there was no sign of the Egyptian army except for some swimming horses. The pillar of fire was on our side of the sea, providing a comforting light for those passing around waterskins and unleavened bread. Soon there were sleeping bodies as far as I could see—some on rugs, some on newly woven mats, but most just collapsed on the uncovered ground. I looked for the elderly woman who'd assisted me, but I saw no one with white hair.

Maratti helped me up onto our wagon, where Shifra was already asleep on the pile of bedding and rugs. I lay down next to her and closed my eyes. I don't know if it was a dream or reality but the last thing I recall hearing him say was, "I will always protect you, Asenet. I wish I could have protected you from my brother."

The sun was high when I woke, and I would have slept longer if it weren't for the savory aroma of cooking food making me realize how hungry I was. Shifra was no longer lying next to me, and I raised myself up on an elbow to look over the wagon's side. I could hardly believe my eyes. I was surrounded by hundreds, maybe thousands, of busy people. Up to their waists in the sea, Eshkar and Gitlam were pulling in nets full of fish, while other men speared fish one at a time. I sighed with relief to see Pua and Ziza's wife, Helah, sitting at a nearby fire roasting fish and tubers of some kind while unleavened dough baked on heated rocks. There were a great many other cooking fires as far as I could see along the shore.

Oh no! How was the goat cheese doing? It should be done by now, but maybe it had stopped curdling. I threw on my shift and jumped out of the wagon to check the goat cheese's progress, but my pan was gone and there was no sign of Shifra. I started to panic, but then I realized someone had already milked the goats and started a new batch of cheese that, by the look of its loose curds, would be complete later in the day. I sighed with relief.

By the time I rebraided my hair and took a seat at my sister's fire, I could see Shifra and Helah's daughter, Haggith, in the distance, struggling with a heavy basket of something they'd collected along the shore. When they got closer, I saw them smiling, smiles that spread to their entire faces when they arrived and emptied the basket of duck eggs into a large pot of water.

The duck eggs would need time to cook, so I went back to stir the coagulating cheese. I was pleasantly surprised to find Maratti asleep in the shade underneath the wagon. I was admiring the freshly woven reed mat beneath him when I noticed our looms were set up between the wagons. Obviously I had been so exhausted yesterday that I hadn't even noticed they'd been taken down from the wagons. I was also appreciating how handsome Maratti looked, his long hair loose and framing his face, when he opened his eyes and smiled.

He yawned and his eyes twinkled at me. "Admiring the view?"

I blushed and averted my eyes, pretending I hadn't been admiring him. "The sea looks lovely when it's calm," I said. "But the food roasting at my sister's fire looks even better." To affirm my words, my stomach growled loudly.

He rolled out from under the wagon. "I haven't eaten since dawn. Shall we join them?"

We ate in silence until Father arrived with a basket of fish. "Look at these beauties." He pointed to some that were bright blue and others that were multicolored.

My mouth was full of boiled duck egg, so I just nodded. But Maratti replied, "They do look good, but the important thing is that they taste good."

Father squatted next to him. "The tide is going out. Will we be fishing for inanimate beauties again?" He winked, and I knew he didn't mean fish.

Maratti nodded. "Alert all the tall men, especially those who can swim. Tell them to particularly look for fallen chariots." He wiped his mouth with his hand and stood up. "They don't weigh much if they're not armored; a single man can carry one."

I stood as well. "What was that about?"

He took my hand. "Come, I'll show you."

Hand in hand, Maratti and I walked to where the wheelbarrows were parked near the shore. Covered with rugs and mats, their contents were hidden. Maratti lifted a rug's corner, and I caught a glimpse of metal reflecting the sun. He put his finger to his lips and beckoned me

36 ASENET

closer. This time he pulled off an entire mat, but I couldn't suppress a gasp. The wheelbarrow was full of swords and shields scavenged from the drowned Egyptians.

"Why so many weapons?" I whispered. "We've defeated the Egyptians."

His answer terrified me. "There are many desert tribes who would love to acquire the treasure we took in lieu of wages from the Egyptians." Before I could question him, he continued, "And don't think that this bounty, including the number of our women, won't soon become common knowledge."

I shivered at the thought of being captured and raped by desert bandits. "But why chariots? We don't have any horses to pull them."

"The Nubians do. They swam into the sea last night and rescued enough to ride." He continued. "But your father wants the wheels to make more wagons."

"Can I help even though I'm short and can't swim?"

"Women and children can stand in the shallows and carry what the men recover onto the shore."

"We can also sort the weapons into different types," I said in agreement.

The salvage operation began well before the tide was at its lowest and continued for hours. Up and down the shore, people went into the water at low tide and brought out what valuables they could. Boys who could swim were bobbing on chariot wheels like rafts, although they had to be reminded that they should be loading weapons onto them. Swords, daggers, shields, spears, and even some armor were heaped on the sand above the high-tide line. I was pleased to see so many daggers, a weapon women could carry, but I tried not to think of what a man had to do to separate that armor from the corpse wearing it. Pharaoh's army

THE MIDWIVES' ESCAPE 37

had consisted of over a thousand warriors and hundreds of chariots, so despite all the spoils we reaped, more were probably buried in the mud below.

Thinking of what else was buried below, I was briefly overcome with sadness. It was one thing for warriors to die in battle, but Pharaoh's intransigence was also responsible for the deaths of many innocent firstborns, including my late husband and son. I may not have been fond of them, but I hadn't wished them dead. I shook my head to dispel these thoughts of death from my mind and returned to sorting the weapons.

We were alive. We had all survived.

Suddenly cheers rang out. A chariot had been found and the strongest men raced to drag it ashore. I was disappointed that we recovered only eight complete chariots in good condition, but Father reassured me that the wagons he could build from them were more than he'd expected. Our men had stripped off their kilts in favor of loincloths, but a number of them had abandoned their loincloths as well. At first I blushed and averted my eyes from the naked men, but eventually I became inured to the sight. I couldn't help but keep a lookout for Maratti, but each time I glimpsed him, I felt disappointed that he still had his loincloth on.

The men, on the other hand, found it impossible to ignore how the women looked in wet tunics that hid none of the flesh underneath. There were catcalls and whistles, which some of the bolder women returned. I found the spectacle more amusing than annoying.

To further gladden everyone as the tide came in and we ceased our efforts, Moses's sister, Miriam, raised a timbrel and led the women in song and dance. Her arms and legs were well muscled, and she danced vigorously with many leaps and twirls. Strands of gray hair escaped from her headscarf, but she made no effort to tuck them back in. I was relieved to see the white-haired woman among the crowd, dancing and singing with Miriam like a young girl:

Sing to GOD, Who has triumphed gloriously

Horse and driver hurled into the sea

Pharaoh's chariots and his army cast into the sea; The pick of
his officers drowned in the Sea of Reeds.

You made Your wind blow, the sea covered them; They sank
like lead in the majestic waters.

Who is like You, GOD, among the celestials? Who is like You,
majestic in holiness,

Awesome in splendor, working wonders!

When the dancers slowed, I asked Pua who the old woman dancing with Miriam was, the one with the long white hair. I explained that
she and I had supported each other through the sea.

Pua looked at me in amazement. "That is Serach bat Asher."

"Bat Asher? Joseph's brother's daughter? Jacob's granddaughter?
Who entered Egypt with him?"

My jaw dropped when Pua nodded. Then I gulped and said, "But
that would make her more than a hundred years old."

"Yes. They say that she showed Moses where Joseph's bones were
buried so Moses could take them out of Egypt with us."

When the first set of dancers slowed, other Hebrew women brought
out timbrels as well. I was amazed at the faith that had led them to
bring these musical instruments along in place of utilitarian necessi-
ties. I wasn't amazed, however, when someone produced wineskins,
after which couples began wandering off into the darkness. I looked
for Maratti without success and forced myself not to wonder whom he
might have gone off with instead of me.

I was still dancing after Shifra and the boys had gone to sleep and
was startled when Maratti appeared at my side, took my hand, and
walked me back to our wagons. He was helping me up when he leaned
closer and said softly, "Some Hittites have a custom that an unmarried
brother of a deceased married man should marry his widow . . . especially if she has children."

I could smell the wine on his breath, but I'd had my share as well, maybe more than my share. "And are you one of those Hittites?" I lifted my face toward his, inviting him to kiss me.

However he merely smiled and replied, "I am, but custom also demands that he wait three months so there is no doubt as to the father of the widow's next child."

CHAPTER SIX

SHIFRA

In the wilderness, the whole Israelite community grumbled against Moses and Aaron.

—Exodus 16:2

WE SPENT TWO WEEKS walking south along the Sea of Reeds before we set up camp, but I saw no more blue lotus plants. I imagined this area was what the shores of the Nile looked like before the land was covered with great cities—just sand dunes for as far as could be seen until rocky hills sprang up. The occasional creek flowing into the sea from those eastern hills ensured that our waterskins were never empty. Thankfully, between the fish, tubers, duck eggs, goat cheese, and unleavened bread, nobody went hungry. Most of the women, and their older daughters, were occupied spinning goat's hair into thread or at their looms weaving that thread into rugs or tent walls and roofs. At the same time, they talked and talked and talked.

Mother, Pua, and the Hebrew midwives could handle the births, which were fewer than we'd attended in Egypt, so Grandfather requisitioned my help to build four new wagons as quickly as possible. When I was younger, Grandfather had taught me the woodworking tasks best suited to small hands with minimal strength. I soon became adept at

THE MIDWIVES' ESCAPE   41

whittling the small fingers and notches at the ends of the side boards so they fit together tightly. But once Mother had me working as her midwife's apprentice, Gitlam took over my woodworking tasks.

Now I was working with Grandfather again. After he traded an old wagon and a wheelbarrow for new tents, we created our own campsite near Pua and Shaul's. Mother and I shared a small tent, while Grandfather and Maratti occupied a larger one with the boys. Grandfather set up the workshop next to their tent and strung up one of my poorer weaving efforts to provide shade. Another curtain shaded our looms, which sat between our tent and the men's.

Making a wagon's wheels and axles were the most difficult jobs, requiring strength beyond my capabilities, but we would be reusing the chariots'. Shaul and Ziza had heavy bronze axes to fell trees for us from those that grew along the creeks. These same axes would also be useful for felling enemies in battle, and thus the two Simeonite men would need no other weapons training. After they hacked off the bark and cut the remaining trunk to the appropriate size, Grandfather and Eshkar used bronze saws to slice the wood into boards that fit between the wheels. Then it was my job to make the box joints that would hold the wagon together more securely than nails alone. Lastly, Gitlam hammered in the bronze nails that attached the boards to form the bottom and sides of the wagons.

I liked woodworking with Grandfather and the boys. Once we had our own campsite, it felt like we were almost a real family.

One would think that having miraculously escaped Pharaoh's army and now being protected by Elohim's cloud by day and fire pillar at night, everyone would be happy. But people still argued and complained. Some, although not the Hebrews, wanted to remain near the sea while others thought that was close enough to Egypt that Pharaoh might be tempted to attack again. Many of the Akkadians wanted to head east to their native country. The Hebrews, of course, were determined to follow Moses to the Promised Land. Nobody asked my opinion, but I had seen enough of Elohim's power that I was content to follow wherever that shimmering cloud led us. Mother and Grandfather would not be parted from Pua's family, while Eshkar, Gitlam, and Uncle Maratti would not be parted from us. The other Hittites followed Maratti, which meant that the Nubians joined us as well. Alas, since there were more men than weapons, there were protests from those who considered the distribution unfair.

I came out of our tent just as Maratti sidestepped that problem by beginning the men's training without any weapons. "The first lesson is that before you learn to use a sword or spear, you must know how to stand." The men looked at him skeptically, but there were no objections.

Maratti led them to a large flat sandy area where they could all see him clearly. Then he crouched slightly into what he called "a simple warrior's stance." His knees were bent and turned sideways, feet far apart, but not too far. "Joshua"—he beckoned the Hebrew leader to come closer—"push me backwards."

"How?"

"Any way you like; just try to throw me off-balance and make me stumble."

Joshua shrugged his shoulders, approached Maratti slowly, and started to shove him back. But Maratti simply knocked Joshua's hands away. Joshua stood up tall and came at him again, but Maratti grabbed Joshua's arm and forced him backward, causing him to stumble.

Maratti pointed to a couple of hefty Judahites. "You two, come help your cousin. Try to force me down."

The two men joined Joshua, but Maratti stepped around their attacks, keeping in between them, adjusting his stance to parry each attempt. He grabbed the first man's arm and yanked him forward, causing the man to trip. He stepped into the second man's shoulder rush, deflecting the attack and forcing him back. Finally, Maratti pulled back as Joshua's arms encircled him, making Joshua fall forward.

THE MIDWIVES' ESCAPE

43

I watched with awe and pride as Maratti remained completely calm, weaving between the three men and adjusting his center of balance. "Successful combat depends on the legs," he yelled as he evaded the attacks, not even breathing hard. "It doesn't matter how fast you are with a sword, how accurate with a spear. If your opponent makes you trip or stumble, or heaven forbid, fall, you'll lose—and losing means dying."

All day and every day that week except the Sabbath, Maratti and his Hittites divided the men into pairs by size and weight to work on their stances: learning how to maintain one, learning how to keep their center of balance, and learning not to lock their knees just as they're threatened. The bare-chested men, wearing either kilts or merely loincloths, proved a great attraction for the women, some of whom set up their looms so they could weave as they watched the training. I was pleased to see Mother's gaze fixed on Maratti, but I knew better than to mention that to either of them.

I liked Maratti; I'd always liked him, though I seldom saw him. He'd come to live with Grandfather and Mother after Father married her. He began as one of the palace night guards, which fit perfectly with Father's daytime occupation. Father was away from dawn to sunset, exactly the time Maratti stayed in our house. Maratti spent much of that time sleeping, of course, but I still saw more of him than I did of Father—particularly if Father stayed out late carousing and Mother was detained in the morning by a lengthy birth. Maratti taught me to read, as well as how to play games like knucklebones, senet, and mehen. I beat him at knucklebones about half the time, which is to be expected since who wins is based totally on chance. I did better at senet and mehen, mostly because Maratti let me cheat.

I used to imagine marrying him, but that was before Eshkar became Grandfather's apprentice. After that Maratti looked like an old man to me, while Eshkar had matured into a handsome swain. As I aged, Maratti began to distance himself from me, and Eshkar paid me more attention. Nobody said anything to me about becoming betrothed to Eshkar, but I'd overheard enough discussion between Grandfather and Mother to know that's what they were planning.

By the following week, it was clear even to me which men would be the most proficient soldiers. They began training with sword and spear in addition to working on their stances. Maratti praised the Gadites for being particularly eager and competent fighters, but he didn't need to extol Joshua—by far the finest swordsman of the Hebrews, in addition to being their leader.

Meanwhile, the Nubians taught a few women, those not occupied spinning goat's hair into thread to weave tents and rugs, how to use a dagger to defend themselves. I was deemed too young to do more than watch, but I could learn more from observing the women train than the men, so I moved my loom to that area.

Grandfather kept two of the new wagons for us and gave the other two to Shaul and Shaul's cousin Ziza. Then he traded our old wagons to the Simeonites' other relatives. Next he and his apprentices built more looms, which he traded for tent wall cloths with intricate, decorative designs. Most Hebrews had been forced to leave their tall looms behind, there being no way to transport them. Reeds were fine for sleeping mats, but rugs and tent walls were woven from goat's wool, which we traded for thread that even small girls knew how to spin.

A month after fleeing Egypt, we turned away from the sea, going east until we reached Elim, an oasis with twelve springs of water and seventy palm trees. We encamped there beside the water for another month before heading into the Wilderness of Zin, our baskets full of ripe dates. I was afraid that we and the other outsiders might be excluded when the Hebrews arranged their tents by tribe, but Shaul and Ziza carefully raised theirs at the edge of the other Simeonites' so that Grandfather and Uncle Maratti could put ours up nearby. That led the other Hittites to settle in near us, with the Nubians just beyond them. I was surprised, and thankful, that none of the Hebrews complained when other foreigners also set up their campsites around the periphery of the tribes'. After all, Elohim had sent all those plagues to free the Hebrews, not any of the rest of us.

Unfortunately there was soon something much more important to complain about. Something that affected both Hebrews and foreigners. Not long after entering the desert, people began running out of food. Our family and Pua's still had grain from what the midwives' clients had paid us, in addition to our goat cheese and dates. But many Hebrews groaned with hunger.

"If only we had died in the land of Egypt, where we ate our fill of bread!" they wailed to Moses. "For you have brought us out into this wilderness to starve to death."

Mother and Pua had a long talk about what to do with our family's excess yet came to no agreement. "We certainly don't have enough to feed everyone," Mother pointed out.

"And if we tried to select those few we were willing to share with, there would be riots," Pua granted.

I said nothing, but it seemed to me that Elohim would not have performed the many miracles that brought us this far only to abandon us in a couple of months. Grandfather and Uncle Maratti also wondered how Elohim could be powerful enough to bring death to all the firstborn Egyptians while sparing the younger ones and the Hebrews, then split the Sea of Reeds so the Hebrews walked through to dry land, yet not be able to provide food for them in the desert.

Ziza's daughter, Haggith, shook her head at all the questioning. "Elohim is testing us," she insisted. "We need to have faith."

She was right. The next day, the last day of the week, Moses announced that "Bread will come down for us from the sky, and the

46   SHIFRA

people shall go out and gather each day that day's portion. But on the sixth day, when you apportion what you have brought in, it shall prove to be double the amount you gathered each earlier day."

"It is GOD," Moses continued, "who has heard your grumblings. By evening you shall eat flesh, and in the morning you shall have your fill of bread—and you shall know that GOD is your god."

Now my family had but one question: Would Elohim provide flesh and bread for all, or only enough for the Hebrews?

We needn't have worried. As the sun set, we heard a whirring noise in the distance, growing louder and louder. "Oh no," Mother cried out. "Elohim has sent more locusts against us. That's our punishment for complaining about not having enough food."

I cupped my ear with my hand. "I don't think so, Mother. That's not what locusts sound like. Besides, if that were locusts, we'd have plenty to eat."

Uncle Maratti squinted to see better. "It looks like some kind of small bird."

The sound increased until it was deafening, and then it ceased abruptly as the birds landed. "They're quails," Grandfather declared. "Quick, grab them before they fly away."

I watched in amazement as the enormous flock of quail flew in for water, so many that they covered the camp. To our, and everyone else's, astonishment, the quail didn't fly away as we approached but sat calmly on the ground as people scooped them up.

Gitlam stood there stroking one. "They're so soft, and cuddly," he murmured.

I picked up two, one in each hand. Their feathers were fluffy and they made little chirping sounds. They were so beautiful, it was almost a shame to eat them.

Mother and Pua were not so sentimental. They, like all the women, rushed to fill pots with water and set them to heat on their fires. At the same time the rest of us—except Gitlam, who hid in his tent—began

THE MIDWIVES' ESCAPE   47

wringing the birds' necks and plucking their feathers. By sunset, the camp was savoring the aroma of cooking quail stew, and when it came time for bed, we not only had full stomachs but feather pillows too.

Later that night, I was awakened by Eshkar pulling on my hand. "Come with me. You've got to see this."

I stifled a yawn. "But it's still dark."

"The sun will rise soon; it might be gone by then." He tugged my hand harder.

"All right." I stood up and stretched. "Show me what's so important."

We walked a little ways to the edge of our campsite. During the night, dew had fallen on the camp, and now it was lifting. Nothing looked unusual, except we two weren't the only people watching the dew lift. Suddenly there was an excited murmur from a small group at a nearby campsite. The dew was gone and there was a white flaky substance on the ground. I gasped with astonishment as the strange stuff appeared everywhere. Moments later when the sun rose, everyone was outside their tents, waiting. None dared touch it, not even the donkey and goats, and no one knew what it was.

We looked around in confusion until Moses appeared, looking tired and relieved. He scooped up a handful of the white stuff and announced, "This manna is the bread that GOD has given you to eat." Then he swallowed it. Eshkar and I each took a handful, looked at it, and shrugged. It didn't look like bread; it more resembled crushed coriander seeds. But we ate it too—and smiled. It didn't taste like bread. It didn't taste like anything I knew. It was delicious.

As a few others tried the "manna bread," Moses continued. "Each household shall gather as much as it requires to eat—an *omer* to a person for as many of you as there are in its tent."

Soon we all did so, some gathering much and some little. Gitlam even collected some for our animals, who downed it greedily. Yet when it was measured by the *omer*, anyone who had gathered much had no excess, and anyone who had gathered little had no deficiency; each household had gathered as much as it needed to eat. In some households, they ate the manna raw and found that while everyone thought it tasted delicious, each person described the flavor differently. Then Moses warned everyone not to leave any of it until morning, but many people paid no attention to him and saved some, discovering in the morning that it had become infested with maggots and stank.

Mother wanted variety, but she didn't want to do anything that angered Moses and drew his attention to the non-Hebrews near the camp. So she encouraged me to boil it with water like porridge or bake it like we would unleavened bread. In the end, no matter how it was prepared, each person's manna tasted different, and wonderful.

There were no complaints from Moses, not even when people gathered double the amount of manna, two *omers* for each, on the sixth day. Instead he looked pleased and said, "Tomorrow is a day of rest, a holy Sabbath of GOD. Bake what you would bake and boil what you would boil, and all that is left put aside to be kept until morning."

So we put it aside until morning, as Moses had ordered, and it did not turn foul, and there were no maggots in it. Then Moses told everyone, "Eat it today, for this day is a Sabbath of GOD. You will not find any manna on the ground today. Six days you shall gather it; on the seventh day, the Sabbath, there will be none." Haggith and I had no doubts that some people would still go out on the seventh day to gather manna, and we couldn't help but laugh when they found nothing.

But Shaul chastised us for finding this so amusing. "How do you think Moses, and Elohim, will feel about people refusing to obey this commandment?"

However, Moses did not seem angry when he addressed everyone. "Remember that it is GOD who, having given you the Sabbath, therefore gives you two days' food on the sixth day. Let everyone remain in their place: let no one leave the area on the seventh day."

Horses eating manna in the Wilderness of Zin

50 SHIFRA

So people rested and remained inactive on the seventh day. I envied all the adults who slept late and took naps, for it was my chore to wake early to milk the goats. Nobody was watching, so Haggith and I sneaked off to admire the horses, who were munching on manna just as our animals had. To our surprise, one of the Nubians beckoned us to come closer. We quietly approached the animals, who gave us curious looks but didn't run away.

The Nubian smiled. "They aren't afraid of girls."

She let us pet them until it was almost midday, when we thanked her and hurried back to eat. It was a pleasure to sleep all I wanted that afternoon while Gitlam did the milking. The goat cheese tasted sweeter, and when questioned, we admitted that we did not prevent the goats from eating their fill of manna each morning.

The whole community continued to move in stages as the cloud led us away from Zin. Wherever we camped, manna fell in the morning. But at Rephidim, there was no water to drink. Haggith came over to our tents to report that people were again quarreling with Moses. We still had goats' milk, so we weren't suffering—yet.

"All the people do is cry out for water," she told us.

"How did Moses reply?" Maratti asked.

"He was frustrated. He asked them again and again, 'Why do you quarrel with me? Why do you try GOD?'"

"Still people thirsted there for water," Haggith continued. "They kept criticizing Moses, 'Why did you bring us up from Egypt to kill us and our children with thirst?' so Moses finally cried out to GOD, 'What shall I do with this people? Before long they will be stoning me!'"

Haggith was still reporting all this to us, when an old woman, her face half hidden by her headscarf, tentatively approached. "May I enter?" she asked.

THE MIDWIVES' ESCAPE

"Welcome." Mother beckoned her in and, always polite to strangers, asked, "Would you like some goat milk?"

When the woman lowered her scarf to drink, I recognized her. "You're Moses's sister," I whispered in awe. "You had a timbrel. You led the women to sing and dance."

She sighed and addressed Haggith. "I need your help. Last night I dreamed how Elohim had already shown Hebrews how to worship and ask for help on the night before we left."

Haggith thought for a moment before replying. "We sacrificed a kid."

This time I didn't whisper. "That is why you're here. You need our kids."

"But we don't have enough for so many people to sacrifice," Mother said.

Miriam shook her head. "I only ask for one male yearling. This afternoon I will sacrifice the kid and start roasting it. When it is cooked, I will gather twelve Hebrew mothers together to eat it, and all the while the women will silently thank Elohim for freeing them and ask for water for their children."

"But one kid is too much food, even for twelve women," I protested.

Miriam smiled at me. "As long as we have twelve Hebrew women, ideally one from each tribe, there's no reason more women, and girls—even outsiders—cannot join us."

I blushed with shame at my direct challenge. I had not meant for my eagerness to attend to be so obvious.

"Would you like to come out to the goat pen and choose the kid?" Mother asked Miriam. I never doubted that Mother would offer one of ours.

"You are very generous," Miriam said in thanks.

I was glad I didn't have to watch the actual sacrifice. I knew that unless one of our bucks needed to be replaced, all the male kids would be sold for slaughter. But Gitlam had named all the kids, and I didn't like to think about killing them. Even so, I appreciated eating roasted meat. At sunset Mother, Pua, and I joined Miriam; her granddaughter, Achsah; and the other women, plus their daughters, at Helah's tent to eat the evening sacrifice and pray for water.

Though Miriam had invited us, I still worried that my and Mother's presence might invalidate the sacrifice somehow.

CHAPTER SEVEN

SHIFRA

Amalek came and fought with Israel at Rephidim.

—Exodus 17:8

THE NEXT MORNING I was surprised to see Miriam at our tent again. She introduced her son, Caleb, and grandson, Uri, who were carrying shovels.

Her face beamed with excitement. "Elohim accepted our sacrifice. Last night I dreamed of three damp areas of sand around the camp."

My enthusiasm made me interrupt her. "Where?"

Miriam apparently wasn't offended. "One of them is nearby. I will know the place when I see it."

Mother offered the men some goat cheese while we anxiously waited. We'd just finished eating when we heard Miriam call out. Nobody told me to stay home, so I followed Maratti and Eshkar, who followed Caleb and Uri.

Miriam had scratched through the surface gravel with a stick, revealing damp sand below. Encouraging shouts reverberated through the narrow canyon as the men dug deeper, but I couldn't see what was happening. All I saw was a pile of dark dirt growing taller. At last there was a cry of triumph when they jumped back as the walls of the hole fell in with a splash. They had reached groundwater; now they needed to dig a proper well—one with stones around the edge and a bucket on a rope to pull the water out.

But Miriam interrupted them. "Let others finish this well. Now that I know my dream was true, I want to find the other two wells."

Word of the well spread quickly. By the time Miriam located the second one, men had nearly completed the first, and a line of people waited to fill their pails and waterskins. This time there were more men eager to dig, but it took longer to reach groundwater. It also took longer to pull all the diggers, some of whom couldn't swim, out of the new, deeper well.

This time Miriam left nearly all the men at the second well to complete it, taking along only those who could swim. "I don't want such a crowd at the third well; nor do I want anyone to drown."

It was a long walk to the third well's location, but as we approached we saw some men already there, none of whom were holding shovels. To my astonishment, Miriam hurried forward and called out, "Moses, what are you doing here?"

I had never seen the great man up close before and was surprised at how ordinary he looked. Unlike his sister, he only had gray hair at his temples, while her entire head of hair was streaked with gray.

He embraced her. "I could ask you the same question."

"Elohim sent me a dream last night showing where I could find water." She said nothing about the women's sacrifice. "And now we have two new wells."

"Today God told me to take some of the elders of Israel with me, along with the staff I used to strike the Nile," Moses began, "and set out toward Horeb. The cloud was hovering over a rock there, and I was told to strike the rock and water would issue from it for the people to drink."

Miriam came closer to watch, but the rest of us stood in back of the elders of Israel. Eshkar and I stayed as far behind them as we could.

THE MIDWIVES' ESCAPE 55

Suddenly Moses lifted his staff and brought it down with a thud. I couldn't see how, or even if, he had struck the rock, but I heard a shout of triumph followed by the gushing of water. Several of the elders stepped back to get out of the way, but Miriam directed her crew to dig a streambed where the water could flow into a pond.

Soon we all had water to drink.

We had several pleasant spring days in Rephidim when the cloud didn't move from its position over the rock whose water we were all so thankful for. Children splashed in the stream, women washed clothes, and men attempted to make beer from fermented manna. Their attempt was a failure, as fermenting manna did not prevent it from becoming infested with maggots. Haggith and I visited the horses every day, and sometimes the Nubians let us groom them. Boys, including Eshkar and Gitlam, climbed rocks and explored the hills that surrounded our camp.

During the evening meal, Eshkar told Maratti that they'd encountered some local boys in the hills. "Strangers who didn't leave Egypt with the rest of us."

"We wanted to be friendly," Gitlam added, "but they ran away when they saw us."

Maratti furrowed his eyebrows. "Could they see our tents?"

Both boys nodded, and Maratti frowned.

"What's wrong?" Mother asked him. "Surely the boys were just having fun."

"The boys did nothing wrong." He put down his bowl of quail stew and stood up. "If my suspicions are confirmed, they've done us a great service. Now I need to consult Joshua."

Maratti returned hours later, after the boys were asleep. I peeked out of our tent to see him talking with Mother near the hearth. He looked even more worried than earlier. "Joshua told me there have been other reports of unfamiliar boys watching our camp."

Tents in the Wilderness of Zin

THE MIDWIVES' ESCAPE

"Who would be spying on us?" Mother gulped hard. "And why?"

"I asked the Akkadians those exact questions, and they warned me that it was likely Amalek."

"I've never heard of Amalek," she interrupted. "Why warn us about them?"

Maratti took Mother's hand. "They are brigands who prey upon caravans that come near their land." His grip tightened as he continued. "They have surely learned about our escape from Pharaoh and that we left with much gold and silver. They likely believe that we'd be an easy target, our troops consisting mainly of escaped slaves."

My stomach tightened when Mother asked, "How soon do you think they'll attack?"

"Joshua says that now that they know we're aware of them, our men should be ready to fight tomorrow. With luck, Amalek will underestimate our strength so we can scare them off."

"Even so, there will be injuries," Mother pointed out. "You will need all the women healers and herbalists among us. Including midwives like me and Pua."

"I don't want you anywhere near the battle—"

Mother cut him off. "And I don't want *you* anywhere near the battle either." She smiled wanly. "But we are needed. You are a warrior and I am a healer."

He sighed his acquiescence. "I will consult with Joshua about how we should distribute the weapons tonight. We need to be ready before dawn."

"I will talk with Pua. She will know who the Hebrew healers are."

As soon as Maratti and Mother disappeared into their tents, Grandfather approached me. "What's all this talk about battles, weapons, and healers?"

I told him what I'd heard. He stroked his beard in thought. "Even if we had enough swords, most men here are not yet adept at wielding one. Shaul and I must make as many cudgels as possible from the wood we have." He donned his sandals and headed for the door.

Amalek attacked the next morning. Even without the Nubian archers and Gadites, whom Joshua wanted to keep in reserve, our men sent them fleeing before noon. Shaul and Ziza wanted to celebrate, but Maratti quashed that idea.

"Joshua says today was merely an initial exploratory attack for Amalek to assess our numbers and strength," he told everyone. "Moses is certain they will return tomorrow to do battle with us, believing the troops they saw today are all we can muster. He has charged Joshua with choosing the best fighters for the next day, while he will station himself on the top of the hill with the staff of Elohim in his hand."

At dawn our men were in position: infantry with swords, spears, and javelins in front, those with cudgels behind, and archers well back of them. The other healers joined Mother, Pua, and me inside a large tent set up for the wounded. The front tent flaps, tied open to easily admit the wounded, gave me a wide view of the battlefield. Suddenly, across the plain, I could see Amalekite banners. Like distant thunder the Amalekites' war chant rose from their throats; it faded and then rose again and crescendoed to a climax. On a hill above us, Moses, Aaron and Miriam's husband, Hur, stood watching. From our ranks came a medley of war cries: Akkadians and Egyptians returned the Amalekite chant harder and more menacingly, Hittites howled like wolves, and the Nubians wailed an undulating yell. Moses raised his staff high, and the Hebrews cheered.

When the Amalekites were within two hundred paces, volleys of Nubian arrows flew out from behind our infantry, each shaft hitting a target. Stung by seeing their friends and kinsmen die with no way to exact vengeance, the Amalek infantrymen quickened their pace. For a moment both infantry lines stared at each other; then Gadites stormed forward and the combatants intermingled, javelins flying from both sides.

THE MIDWIVES' ESCAPE

All order vanished as squadrons, smaller groups, and even individuals charged, wheeled, retreated, and then charged again. The din hit me like a blow: one enormous noise, louder than a pyramid collapsing, made of many smaller noises—sword on shield, metal on wood, trumpets and rams' horns blaring, men yelling, men screaming.

The number of wounded men in our healing tents increased. Those bleeding had their cuts cleaned, then either immediately bandaged with a strip of clean linen or sutured first and then bandaged. Pua and Mother were experts at suturing women whose birth canal tore during birth, so they attended the heavy bleeders. We had three war surgeons who were either too old to fight or had a previous injury that now kept them off the battlefield. They were experienced at setting broken bones, but I was appalled at how often they would amputate a limb rather than try to deal with a compound fracture. At those times I pleaded to at least let me clean the wound first—and that was when I especially appreciated the separate surgery tent.

The Gadite men were indeed fierce warriors, and their women were fine herbalists. Their pain-relieving potions were very effective, and I resolved to learn whether they would be equally effective, and safe, for use during childbirth. Women from other tribes tirelessly filled and carried waterskins to the battlefield, then returned them empty to refill. The bravest ones, usually Gadites, brought water right to thirsty men's lips and were able to report where an injured man lay. Even the worst fighters were capable of helping get injured comrades back to the healing tents, a task equally as dangerous as armed combat.

CHAPTER EIGHT

ASENET

*Moses said to Joshua, "Pick some troops for us, and go out and do
battle with Amalek. Tomorrow I will station myself on the top of the
hill, with the rod of GOD in my hand." Joshua did as Moses told him
and fought with Amalek, while Moses, Aaron, and Hur went up to
the top of the hill. Then, whenever Moses held up his hand, Israel
prevailed; but whenever he let down his hand, Amalek prevailed.*

—Exodus 17:9–11

AS THE BATTLE CONTINUED, each man looked to attack further or seek
safety as his courage or circumstance directed. Whenever Moses held
up his hand, our people prevailed, but whenever he tired and let it fall,
Amalek prevailed. So Aaron and Hur, one on either side, held up his
arms. Thus Moses's hands remained steady until it was nearing sunset.
By then the Amalek line had thinned. Officers at the rear threatened
and cajoled, even forced the Amalekite men back into position with the
flats of their swords.

Suddenly, the Amalekite cavalry charged. I had to remind myself
what the Nubians had told me about horses; once running, they were
almost impossible to stop, but they would not run into solid obsta-
cles. A line of men holding shields shoulder to shoulder was a solid

Battle with Amalek; Hebrew men on a hill, Amalekites fleeing below

62   ASENET

obstacle. Unless our infantry fell, the Amalekite horses would pull up short, wheel, and throw their riders. When that happened, the Nubians would gallop out and take hold of the riderless horses' reins and lead them away from the battlefield. When I had a free moment, I watched through the tent flaps in horror, but with some satisfaction, as that was exactly what occurred. But soon I had to turn away from the chaos; there were injured men to treat.

When the sun set, most of our injured troops had been attended to, so I sent Shifra and the other younger healers back to their tents to rest. This gave the remaining healers more opportunity to see what had happened. Half the Amalekites had disappeared into the bush, and the rest had broken into a mob fleeing for their lives. Where there had once been a battle, now it was a rout. Where there had been fighting, now there was only killing. The waxing gibbous moon illuminated hacked shields, bent and broken swords and spears, and snapped cudgels strewn on the dusty field. Some of our men salvaged bent weapons that could be repaired and arrows the Nubians would reuse. Others buried our dead, but we left the Amalekite corpses on the field for the carrion eaters.

All night Pua and I dressed wounds and administered pain-relieving potions. The morning before we left, we explained the symptoms of infection and the importance of looking carefully for them to our replacements. "When you observe a wound with redness, swelling, drainage, or pus, alert one of the herbalists so they can treat it."

"Be sure to check for fever." Pua put her hand on a wounded man's forehead. "Also does the area around the wound feel hot? Does touching it gently cause the man pain? Hurry to alert an herbalist if these signs are present." She then yawned widely.

I yawned as well, and when none of the women had questions, we plodded back to our tents. As I crawled into my bedding, I gave thanks to Elohim for our victory, and even more that Maratti had returned uninjured.

It was only the next day that the enormity of the violence I'd witnessed hit me. I could barely eat with all the horrific memories of what I'd seen still in my head. I knew we hadn't destroyed the Amalekites, and I was terrified they could attack us again at any time.

We waited at Rephidim a week for enough of our injured men to recover sufficiently to travel. But not all our warriors healed from their wounds. Maratti, Joshua, and Hur didn't know what to do for the disabled casualties that would both reward them for their valor and enable their families to earn a living when we reached the Promised Land. To my surprise, it was the children, Shifra and Gitlam, whose constant complaints over who had more work to do tending the goats exasperated me, who inadvertently suggested a solution.

They were in the middle of a maddening argument when I lost my temper. "So what do you two want?" I yelled. "To rid ourselves of the goats so you don't have to care for them?"

The words were just out of my mouth when I had the epiphany. The children were right. We did have too many goats for just the two of them, especially with Shifra training to be a midwife and Gitlam a wainwright. We could, however, get rid of some of the goats. Perhaps it was the diet of manna, but our does had been unusually fruitful. In the past most pregnancies resulted in twins, but this season the majority of does birthed triplets.

I waited until after the midday meal to share my idea with Maratti. "It has come to my attention that we have more goats than we need," I began. "Do you think we could offer some of our excess kids, say two doelings and a buckling, to each disabled man's family? Even a man who limps or needs a walking stick can tend goats."

Maratti gazed at me with a look that was a mixture of surprise, admiration, and relief. "Especially if he has children who can help."

My excitement grew. "We must ensure that one of the doelings is old enough to be bred in the fall. Then she'll give birth next spring."

"And the family will be able to make cheese in a year too."

"We'll only be able to help six or eight families now, but hopefully we can give more next season."

Maratti squeezed my hand. "We're not the only ones raising goats here. I'll ask Joshua to approach the Hebrew goatherders."

I pulled my hand out of his and threw my arms around him. "Shifra and Gitlam will be so happy."

Maratti kept me in our embrace, and after the rest of the family had returned to their work, I got my nerve up. "Maratti, your brother died almost three months ago. Don't you think it is finally time for us to marry?"

The next thing I knew, he was kissing me, and I was returning his kisses with equal fervor. It seemed like forever until I caught my breath and said, "I assume that is a yes."

He laughed softly. "Most definitely."

I looked around and was mortified to see our entire household grinning at us.

Father broke the silence. "So when shall we have the wedding?"

The three of us agreed that, my being a recent widow, the feast would be modest compared to what Father would have served if I'd been a maiden. Even so, we served two roasted year-old bucklings in addition to the usual quail. Somehow Father obtained enough wine that everyone jumped up to dance when the music began. Maratti's Hittite comrades treated us to a large number of increasingly ribald songs and stories, continuing even after he and I fled to our new marital tent.

My mouth dropped in delight when I saw the beautiful new bedding Pua had gifted us with, expertly woven by her own hands. It incorporated multicolored ankhs, the key of life, as a decorative motif, making it a powerful Egyptian symbol of fertility. Even if someone was unfamiliar with the ankh's symbolism, it was still a stunning design. In any case, it brought no memories of my former husband.

Yet I was haunted by my first wedding night. I shouldn't experience that level of agony, but would coupling with Maratti provide pleasure or merely the boredom of lying underneath him until he finished with me? If the latter, should I pretend to enjoy it or not? But maybe he'd realize I was pretending and be angry.

I expected that Maratti and I would undress and immediately get into our bedding, as had happened with his brother. But my new husband was in no hurry. He drew me close and slowly unbraided my hair until it fell long and loose to my hips. Then he kissed my cheeks before making his way to my lips. That felt so good, I would gladly have stood there simply kissing, when he surprised me by working his tongue between my lips and into my mouth. Somehow I sensed that my tongue should reciprocate.

Maratti gave a small shiver, and without moving his mouth from mine, he pulled down my shift and stripped off his kilt. The nearly full moon provided more than enough light for him to admire my nakedness; I blushed with embarrassment and quickly averted my gaze from his lower body's obvious arousal. I kept my eyes closed and concentrated on how his hands felt caressing my shoulders and torso while he gently eased me onto my back. I expected him to force my legs apart and thrust into my hidden place, thus making me his wife and him my husband.

But instead he lay down next to me. His fingers made their way to my breasts, circling the skin until they reached my nipples. Then his lips replaced his fingers, but it felt nothing like a baby nursing. That had been pleasurable, but this produced a burning, itching feeling between my legs that wouldn't let me hold still, and the feeling intensified when his fingers found it. I moaned, but I wasn't in pain. Was this what desire felt like?

Without taking his lips away, Maratti rolled on top of me, but he didn't enter until I lifted my hips toward his. As he moved, what I felt was beyond pleasure. Later I would describe it as delight and bliss, but now my mind was entirely focused on the sensation, not naming it. I knew he was feeling pleasure too, but he was holding back. It was only when I thought I would scream with frustrated desire that I forced his hips toward mine. Abruptly he began moving faster and more vigorously. Then it was as if something boiled over inside me as spasm after spasm of ecstasy cascaded through me.

I lay there astounded that lying with Maratti could feel so different, so wonderful, compared with his brother. I wasn't even aware of falling asleep, but when I woke, he was gazing at me. This time I was the one to urge his head down to kiss him, to caress his body, and ultimately to pull him on top of me and into me.

Later that day Moses announced that we would enter the wilderness of Sinai by the new moon and then encamp there in front of the mountain. On the way we would stop at an oasis near some copper and malachite mines worked by Amalek's Akkadian slaves. While the rest of us tarried there, our warriors would attack the mines and plunder the gemstones and then kill the Amalekite taskmasters and free the slaves.

The Gadites, particularly those the Nubians had taught to ride the captured Amalekite horses, were greatly enthused by the prospect. They returned well before sunset with proof of their success, a severed hand from each slain Amalekite and much booty. Personally, I found this defiling of the dead a vile practice, but it was a customary way of keeping count of the enemies killed.

They also brought back the Akkadian slaves, robust men who spoke a Semitic language the Hebrews understood. Moses freed them and gave them a choice: return to their native land or join the Akkadians traveling with us and worship Elohim.

THE MIDWIVES' ESCAPE

67

After experiencing the miracle of manna the next morning, the slaves needed no further inducements to remain with us. However, those Hebrews who had objected to any foreigners joining their flight from Egypt were even angrier at additional ones.

Fortunately, my husband was not pressed into duty. Joshua took him aside and told him, "Elohim declares that when a man takes a bride, he shall not go out with the army; he shall be exempt one year for the sake of his household, to give happiness to the woman he has married."

I was so pleased with this law that I told my sister to let the rest of the Hebrew women know about it. Then I swore to thank Elohim every night for this kindness to me and Maratti—which should ensure that we beget a child before he had to rejoin his men.

CHAPTER NINE

ASENET

So Jethro, Moses' father-in-law, took Zipporah, Moses' wife, after she had been sent home, and her two sons—of whom one was named Gershom . . . and the other was named Eliezer. Jethro brought Moses' sons and wife to him in the wilderness, where he was encamped at the mountain of Elohim.

—Exodus 18:2–5

SHIFRA AND I HAD just returned from a grueling yet ultimately successful delivery. The baby boy was large, which pleased his parents, but it took a long time for him to be born. Shifra headed straight for her bed, but I sat down to eat some manna and cheese.

Suddenly Eshkar raced in and called out, "Father, Grandfather, come quickly. A Midianite caravan is coming."

"You go without me," I told the males. "Later you can tell me what they have to sell."

I had just about finished my meal when my sister, Pua, burst in. "I've seen one of the Midianite women and her two boys before," she confided. "They are Moses's sons, Gershom and Eliezer, and his wife, Zipporah."

"Are you sure?" I didn't hide my skepticism. "But you've never been to Midian."

"I saw them in Egypt. They were staying at an inn outside Goshen, where I'd been called to attend a woman in labor." She paused to think. "It was while the plagues were happening."

"What were they doing there?"

"She was arguing with Aaron. The boys were watching, I guess."

My frustration increased. "Just tell me what you saw and heard already." Now that I was done eating, I just wanted to get some sleep.

My sister looked pleased at having irritated me. "Zipporah kept badgering Aaron about why her husband couldn't come see her and their sons after they had come all this way."

When I remained silent, Pua continued. "Aaron had all sorts of excuses—Moses didn't have time to travel to Goshen; he was busy dealing with Pharaoh; he didn't need any distractions now; it was too dangerous, both for him and for them." She barely paused before continuing, "And when Zipporah offered to go see Moses herself, Aaron just repeated the same excuses as before, this time emphasizing how dangerous it would be for her and the boys if their identities were discovered."

"I suppose all those reasons were true. But surely Aaron could have arranged something." I gave her a sly look. "Maybe Aaron didn't want Moses to see his family. Maybe he didn't even tell Moses they were there."

Pua nodded slowly, savoring this criticism of Aaron. "He was insistent that she and the boys return home as soon as possible. He told her their room was only reserved through that night and that there was a caravan going to Midian in the morning." She added, "Aaron said he didn't know when the next one would be there, what with all the disruptions Moses's plagues were causing in Egypt."

"That's right." I frowned. "Blame it all on Moses." Then I brightened. "But his family is here now. He'll have to see them."

70 ASENET

However, the one who had come to see Moses was his father-in-law, Jethro. According to the gossip, Moses went out to meet his father-in-law and bowed low and kissed him, after which they went into Moses's tent while Zipporah and the boys stayed in Jethro's tent. Moses then told Jethro everything that Elohim had done to Pharaoh and to the Egyptians. Apparently Jethro was so impressed that he brought a burnt offering and sacrifices for Elohim, and Aaron asked all the elders of Israel to partake of a meal with Jethro the next day.

I asked Maratti to confirm or deny the gossip. "What about Zipporah and the boys?"

"From what I heard, they weren't invited."

Outraged, I charged off to Pua's tent. "You and I must insist that Zipporah and her sons dine with us while Jethro is with the men."

Pua immediately agreed. "We can't have her thinking our women know nothing about hospitality to strangers."

We had to press Zipporah to accept our invitation, which she did only when we agreed to limit attendance to her family and ours. She insisted on not including any Hebrews, especially not any Levites. However, she agreed for Pua to bring Rephaiah, who was between the ages of Gershom and Eliezer, so the boys could play together.

Gitlam also ate with us, but Eshkar went off with Father, Maratti, and Shaul to eat with the soldiers. Gitlam let the boys watch while he milked the does and then rode the big bucks. Gershom, the eldest, proudly declared that his family raised sheep, but nobody could ride them, not even little children. The boys argued a bit over whether goats or sheep were better until Zipporah stepped in and praised both animals, sheep providing better wool and goats better cheese.

"Sheep need rich grassy pastures," she explained. "While goats can survive in the desert where the soil is poor."

I offered everyone more cheese, including some that I'd made fresh that morning, and we all agreed that both animals were very good.

THE MIDWIVES' ESCAPE

The next day, Maratti told me that Jethro had watched as Moses spent all day judging the people's disputes. Finally, when Moses was finished, Jethro told Moses that he would surely wear himself out, and these people as well. He urged Moses to seek out capable individuals who fear Elohim—trustworthy ones who spurn ill-gotten gain—and let them judge the people.

"Jethro is a wise man," I said. "I hope Moses heeded his counsel."

"He did." Maratti sighed. "Then to my surprise, Moses bade farewell to Jethro, who then took his daughter and grandsons back to Midian."

"Surprised!" I blurted out. "I'm shocked that Moses didn't even share a meal with his wife and sons. He just sent them back to Midian. What kind of leader sets such a poor example of how to treat his family?"

I soon learned that many Hebrews were pleased that Moses had apparently divorced his foreign wife. Others, especially those like Shaul who had married Egyptians, were angry at Moses or felt sympathy for Zipporah—or both. Pua and I both suspected that Aaron was behind the separation and felt sorry for all four of the victims of his machinations: Moses, Zipporah, and their two young sons.

By the third new moon after we had gone out from the land of Egypt, Jethro and Moses's family were no longer on people's minds. For on that day, we entered the wilderness of Sinai. There was little vegetation, just a plateau covered by sand and rocks as far as the eye could see. In the distance a ring of mountains surrounded us, one higher than the others. It was almost midsummer, and we sweltered in the lack of shade as we encamped in front of Elohim's mountain.

Everyone watched as Moses went up to the mountain. I held tight to Maratti's hand as my feelings fluctuated between excitement, anxiety, and most of all, fear.

72   ASENET

To my relief, Moses soon came down and addressed the people. "This is what GOD told me to say to the house of Jacob and the children of Israel: 'You have seen what I did to the Egyptians, how I bore you on eagles' wings and brought you to Me. Now, if you will obey Me faithfully and keep My covenant, you shall be My treasured possession among all the peoples.'"

I was astonished when all those assembled, including me and the other outsiders, answered as one. "All that GOD has spoken we will do!"

How could I have no doubts whatsoever?

Then Moses warned everyone to be ready for the third day, to wash their clothes, and, to stay pure, the men should not go near a woman. "For on the third day GOD will come down, in the sight of all the people, on Mount Sinai." He continued. "Beware of going up the mountain or touching the border of it. However, when the ram's horn sounds a long blast, you may go up to the mountain."

So I washed our clothes and kept my distance from Maratti. As long as I had wash water, I washed my hair and had Shifra cut it so it hung only to my shoulders. I had no idea what it would be like to see Elohim or if outsiders would even be able to see the Hebrews' god, but I did what Moses told us. I didn't remember ever feeling this nervous, except maybe before my wedding. I kept far back from the mountain.

On the third day, as morning dawned, I woke to thunder and lightning, but it wasn't raining. Curious, I peeked outside the tent and saw a dense cloud on the mountain. But it didn't look right; it whirled and churned. Jagged spears of lightning flashed within it, each followed by an exceedingly loud horn blast that made me, and likely everyone else, tremble. Yet no lightning hit the ground.

I hurriedly dressed and followed as Moses led us out of the camp to stand at the foot of the mountain. Now Mount Sinai was smoking like a

Lightning in clouds over Sinai

74   ASENET

kiln, for Elohim had come down upon it in fire. I was thankful that my family, along with many other outsiders, stood at the rear. Heat rose as if from a giant hearth, but there was no ash in the air or on the ground. The mountain shook violently—as did many people, me included.

The blare of the horn grew louder and louder as Moses went down and spoke gently to the people to calm them. When he finished, there was a vast silence, as if even the land was waiting in suspense.

Then Elohim answered in thunder, saying:

I GOD am your god who brought you out of the land of Egypt, the house of bondage: You shall have no other gods besides Me.

You shall not make for yourself a sculptured image, or any likeness of what is in the heavens above, or on the earth below, or in the waters under the earth. You shall not bow down to them or serve them. For I GOD am an impassioned god, visiting the guilt of the parents upon the children, upon the third and upon the fourth generations of those who reject Me, but showing kindness to the thousandth generation of those who love Me and keep My commandments.

You shall not swear falsely by the name of GOD your god, for GOD will not clear one who swears falsely by that name.

Remember the Sabbath day and keep it holy. Six days you shall labor and do all your work, but the seventh day is a Sabbath of GOD your god; you shall not do any work—you, your son or daughter, your male or female slave, or your cattle, or the stranger who is within your settlements. For in six days GOD made heaven and earth and sea—and all that is in them—and then rested on the seventh day; therefore GOD blessed the Sabbath day and hallowed it.

Honor your father and your mother, that you may long endure on the land that GOD your god is assigning to you.

You shall not murder.

You shall not commit adultery.

You shall not steal.

THE MIDWIVES' ESCAPE   75

You shall not bear false witness against your neighbor.

You shall not covet your neighbor's house: you shall not covet your neighbor's wife, or male or female slave, or ox or donkey, or anything that is your neighbor's.

At first I was too overwhelmed to move or open my eyes. I lay there, face down in the sand, every limb shaking, until I was certain Elohim had finished addressing me. I had no doubt that the words had been directed to me, for it was my mother's voice I'd heard in my head. Tears in my eyes, I slowly looked up and gazed around me in wonder. Some people stood like statues, others were on their knees, but most were lying flat in the dirt.

The mountain's smoking ceased, and the thunder and lightning quieted, and as people recovered, they moved back and stood at a distance from the mountain. Many were crying or had been. I was too stunned to move, but the unborn child in my womb was kicking vigorously.

I heard a woman cry out to Moses, "You speak to us, and we will obey; but do not let Elohim speak to us, lest we die." I lifted my head briefly and saw that it was the white-haired old woman, Serach bat Asher.

"Be not afraid," Moses answered gently. "Elohim has come only in order that you will remember this miraculous day on which you stood before GOD your god, and in order that the awe of Elohim may be ever with you so that you do not go astray."

Then Moses stood quietly, apparently listening to Elohim, for Moses next said to us, "You yourselves have seen and heard Elohim speak to you from the very heavens. Therefore, you shall not make any gods of silver, nor any gods of gold."

When my subdued family shared our evening meal with Pua and Shaul, nobody spoke until I asked, "When Elohim spoke to you, what did you hear?"

76 ASENET

Father replied first. "I heard nine things not to do, and only two that we should." When I gave him a skeptical frown, he replied with a small smile and continued, "One: remember the Sabbath day and keep it holy. Two: honor your father and your mother."

The adults broke the tension by chortling, while I turned to Father and said, "I didn't mean what exactly you heard, but how you perceived it, what voice Elohim used."

There was silence as they each considered this question. "Elohim's voice wasn't always the same," Shifra answered first. "Sometimes—most times—it was loving and encouraging. There was also disappointment and sadness over the commands I'd broken. But there was no anger."

We learned that each of us had received an identical message from Elohim in the voice of a beloved and revered ancestor. Pua had also recognized our mother's voice, as had my daughter, Shifra. Father, Maratti, and Shaul had each heard their own father's voice. The men were surprised that none of us had felt any anger, only disappointment.

"No anger?" Maratti asked in surprise. "Elohim was very angry with Pharaoh."

"That was different," Shaul replied. "We are Elohim's people."

I wasn't quite convinced of that, but Eshkar interrupted my thoughts to say that he and Gitlam weren't sure if it had been their father or uncle talking to them, but we all assured the boys that it had actually been Elohim.

Father smiled at the children and asked if they understood what Elohim had said.

"So nobody is allowed to work on the Sabbath, not even animals?" Gitlam asked.

Shaul nodded and added, "Not even slaves."

Almost simultaneously Shifra and Eshkar asked, "What is adultery?"

THE MIDWIVES' ESCAPE 77

There was a lengthy silence until I replied, "When a man and woman marry, they are only allowed to lie together with each other. If the woman lies with a man who is not her husband, it is adultery."

"Forbidding adultery ensures that a husband is the man who fathers his wife's children," Pua explained.

Shifra looked like she had more questions, but I quickly declared that it had been an exhausting day and we should all make ready for bed. "Poor little Rephaiah can barely keep his eyes open," I whispered. In truth, I couldn't either.

When Maratti and I finally retired to the privacy of our tent, I was still having trouble accepting that the Hebrew god had spoken to me personally and individually. No Egyptian god had ever spoken to me or acknowledged me in any way. It was both an honor and a responsibility. Though the air was warm, I shivered.

Maratti put his arms around me and pulled me close. "Are you chilled?"

I put my arms around him. "No, but I feel less frightened when you hold me."

"Today was quite an awesome, and terrifying, experience," he whispered in my ear. "Not that I'd admit that to anyone except you."

Neither of us pulled away, and Maratti began kissing my ear. When I moaned softly, his lips slowly trailed their way down my neck to my breasts. I pulled him down onto our bedding and, though the waxing moon hadn't yet risen, I closed my eyes.

For the next two weeks, I could tell that people were subdued. Moses and Joshua had gone up the mountain to receive more laws from Elohim, and it was as though our father had left on a journey. It was too soon to receive messages, yet he was missed. When a month had passed with no sign of or from Moses, rumors that he was dead or gravely injured spread through the camp. I didn't know what to believe.

I tried to quell my and the children's anxiety by reminding them, "See, the cloud remains in position above the mountain, and manna appears for us in the morning like usual. The creeks continue flowing down the mountainside to provide us plenty of water." Gitlam sniffed back tears, and I held him close. "Surely Elohim still watches over us."

But the longer Moses was gone, the more men begged Aaron, "Come, make us a god who shall lead us, for Moses—the man who brought us from the land of Egypt—we do not know what has happened to him."

When Aaron saw how enraged the Hebrew men became when he made excuses for his brother's delay, he became afraid and attempted a subterfuge. He told them, "Take off the gold rings that are on the ears of your wives and bring them to me."

I thought he expected that the women would refuse to give their rings up, especially for such an egregious purpose. "Heaven forbid we should make an idol and betray Elohim." We women supported each other. "Who wrought such miracles and mighty deeds on our behalf."

So while some of the Hebrew men took off their own gold earrings and brought them to Aaron, most of the outsider women, including me and Pua, insisted that our husbands not join the increasingly frustrated and angry mob.

I had no difficulty persuading Maratti, who whispered to me, "Don't worry. Joshua will go up the mountain to find Moses and inform him of the danger."

A few days later, Pua ran into our tent, crying. "Can you believe that Aaron, Moses's only brother, has taken the men's jewelry, melted it down, and built a mold to fashion a golden calf?" She sank down on the rug and put her head in her hands.

I didn't want to believe her, until I heard the men chanting, "This is your god, O Israel, who brought you out of the land of Egypt!" I was

THE MIDWIVES' ESCAPE

desperate to see what was going on, but I had been gone only a few moments when Maratti grabbed my arm and pulled me back into our tent.

"Are you out of your mind, Asenet?" His face was red and he was breathing heavily. "You have no idea how dangerous it is down there. Miriam's husband, Hur, couldn't stand it any longer. He rushed into the crowd of men and rebuked them, 'You stiff-necked people! Do you not remember how many miracles Moses performed on your behalf? Did not Elohim command you, "You shall not make any gods of silver, nor any gods of gold"?'"

"I'm sorry." I started to cry. "I'm so frightened I can't think properly."

Then we heard Miriam screaming. "Those evil men, they've slain my husband!"

CHAPTER TEN

SHIFRA

And let them make Me a sanctuary that I may dwell among them.

—Exodus 25:8

NEXT THING WE KNEW, Miriam's granddaughter, Achsah, was leading Miriam back to where the terrified women waited. "The men have gathered against Aaron," Achsah reported. "They warned him, 'If you make a god for us, well and good; but if not, we will do to you what we did to Hur.'"

That evening, to my dismay, Maratti reported that Aaron had not only created a golden calf but had also built an altar before it. "Tomorrow," Aaron had announced, "shall be a festival of GOD!"

Thankfully, nearly all the women, both Hebrew and outsider, either refused or were afraid to attend. As curious as I felt, I made sure to stay away as Hebrew men began bringing sacrifices and burnt offerings to Aaron before dawn. Mother made sure that the four males in our tents stayed away as well.

But my curiosity was too great. After a few days I had to see what the golden calf looked like and how the men were worshipping it. So I slipped away to spy on them.

THE MIDWIVES' ESCAPE

In the camp men were eating and drinking, and some rose to dance around the golden idol. I hadn't seen them earlier, but now there were women dancing too—ones Mother and Pua had called harlots. I didn't know much about them except that they lived together in their own tents without husbands. Suddenly I knew I had to intercept Moses and alert him of the danger. I dared not ask Mother's permission, for she would forbid me to go.

There was only one path up the mountain from the camp, but it took me a while to reach it without letting the men see me. If there was a fork in the trail farther up, hopefully I'd reach Moses first and not have to choose which way to go. I was glad I'd brought a waterskin, not only to slake my thirst, but Mother would see one was missing and understand that I'd taken it.

The sun was almost at its zenith when I saw a good-sized flat stone under a tree ahead. I abruptly realized I was hungry and convinced myself that this would be a good place to eat some cheese and manna. I sat down in the shade and turned my attention to not dropping any food. I was almost finished when I heard an ominous growl. I slowly stood up and looked around.

But I immediately sat down when I saw the two hyenas in the brush. They would catch me if I ran, but perhaps I could climb the tree first.

I was gradually sliding closer to the trunk when an authoritative female voice called out, "Don't move."

I stiffened into a statue, and suddenly the two hyenas lay on the dirt, one with an arrow in its eye and the other with an arrow through its throat. Standing behind me, wiping her hands with satisfaction, was Gudit the Nubian. She wore a man's kilt below her waist. Above was a long cloth wrapped around her back and over her breasts in such a way that it both supported and concealed them.

"What are you doing here?" we each asked the other.

Dead hyenas on the trail up to Mount Sinai

THE MIDWIVES' ESCAPE   83

My mouth was so dry I could barely speak. "I had to find Moses and warn him."

"I saw you sneak off and decided to follow . . ." She looked at me askance. "Just in case. Apparently you didn't know that Joshua headed up this way an hour before you."

I remembered my manners. "Thank you . . . so very much."

Gudit smiled. "Don't worry, I won't tell anyone about meeting you here. You can thank me by retrieving my arrows."

It was a gruesome business, but it was fascinating to examine an arrow up close. Thankfully neither arrow was damaged. I was likely in enough trouble already. I washed my hands in the creek that bordered the trail and was refilling the waterskin when I heard a man's voice coming from around the bend.

It was Joshua. "Do you hear all those boisterous people?" he asked. "Men are shouting and yelling in the camp."

An older man, undoubtedly Moses, answered. "No, it is singing that I hear! Men and women singing."

Their conversation ended abruptly when they saw me and Gudit. Moses was carrying two enormous stone tablets, one in each arm. I could see there was something inscribed on them, but the writing was mostly hidden by Moses's arms. Both men stared at Gudit with identical admiring expressions, the same look Maratti wore when he watched Mother preparing for bed. Somehow I knew I had seen too much and averted my eyes.

As soon as we came close enough to see the calf and the people dancing around it, Moses flew into a rage. He hurled the tablets from his hands and shattered them at the foot of the mountain while the men groveled before him. He stomped into camp, and though I never imagined that he, being so old, could be that strong, he picked up the golden calf and threw it in the fire. By this time most of the women had crept back to see what was happening, as had the men who had not joined the revelers.

I was filled with relief to see that instead of worshipping the idol with the men, Maratti and Grandfather were standing next to Mother along with Shaul's and Zizi's families. I hurried to join Mother, who gave me a look that said I would be in trouble later. So I stood next to Haggith. We all watched in awe as Moses ground the remains of the burnt idol to powder and strewed it upon the creek's water so everyone had to drink it.

Then Moses turned to Aaron. "What did this people do to you that you have brought such great sin upon them?"

Aaron's face paled. "Don't be enraged. You know this people is bent on evil. They said to me, 'Make us a god who shall lead us; for Moses— the man who brought us from the land of Egypt—we do not know what has happened to him.' So I told them, 'Whoever has gold, take it off!' They gave it to me and I hurled it into the fire and out came this calf!"

I knew for a fact that Aaron had made the mold that formed the golden calf, and I expected that many other people knew this too. It made me angry that nobody challenged Aaron's word that he had merely collected people's gold and then, after he'd thrown it in the fire, the calf had suddenly appeared. Now I trusted him even less than when I learned he'd sent Zipporah and her sons back home without telling Moses.

We were still camped at the foot of Mount Sinai when a plague came from drinking water containing the powdered remains of the golden calf. Our family viewed this as a punishment for sinning with the calf that Aaron had made because their symptoms were clearly in proportion to their sinfulness. The men who collected the gold but didn't worship the calf suffered agonizing intestinal distress for weeks. Other men, who hadn't participated in building the calf, but neither had they protested against building it, were ill only until the following Sabbath.

THE MIDWIVES' ESCAPE

Most of the women and all the children were spared any suffering. However, Mother and Aunt Pua quickly ascertained that the women, including themselves, whose symptoms were primarily vomiting, were not being punished, but conversely, were in the early weeks of pregnancy. My apprentice midwife duties now took up most of my time as I treated the most severely afflicted. Many of these women had previously been barren, and they rejoiced over their nausea when I explained that such women usually bore the healthiest babies.

I soon discovered that the husbands of the pregnant women, like Maratti and Shaul, had not participated in the golden calf debacle. I also learned that women who had given gold to the worst of the revelers had miscarried. Elohim had thus rewarded those who refrained from evil and punished the others.

What I never learned or understood was why so many Hebrews who'd experienced Elohim's power and miracles firsthand demanded a golden idol to worship instead.

Mother may have wanted to restrict me to our tents to punish me for going up the mountain by myself, but she needed me to help the pregnant women. Thus I enjoyed free access throughout the camp, where I overheard much grumbling that none of the Levites had been punished, though they had not tried to prevent Aaron from making the calf. Rumors even spread that Levites would be appointed priests to serve in Elohim's Tabernacle when Moses returned. But I heard no one dare voice their fiercest fury against Aaron, who had actually built the calf and led people into sin yet had not been punished at all. The closest thing to condemnation came from his sister, Miriam, who, gossip held, shunned Aaron as much as possible to keep from breaking down and publicly accusing him of responsibility for Hur's death.

She took to frequenting the area outside the camp where we outsiders had our tents to the dual effect of meeting some of the various peoples who'd left Egypt with the Hebrews and of avoiding those involved in building the calf. She took an interest in our goats, saying

86 SHIFRA

she found it soothing to sit and spin the kids' soft inner hair into supple wool thread.

"Miriam just needs some peace and quiet, away from all the Hebrews who wanted her to intercede for them with Moses or Aaron," Mother told me.

One morning Miriam was already here when I returned from bringing a strong antinausea potion to a pregnant woman who could barely keep any food down. Miriam and Mother were sitting close to each other on floor cushions near the hearth, having what looked to be a private conversation while they shared a bowl of cheese. Hoping to eavesdrop, I walked to the farthest loom and continued weaving where someone else had left off.

"You don't need to go away, Shifra," Mother called to me. "What Miriam is saying will interest you too."

I pulled a cushion near them and sat down. "When I first heard your mother called Asenet," Miriam began, "I knew the name sounded familiar, but I couldn't place it until today when I asked her about its history."

"I told her that my great-grandmother was also named Asenet," Mother said. "I never knew her, but my mother took great pride that Asenet was the adopted daughter of Potiphar, captain of the Pharaoh's guard."

"Like I'm the adopted daughter of Maratti," I interrupted proudly, "who used to be captain of the Pharaoh's guard."

Miriam smiled and nodded. "That Asenet was adopted as an infant because Potiphar's wife was barren. She was born to Jacob's daughter Dinah, whose intended husband was killed by her brothers Simeon and Levi. Dinah concealed her pregnancy and gave birth after Jacob's family reached Egypt. There Dinah set baby Asenet down beside a wall where Egyptians left foundlings for barren women to adopt."

Mother shook her head in astonishment. "You mean my great-grandmother Asenet was a Hebrew?" Then she turned to me. "Shifra, go get Pua. She needs to hear this too."

I didn't give my aunt any explanation, only that she needed to come to our tent right away. When we returned, Maratti and Grandfather were also waiting.

Miriam repeated what she'd already told the rest of us before continuing. "One day Potiphar went for his usual walk near the wall, hoping as always that he'd find a baby his wife would like. When he heard the infant crying, he called for his servants to bring the child to him. Even then, Asenet was beautiful."

Grandfather blinked back tears. "Yes, my grandmother was a stunning woman. No wonder a high official like Yusuf married her." He sighed and turned to Miriam. "Sorry for interrupting you. Please continue."

"Potiphar brought her home to his wife, and they found her a wet nurse. As she grew, Potiphar and his wife raised Asenet as their own daughter. When she was grown, Potiphar married her to a man named Joseph, one of Pharaoh's counselors, whom you knew as Yusuf." Miriam paused and locked eyes with Grandfather. "We Hebrews know they had two sons, Menachem and Ephraim, but until today I didn't know they'd also had a daughter."

"My mother, Shifra," Grandfather acknowledged. "She married an Egyptian wainwright, who taught me his trade."

"Our greatest warrior, Joshua, is an Ephraimite," Miriam said. "Your family should be proud to be his cousins." Then she turned to Mother. "This cheese is delicious, Asenet. You should be proud of that too."

Mother blushed. "My daughter, Shifra, makes more of it than I do. Shifra should teach the women we gave our excess doelings to how to make cheese."

When Miriam looked at her questioningly, Mother reminded her, along with Maratti and Grandfather, that we had donated some of our goats to the families whose men had been disabled in the battles with the Amalekites.

Two days later, six women met at our tent, each with a clay pot of fresh goat's milk, a pot holder, a long wooden spoon, and a length of cheesecloth. I helped them place their pots on the hearth, which was banked to a low heat, and sit down nearby.

"Watch carefully that the milk does not reach a full boil," I advised them. "Nor do you want the milk to burn on the bottom of the pot, so keep the heat low and be patient. Once the milk reaches the right temperature, gentle bubbles will start to form."

Each woman took hold of her pot holder, and we waited for the bubbles to appear. "There, now remove your pot from the heat," I told them. "Place it here on the table, add a small cup of vinegar, and give the mixture a quick stir with your wooden spoon." I demonstrated with our pot while I observed the other women, correcting those who stirred too slowly or too vigorously.

"Now let it sit undisturbed until loose curds form on the surface. During this time, drape your cheesecloth into several layers, leaving it large enough that you can pull the sides up around the curds," I said as I showed them how to do it. "Then hang the cheesecloth over a large bowl and pour the pot of goat milk into the cheesecloth to catch the solid curds."

Once they had done that to my satisfaction, I continued. "Now pull the sides of the cheesecloth up and around the curds, forming a pouch. Then tie the pouch to hang from your spoon's handle, and balance the spoon handle over a pot or a tall jar. Let the cheesecloth pouch full of curds hang like this, undisturbed, for an hour or so while the remaining moisture drips out."

Good hostesses, Mother and I served a small meal of lentil stew and baked manna while the women exchanged gossip. Who was pregnant; who wanted to be but was not; whose baby girl had been weaned at two years so the mother could quickly become pregnant again, hopefully with a boy; and who hoped to nurse her son until his fourth year to avoid another pregnancy. I eagerly listened to learn whose daughter had become betrothed to whose son, but to my disappointment, the subject never came up.

After all the whey had dripped out, we gently squeezed our pouches to force a few more drops of moisture out. Then we spooned the curds back into our bowls and seasoned them with salt and herbs.

"Now massage the salt and seasonings into the curds with your hands, almost like you're kneading dough. This helps the texture of the curds become softer, smoother, and creamier," I explained. "Use your hands to pat and roll the curds into whatever shape you like. Or you can just smooth them back into your bowl."

"When can we taste them?" a young woman a few years my senior asked.

"You can eat the cheese now," I replied. "But the flavor improves if you let it sit overnight in the cold."

No one could resist the temptation to taste their cheese immediately, and when we were finished eating, we pulled out our distaffs and spun wool thread as the subject changed to Elohim's latest instructions to Moses: that everyone whose heart is so moved should bring gifts of materials needed for the Tabernacle. The list was long: gold, silver, and copper; blue, purple, and crimson yarns; fine linen; goat's hair; tanned ram skins, tachash skins, and acacia wood; clear oil of beaten olives for lighting and kindling the lamps; spices for the anointing oil and the aromatic incense; lapis lazuli and other gemstones for the ephod and breastplate.

I gasped in amazement. So many items depended on women's generosity. "What are tachash skins?" I asked. I'd never even heard the word before.

Most of the woman shrugged, revealing that they didn't know either. However one older woman said she thought it was some kind of sea creature with waterproof skin that Moses could use for the Tabernacle's roof.

"That's a lot of things," Mother whispered. "We will need more wagons if we're going to haul the Tabernacle with us from one camp to the next."

Everyone quieted when I asked, "It will be difficult enough to find tachash skins. Where are we going to find enough skilled artisans to make all that Elohim has commanded?" I wasn't skilled enough to provide anything on Moses's list except goat's hair, which didn't require any skill beyond knowing how to use a scissors.

I was ashamed of being so useless.

CHAPTER ELEVEN

SHIFRA

Now Aaron's sons Nadav and Avihu each took his fire pan, put fire in it, and laid incense on it. And they offered before GOD alien fire, which had not been enjoined upon them. And fire came forth from GOD and consumed them; thus they died in the Presence of GOD.

—Leviticus 10:1–2

To most people's surprise, including mine, within a week everyone who excelled in ability and everyone whose spirit was moved, both men and women, began to bring offerings for making the Tent of Meeting. Grandfather and Shaul brought in two wagonloads of acacia wood, the boards cut to the needed sizes. Mother and Pua discussed how many of the gold items taken from their deceased Egyptian clients they should give without impoverishing our families.

I was relieved when Mother said that we would keep any truly beautiful or ornamental pieces that were worth far more than just the weight of their gold. There was a beautiful gold cup encrusted with gemstones that I hoped would be part of my dowry.

Pua nodded. "Plain gold plates or bowls should be the first to go."

"Along with simple earrings or other unadorned jewelry," Mother agreed. Eventually they decided to give about half the gold they'd acquired, with the idea that they could give more later if necessary.

But that wasn't necessary. The following week Moses proudly announced, "People are bringing more than is needed. Let no man or woman make further effort toward gifts for the sanctuary!"

That very day work on the Tabernacle began. All the skilled women brought what they had spun with their own hands, in blue, purple, and crimson yarns, and in fine linen. The women who excelled in the skill of spinning goat's hair brought that yarn.

I was certainly not in the first category of skilled women, but maybe I could qualify in the second. To my distress, when I saw other women's goat's hair thread, I knew I would never be able to match its quality. All I could do was slink back to my bed in shame.

I'd lain there for maybe an hour when I heard Eshkar at the entrance. "Shifra, are you in there?"

"Go away," I called out.

"What's wrong? Are you hurt or ill? Should I get your mother?"

"I'm not hurt or ill. And I certainly don't need Mother."

"But something's wrong. If you don't tell me now, I'll stay here until you do."

I would be even more ashamed if anyone saw Eshkar standing outside my tent. "I'm coming out," I told him, and I sat down near the hearth. He sat near me and waited patiently for me to speak.

I couldn't stand the silence. "I'm completely useless. All the other women's gifts are better than mine. I can't even spin decent goat's hair thread." I stopped talking when I felt tears welling in my eyes.

"But any female knows how to spin," he protested. "You know how to make goat-milk cheese, and more important, you know how to heal injured people and deliver babies. Think of all the warriors, the mothers and infants, whose lives you've saved."

His expression was so earnest my heart swelled with gratitude. "Thank you. I needed that." I reached out my hand and he pulled me up to stand.

THE MIDWIVES' ESCAPE   93

He asked me, "Shall we walk down and see all the other gifts?" But he did not let go of my hand.

Everyone worked so diligently that, five months later, in mid-Adar, all the work of the Tabernacle and the Tent of Meeting was complete. Everyone, including my family, came to watch as the Levites brought the pieces of Tabernacle and all its furnishings to Moses: clasps, planks, bars, posts, and sockets; the coverings of tanned ram and tachash skins, and the curtain for the screen; the Ark of the Covenant and its poles and cover; the table and all its utensils; the pure lampstand, its lamps, and all their fittings, and the oil for lighting; the altar of gold, the oil for anointing, the aromatic incense, and the screen for the entrance of the tent; the copper altar with its copper grating, poles, and all its utensils, the laver and its stand; the hangings of the enclosure, its posts and sockets, the screen for the gate of the enclosure, its cords and pegs—all the furnishings for the service of the Tabernacle. Last of all, the sacral vestments that Aaron and his sons would wear during their priestly services.

When Moses saw that people had performed all the tasks—as GOD had commanded—Moses raised his hands to bless us. I closed my eyes and felt a warm sensation on my shoulders, as if I were standing in sunshine. Only it was winter.

"May GOD bless you and protect you!

"May GOD deal kindly and graciously with you!

"May GOD bestow [divine] favor upon you and grant you peace!"

Slowly the warmth faded away, and when I opened my eyes, Moses's hands were down at his sides.

On the eighth day Moses called Aaron and his sons and the elders of Israel. He told Aaron to speak to the Israelites, saying: "Take a he-goat for a sin offering; a kid and a lamb, yearlings without blemish, for a burnt offering; and a meal offering with oil mixed in. For today GOD will appear to you."

The crowd watching Aaron approach the altar and slaughter his he-goat sin offering was much smaller than when the Tabernacle was consecrated, but Eshkar, Gitlam, and I went to see the ceremony anyway. I was so squeamish that I closed my eyes as the knife was lowered, and I did the same when Aaron slaughtered the goat for his sin offering. By the time he brought forward the people's offering, the altar was covered in blood, and I was getting bored. I was relieved when finally he brought out the meal offering, which he turned into smoke on the altar. Finally Aaron presented the burnt offering.

Suddenly the Presence of GOD appeared, and immediately fire came forth and consumed the burnt offering. There was utter silence for a moment after people saw this. Then they gave a great shout and fell to the ground.

Now Aaron's sons Nadav and Avihu each took his fire pan, put fire in it, and laid incense on it, and then they offered an alien fire before GOD, which had not been enjoined upon them. We watched with horror as two tendrils of fire came forth from GOD and entered Aaron's sons' nostrils, consuming them. Thus they died before GOD.

I couldn't believe my eyes. The corpses' skin was burnt black and their eyes were solid white like boiled eggs, but their tunics were not even singed. Men and women both began to scream and cry, and some people fainted. Aaron's wife, Elisheva, tore her hair and collapsed on the ground, while her daughter sank down beside her weeping in terror. I had to grab hold of Eshkar's arm to keep from falling myself. Poor Gitlam was crying, having vomited all over his new tunic.

But Aaron stood there staring at his dead sons' bodies, silent and motionless as a statue.

Moses called to two of his cousins. "Come forward and carry your kinsmen away from the sanctuary to a place outside the camp."

THE MIDWIVES' ESCAPE   95

They came and carried them away by their tunics, so as not to touch the bodies' unclean flesh.

Then Moses warned Aaron and his sons Eleazar and Ithamar, "Do not bare your heads, dishevel your hair, or rend your clothes. But your kin, all the house of Israel, shall bewail the burning that GOD has wrought." Then he added, "When you have finished purging the altar, a live goat shall be brought forward. Aaron shall lay both his hands upon the head of the live goat and confess over it all the iniquities and transgressions of the Israelites, whatever their sins, putting them on the head of the goat; and it shall be sent off to the wilderness. Thus the goat shall carry all their iniquities to an inaccessible region."

There was a universal sigh of relief from everyone still standing. Then Moses concluded, "This shall be to you a law for all time: In the seventh month, on the tenth day of the month, you shall practice self-denial; and you shall do no manner of work, neither the citizen nor the foreigner who resides among you. For on this day atonement shall be made for you to purify you of all your sins, for GOD is compassionate and gracious, slow to anger, abounding in kindness and faithfulness, extending kindness to the thousandth generation, forgiving iniquity, transgression, and sin. It shall be a Sabbath of complete rest for you, and you shall practice self-denial."

The next night Mother went into labor. She was confident I could handle the delivery by myself, but Pua came over anyway, insisting it was only a precaution.

"Do you want my Taweret amulet?" Pua held out the small greenish-turquoise stone carved to depict a bipedal female hippopotamus with pendulous female human breasts, limbs and paws of a lion, and the back and tail of a Nile crocodile.

I immediately recognized the ancient Egyptian goddess of childbirth and fertility. I'd never assisted at a birth where the laboring woman

Taweret amulet

THE MIDWIVES' ESCAPE 97

didn't hold one of the protective amulets. We'd just been blessed by Elohim, however, who forbade the worship of idols and other gods. How could Pua, married to a Hebrew, suggest such a transgression?

More importantly, would Mother give in to tradition and take the Taweret stone?

But Mother raised her hand and beckoned away the amulet. "Why don't you go sit with Maratti and Grandfather to keep them calm?" she suggested, although it sounded like an order to me.

Truthfully, I'd have felt calmer if Pua weren't there watching me.

For the first few hours, there wasn't much for me to do. Mother joined me in counting the time between contractions, ostensibly as part of my training. But soon their frequency increased so rapidly, along with her pain, that she was forced to focus all her attention on relaxing in between contractions. With my hand on her belly, I could feel them growing stronger along with her screams.

Mother had always made me step away when it was time for her patients to push, but this time she grasped my hand and held it tightly. "Should I call Pua?" I asked, trying to hide my anxiety.

Mother wasn't deceived. "Not yet," she whispered between gasps. "Wait until the head is born."

Until the head is born! How long will that be?

Thankfully it wasn't long until she squeezed my hand hard, took a deep breath, pushed, and then loosened her grip. I was familiar with this step; it had been my task to keep the woman calm while Mother observed the womb's opening. Now it was my turn to watch for the first glimpse of my new sibling.

"I see dark hair," I squealed. I'd wanted to keep my voice down but I was too excited. "The baby is facing down," I told her, then let my breath out in relief. Most babies were born face down; it was the easiest position for mothers to push one out.

It was only two hours later when Mother clutched my hand so tightly I thought my bones might break. But abruptly the pressure

98   SHIFRA

ceased as the baby's entire head popped out. As I'd been taught, I cradled it gently with one hand, my other hand ready to catch the rest of the body. My emotions were at odds as I eagerly waited to catch sight of the infant's genitals. I wanted a sister, but I knew that Mother, Grandfather, and most of all, Maratti, wanted a son. I called for Pua to come in; let her deliver the news to those waiting outside.

My heart swelled with happiness when I saw that my desire had been granted. But it swelled further when Mother brought my new sister to her breast and I saw the baby girl latch on and begin suckling. That meant Mother was safe and well and that the infant was too.

Not that the situation couldn't change at any time.

I smiled when I heard Pua addressing the others. "Don't fret that it's a girl. An elder daughter is a blessing for more sons to come, so she can help raise them." I'd heard Mama and Pua agreeing that if this baby was female, they would name her Tantana after Maratti's mother and arrange for her to marry Pua's young son, Rephaiah. Then their grandchildren would be Hebrews.

I could help raise this child too. Although by the time Mother had given Maratti several sons, I hoped to be too busy raising my own children to help her much.

On the first day of Nisan, almost a year since we'd fled Egypt, Moses finished setting up the Tabernacle. We were still on the plain below Mount Sinai, and it seemed to me that the entire population had come to watch as Moses brought Aaron and his sons forward to the entrance. No one made a sound while Moses placed the white sacral vestments on Aaron and then anointed him and consecrated him that he would serve Elohim as high priest. Next Moses brought Aaron's sons forward and put the blue robes of Levitical priests on them. These were seamlessly woven garments trimmed on the bottom hem with alternating bells and pomegranate tassels of sky-blue, dark-red, and crimson wool, the most beautiful men's garments I'd ever seen. Once their tunics were on, Moses anointed them as he had anointed their father.

After this, the chieftains of the tribes approached and brought their offerings: six beautifully polished draft carts and twelve magnificent oxen. I felt so proud when they brought them before the Tabernacle, for Grandfather and Eshkar had made those carts—although I had helped. Moses took the carts and the oxen and gave them to the Levites for when it was time to move the Tabernacle to a new camp.

As soon as the Tabernacle was set up, the cloud moved to cover it, and in the evening it rested above the Tabernacle as a pillar of fire until morning. Then the Israelites set up camp around the Tent of Meeting, under the banners of their tribe. It was a grand, and impressive, procession. The tribe of Judah, whose banner had a proud lion's head in the center, camped on the east side. The tribe of Issachar camped next to them, a donkey on their banner, and below them was the tribe of Zebulon with a tall ship on their banner. To the west camped the tribes of Ephraim, Manasseh, and Benjamin. The tribes of Dan, Asher, and Naphtali camped on the north, with the tribes of Reuben, Simeon, and Gad on the south side. I was very proud of Simeon's banner, which we could see from our tents. It depicted a splendid castle surrounded by water.

The Levites camped in the center, surrounding the Tabernacle. "Should the Tabernacle be attacked and the other Israelites fall defending it, the Levites are supposed to be the last guards to protect it," Maratti told me. Then he rolled his eyes and added, "Except that the Levites are no warriors; most don't know one end of a sword from the other. If and when our camp is attacked, it will be my troops who defend us."

The next afternoon, Haggith asked me to meet her outside the Tabernacle at sunset. Her voice was shaking, and she kept looking around as if she expected someone to interrupt us.

"What is the matter?" I asked, and when she said nothing, I said, "What happened? You can tell me."

"Walk around the Tabernacle," she told me. "Make sure nobody is nearby."

Now I was more concerned than curious. I did as she asked and said, "I don't see or hear anyone."

"Sit with me." Haggith lowered herself to the ground. "Fewer people will see us."

I joined her on the sand and waited silently. As I hoped, she started talking.

"You must believe what I'm going to tell you."

"Of course," I replied. "And I won't tell anyone else."

She took a deep breath before continuing. "Today I saw what is inside the Tabernacle—the curtains, the twenty-eight cubits of fine linen cloths with blue, purple, and crimson yarns worked into designs of cherubim. They were coupled together by fifty gold clasps so that the Tabernacle became one whole piece." She sighed with awe. "It was magnificent."

"But only priests are allowed in there," I protested. "How did you get in?"

"While the other priests left to eat their midday meal," she began, "one of them—I don't know his name—stayed behind with me at the gate." She stopped and blushed.

"And?" I urged her to continue; I had a bad feeling about this.

"He asked if I wanted to see all the beautiful things inside the Tabernacle." Haggith averted her eyes, and her voice quickened. "He said it wouldn't be sinful because he, a priest, was with me. He could tell I did want to see them because he told me that if I would lie with him, he would bring me in."

I gasped in alarm. "Don't tell me you did what he wanted."

She shook her head. "I'm not that gullible. I agreed to lie with him *after* he took me in and I'd seen everything."

THE MIDWIVES' ESCAPE   101

"You were inside the Holy of Holies!" When she nodded, I demanded, "How is it that you're not dead? I thought only Moses and Aaron are allowed in there."

"Only he was completely inside. I looked in where he unclasped the curtains."

"So what did you see?"

"The most important thing inside the Tabernacle is the Ark, which contains the Tablets of the Covenant." Haggith's voice softened. "A big box made of acacia wood and overlaid with pure gold—inside and out—it is amazing. There are four gold rings attached to its four feet."

"Whatever for?"

"For carrying the Ark—which the priests do with acacia-wood poles, also overlaid with gold," Haggith replied, her eyes wide at the memory. "Even more beautiful, there were two golden cherubim facing each other on the Ark's cover, their wings spread out to shield it." She sighed with pleasure. "In the anteroom going into the Holy of Holies there were seven lamps mounted to light the Ark's front side—all of pure gold. The way the gold glinted in the sunset was incredibly beautiful."

I had difficulty visualizing the six-branched gold lampstand with three branches on each side, each branch with three cups shaped like almond blossoms with calyxes and petals, but I didn't ask for Haggith to describe it again.

"The final piece, one of the most beautiful items there, was the curtain," she concluded, "made of fine twisted linen with a design of cherubim woven from blue, purple, and crimson yarns. It hung from gold hooks on four posts of acacia wood overlaid with gold, making a partition between the Holy, where regular priests go, and the Holy of Holies, where the Ark sat behind it."

"I thought only Moses and Aaron were permitted to go there," I interrupted. Then I asked, "How did you avoid the priest?"

"I didn't have to do anything. I backed away from the curtain, and when he came after me, he dropped dead. I ran as fast as I could and

102   SHIFRA

here I am." She heaved a sigh of relief. "I guess Moses or Aaron will find him in the morning."

But there was no alarm in the morning, nor any time that day. Two days later the camp was gone, replaced by flat desert sand. Levites had taken down the Tabernacle and carted it away. Families like mine, who had wagons and donkeys to pull them, carried little in their arms besides the infants born that spring. The majority, who had no wagons or carts, were forced to carry their babies and small children in addition to their tents and contents.

As before, we and Maratti's men, many of whom were now married, set up our tents to the south of Simeon and Gad, just outside the camp. We also provided several empty tents nearby for women in childbirth, whom Moses said were impure for seven days if they bore a male and for fourteen days if a female, and thus they had to dwell apart outside the camp. For my family and other foreign women, this was no inconvenience. We lived outside the camp all the time.

A short distance away were tents for menstruants, who were impure for seven days after their regular bleeding began. From what I'd seen, these women were glad to live apart for a week. I could hear them singing, dancing, and telling stories—it sounded like a weeklong party. I looked forward to my first menses, when I could join them.

Moses hadn't specified where outside the camp these unclean people had to dwell, so Mother and Pua took advantage of their midwife status to situate the childbirth tents near ours. They also insisted that those unclean from skin diseases such as leprosy should dwell as far away from these women and their babies as possible. Unfortunately there was nothing any of us could do about where the latrines were located. Just beyond each of the four sides of the camp, behind the three tribes' tents, were long trenches littered with shovels stuck into

THE MIDWIVES' ESCAPE   103

the ground. Everyone, even the priests, was expected to dig holes for their own excrement and then cover them over afterward.

In the second year, on the twentieth day of the second month, the cloud lifted from the Tabernacle and the Israelites prepared to leave the Sinai wilderness. Moses came to where Hobab the Midianite, son of Moses's father-in-law, was staying with the unmarried Hittites outside the camp. The Hittites and Gadites were outside training, so, curious as usual, I stole up behind the tent to watch and listen.

Earlier I would have expected Haggith to join me, but she was of marriageable age now, so she had joined widows and other unmarried young women who performed the task of washing the feet of priests and other men bringing sacrifices at the entrance of the Tabernacle. So many men had died in battle or in the golden calf massacre the previous year that this was a single woman's best hope for enticing one of the men to marry her. Haggith would have preferred an unmarried man, but she sadly accepted that many men would be taking second wives.

I recognized Moses's voice. "We will soon be setting out for the place that GOD has promised us. Come with us, Hobab, and we will be generous with you, for GOD has promised to be generous to Israel."

"I cannot go," Hobab replied. "I must return to my land and my kindred."

"Your kindred? You told me Jethro and Zipporah were dead."

I barely stifled a gasp of surprise. Jethro was old, but Zipporah was—my thoughts were interrupted as Hobab continued. "Your sons live with me now."

I expected Moses to ask after them, but he said instead, "Please do not leave us. You know where we should camp in the wilderness and can be our guide."

I couldn't hear Hobab's reply, but I did hear Moses exit the tent and head toward the Levites' camp. When I no longer heard his heavy footsteps, I stood up and turned to go back to my family's tent.

But Gudit the Nubian blocked my path and gave me a stern look. "Tell no one what you heard," she warned me. "Not even after Hobab has left."

My anger kindled at her distrust. "I am not a child who babbles everything she hears to others. I am a midwife's apprentice, so I hear women in labor disclose all sorts of secrets." I stood tall and glared at her. "My mother has trained me well to never share any secret I learn in the childbirth tent, or elsewhere."

CHAPTER TWELVE

SHIFRA

There GOD spoke to Moses, saying, "Send agents to scout the land of Canaan, which I am giving to the Israelite people. Send one partici- pant from each of their tribes, each one a chieftain among them."

—Numbers 13:2

WE MARCHED FROM THE mountain of GOD a distance of three days. GOD's cloud kept above us by day, as we moved on, but it was small protection against the heat and bright sun. From dawn to dusk we kept walking until we stopped to set up the Tabernacle. After over a year of doing nothing strenuous, most people were not as strong as when they were slaves, especially the Levites—who now erected the Tabernacle and took it down every day. Yet to be fair, neither the Levites nor other people had carried as much when we fled Egypt, whereas now they lugged heavy tents, tent poles, and rugs. People took to complaining bitterly, though instead of groaning about their sore feet and backs, they longingly recalled the fish they used to eat in Egypt and remi- nisced about the cucumbers, melons, leeks, onions, and garlic they had enjoyed there.

Apparently GOD heard and was furious, because a fire broke out against the ones who groused the most. But people cried out to

Cloud over the tabernacle in the Sinai wilderness

THE MIDWIVES' ESCAPE   107

Moses, Moses prayed to GOD, and the fire died down. The next day we stopped to camp at Hazeroth, where Grandfather and Eshkar were overwhelmed by orders for wagons and handcarts.

That day Moses sent out men of consequence, leaders of the Israelites, saying, "Go up into the Negev and on into the hill country and see what kind of land it is. Are the people who dwell in it strong or weak, few or many? Is the country in which they dwell good or bad? Are the towns they live in open or fortified? Is the soil rich or poor? Is it wooded or not? And take pains to bring back some of the fruit of the land."

It was time to begin taking possession of the Promised Land.

Finally, I thought.

While the scouts were away, there was little else to do but wait and gossip. For weeks I listened to all the varied speculations as to why Nadav and Avihu had died. The fire had consumed Aaron's sons so quickly, so suddenly, that only priests were close enough to see what had happened. Most priests were too traumatized to recall the details of what they'd seen, though that didn't stop them from insisting that Nadav and Avihu must have done something wrong that led to their deaths.

"Elohim declared to Moses that He would send His own fire to consume the sacrifice as a sign of His Presence," these priests reminded everyone who would listen. "But when Nadav and Avihu lit the offering themselves, they had prepared the incense on kindling of their own, not on the holy incense from the sacred altar. Don't you understand?" they challenged everyone. "Aaron's sons spurned the command to wait for holy fire and offered incense with profane fire. That is why they were punished."

The mystery fascinated me, although it bored the rest of my family. I tended to agree with the seventy elders who had accompanied Moses, Aaron, Nadav, and Avihu up Mount Sinai. They reported that Nadav and Avihu had seen Elohim with great clarity, walking on a pavement of sapphire stone. They had even shared a meal in Elohim's presence without being harmed as a result. Surely their great enthusiasm to offer the Tabernacle's first sacrifice had caused them to err, but just as surely Elohim would not have killed them for that.

I noted that when their bodies were carried away by their tunics, Nadav and Avihu were naked underneath. Yet Elohim had commanded that linen breeches must be worn by Aaron and his sons when they entered the Tabernacle or approached the altar. These breeches should extend from the hips to the thighs to cover their nakedness so they do not incur punishment and die. But some old men chastised me, saying that the breeches were there originally but had been burnt off by Elohim's fire.

Women, on the other hand, suggested that Nadav and Avihu had been punished for not marrying and procreating as Elohim had commanded, and their very public deaths came as a clear warning to the remaining unmarried men not to be too picky in choosing wives. A pious minority disputed that Aaron's sons' deaths were a punishment at all. Nadav and Avihu's dying had been painless and, having seen Elohim and the heavenly sapphire pavement, they could no longer abide in the earthly realm.

I ended up agreeing with the many who whispered that it was Aaron who was being punished for instigating the golden calf—by having his sons die before his very eyes.

Eventually I lost interest in the bored men's speculations. My aunt Pua gave birth to her second son. Meanwhile, Mother needed to nurse Tantana every few hours and to try to get as much sleep as possible, while Pua had not only a newborn but also her son Rephaiah, who was too young to be left alone. So they were forced to rely on me to take on more of our midwife duties, a responsibility I relished. Still, Mother and I were regularly away from our own tents during the night.

So it happened that one night I had no sooner stepped outside after cleaning up from another uneventful birth than I heard hoofbeats. I stood still until I knew they were coming in my direction. Then I

THE MIDWIVES' ESCAPE   109

hurried toward the sounds, hoping I could encounter the rider and beg a ride back to my tent. The only people who possessed horses were the Nubians, and I had no fear of sharing a horse with a woman. Mother had often done that at night to avoid walking to our tent in the dark.

The moon was nearly full so I easily recognized Gudit as her horse slowed for me. Mother had told me in confidence that Gudit spent many evenings in Moses's tent, learning Elohim's commandments so she could bring them back to her people. I said nothing more than thank you when Gudit helped me up to sit behind her.

After a little while, during which time I said nothing, Gudit asked me, "Aren't you curious about where I go at night?"

"Of course," I admitted. "I like secrets."

We rode in silence until we neared the Nubians' tents. "There has been much talk about my nocturnal rides, so I have decided to inform you. Can I can trust you to spread the truth and defend my honor?"

"Gladly." I leaned forward to hear her better.

"I am my people's oldest princess," Gudit began, "and I expect to become queen when my mother dies. During the last few years, I have seen that the Hebrew god, Elohim, is more powerful than any other people's gods. I have personally experienced the miracles and wonders He did for His people."

"As have I," I agreed.

"To get back to why I'm riding around the camp at night," Gudit continued, "I spend most evenings with Moses studying Elohim's teachings: His laws and commandments, what He expects from His people, how they can best follow His ways. Then I can teach these things to my people when I return so Elohim can be our god too."

My jaw dropped. "Return to Nubia? But I thought you and Moses were married."

"Why should we not marry? Zipporah is dead," Gudit challenged me. "Any children I had with Moses would be Levites and thus suitable to be our priests."

I thought about this for a while before replying. "Moses is a grown man; what he does is his own business. He answers only to Elohim.

"Moses is a profoundly unhappy and lonely man. He was content to remain a shepherd in Midian with his wife and sons. He never wanted to return to Egypt, and he wanted even less to lead the Hebrews out of slavery to freedom in another land. Except perhaps for Joshua, he has no friends. The other Levites resent him, especially Aaron."

"But Aaron is his brother," I protested.

"His *older* brother," Gudit countered. "Hebrews privilege the eldest son. Among other perquisites, they inherit twice what other sons do. Yet Elohim has chosen Moses as his favorite and speaks through him. It is a heavy burden."

"Which you help lighten."

"True, I lighten his burden, but I also give him some pleasure." She quickly added, "Not just physical pleasure, but the pleasure of teaching a student who is eager to learn. Levites learn Elohim's laws and commandments because they must; I learn them because I love learning."

Gudit's face lit up as she described her studies with Moses. No wonder they spent nights together. Until now I had never thought of him as a real person, as a human being with needs like other people. Suddenly I felt sorry for him.

I felt even more sorry for Moses when the scouts came back.

CHAPTER THIRTEEN

ASENET

At the end of forty days they returned from scouting the land. They went straight to Moses and Aaron and the whole Israelite community at Kadesh in the wilderness of Paran. They made their report to them and to the whole community.

—Numbers 13:25–26

MARATTI AND I were eager to hear the scouts' report. I enthusiastically squeezed Maratti's hand when they showed off the land's large fruit and reported that the land indeed flowed with milk and honey. But I dropped his hand when, instead of being eager to conquer the land, they demurred.

"The people who inhabit the country are powerful," the Zebulon chieftain opined. "The cities are fortified and very large; moreover, we saw Anakites there."

"Jebusites and Amorites inhabit the hill country," a Danite scout added, "while Philistines dwell by the sea and Canaanites along the Jordan."

All around me people's faces fell, and some began to cry. Caleb hushed the crowd and declared, "Let us by all means go up, for we shall surely overcome the land and gain possession of it."

But the other scouts who had gone up with Caleb insisted, "We cannot attack that people, for they are stronger than we."

Over the next few days Maratti's frustration grew as these cowardly scouts spread calumnies about the land, saying, "The country that we traversed and scouted is one that devours its settlers. All the people in it are of great size; we saw giant Anakites and must have looked like grasshoppers in comparison to them."

In a week, the entire community was in despair. The Israelites broke into loud cries and railed against Moses and Aaron. "Why is Elohim taking us to that land to fall by the sword? Our wives and children will be carried off! It would be better for us to go back to Egypt!"

Maratti was furious that, of those who had scouted the land, only Joshua and Caleb exhorted the Israelites, "The land that we traversed and scouted is an exceedingly good land. If pleased with us, Elohim will bring us into that land, a land that flows with milk and honey, and give it to us. Only you must not rebel against Elohim. Have no fear of the people of the country, for they are our prey: their protection has departed from them, for Elohim is with us."

I was terrified when the community threatened to pelt Joshua and Caleb with stones, until the Presence of GOD appeared in the Tabernacle before them. All around us people fell on their faces in fear as Moses begged, "Pardon, I pray, the iniquity of this people with Your great kindness, as You have forgiven this people ever since Egypt."

And the voice of GOD answered, "I pardon, as you have asked. Nevertheless, none of those who have seen My Presence and the signs I have performed in Egypt and in the wilderness and who have continued to try Me and disobey Me these many times; none of you shall see this land." There was a great gasp from those around us.

Then GOD concluded with, "In this very wilderness shall your carcasses drop. Of all of the Israelite men who are older than twenty years, not one shall enter the land in which I swore to settle you—save Caleb and Joshua."

THE MIDWIVES' ESCAPE 113

People began to weep and wail as GOD continued. "Only your children whom you said would be carried off—these will I allow to enter, and they shall know the land that you have rejected."

Early the next morning my sleep was interrupted by an Israelite fighting force setting out toward the crest of the hill country chanting, "We are prepared to go up to the place that GOD has spoken of, for we were wrong."

But Moses warned them, "Why do you transgress GOD's command? Do not go up, lest you be routed by your enemies, for they will be there to face you. You will fall by their swords since GOD is not with you."

Maratti consulted with Joshua, who agreed that their warriors would stay in camp. I shook my head in disbelief that the Israelites could be so disobedient as to defy Moses's and Elohim's clear caveat. What a foolish and stubborn people, to go to battle without the leadership of Joshua and Caleb.

Still, many Israelite men defiantly marched to the hill country. The Amalekites and Canaanites who dwelt there came down and dealt them a shattering blow. The few men who managed to return were gravely injured, and while Pua, Shifra, and I used all our healing skills, many of the wounded did not survive. The Israelites went into mourning over all the dead, but I was angry at such a wanton waste of life.

Maratti was angry too. "A soldier who doesn't follow his commander's orders is bad enough, but one who encourages others to disobey them is worse—a traitor who deserves punishment, not a reward."

We agreed that Elohim was right to limit entrance to the Promised Land to those who had trusted and followed the Hebrews' god's orders.

A few days after the mourning period was over, Pua reported that a man named Zelophehad had been gathering wood on the Sabbath day. Those who found him gathering wood brought him before Moses and the community leadership.

Then GOD said to Moses, "The man in question shall be put to death; the community leaders shall pelt him with stones outside the camp."

I understood that this was the law, but I asked Maratti, "Doesn't it seem odd that a man would so obviously violate one of Elohim's ten commands when he knows the penalty is death?"

"Let me ask Moses if there are any extenuating circumstances," he replied.

I accompanied Maratti to the interview, but Zelophehad didn't appear the least bit ashamed. "My intent was for the sake of heaven," he began. "The Israelites are saying that since it was decreed for us not to enter the land, we are not obligated in the commandments. So I went and violated Sabbath publicly in order to be executed, to demonstrate that Elohim's warning of the penalty dealt out to a deliberate transgressor is not an empty threat." He paused and took a deep breath. "I did not want my peers to think that just because they would not enter the Promised Land, it meant that Elohim's laws no longer applied to them."

Maratti sighed. "But the penalty is death."

"I understand. I have no sons, only daughters, so I will have no descendants to inherit my portion in the Promised Land or to continue my name," Zelophehad said. "I ask only for my death to be as painless as possible."

Returning to our tent, Maratti and I got into one of our few arguments. "Do you feel the same as Zelophehad, that a man without sons has no point in living? I think it's appalling."

"I would like to have some sons," Maratti replied, then quickly added, "There is still time for us to have more children."

"But what if I have no sons?" I pressed him. "Would your life not be worth living unless you took a second wife and had sons from her?" I was almost crying.

He took me in his arms. "I admit I would like to have sons, Asenet, but there is more to life than that."

THE MIDWIVES' ESCAPE   115

The next day Maratti told me that Moses had consulted with Joshua. "We must ensure that this execution is a signal to the other Israelites not to consider Elohim's laws as no longer binding for the adults who would not enter the Promised Land. Moses had whispered to Joshua, "I want you to find the two best stone slingers among our warriors, the strongest and most accurate."

"I understand," Joshua replied. "They must be able to render Zelophehad unconscious immediately with only one stone each or to kill him outright. Even so, I suggest that he be given a great deal of strong wine first."

"Agreed. In addition I will explain to his daughters that since he is actually a martyr, not a sinner, he will be executed at sunset so they may bury his body after dark. Then everyone will assume some animal took it away when it is gone in the morning."

So the community leadership took Zelophehad outside the camp and stoned him to death—as GOD had commanded Moses.

Which is how Joshua explained it to Maratti, who explained it to me.

However some complaints grew into actual rebellions. First Dathan and Abiram rose up against Moses, saying, "You have gone too far! For all the community are holy, all of them."

It didn't seem to me that all the community were holy. Some were just fomenting trouble. Again I wondered why the Hebrews were so obstreperous.

So Moses sent for Dathan and Abiram, but they said, "We will not come! Is it not enough that you brought us from a land flowing with milk and honey to have us die in the wilderness, that you would also lord it over us?"

Moses was aggrieved and said to GOD, "I have not wronged any one of them."

Then he rose and went to Dathan and Abiram, with the elders of Israel following him. Moses addressed the community, saying, "Move

116 ASENET

away from the tents of these wicked men and touch nothing that belongs to them, lest you be wiped out for all their sins."

As people withdrew from about the abodes of Dathan and Abiram, Moses said, "By this you shall know that it was GOD who sent me to do all these things, that they are not of my own devising. If these people's death is like that of every human, if their lot is humanity's common fate, then it was not GOD who sent me." Then he continued. "But if GOD brings about something unheard-of so that the ground opens its mouth and swallows them up and they go down alive into Sheol, you shall know that they have spurned GOD."

This I had to see, and I brought Shifra along to be another witness. Scarcely had Moses finished speaking when the ground under Dathan and Abiram burst asunder, and they went down alive into Sheol with all that belonged to them. I would have said, "I told you so," but I was shocked speechless.

I thought the rebels would have learned their lesson, but no. Only a week later, Korah the Levite together with two hundred and fifty Israelites—chieftains of the community—assembled against Moses and Aaron and protested, "Why do you raise yourselves above GOD's congregation?"

Outraged, Moses addressed Korah and his company, saying, "Come morning GOD will make known who is His, who is holy, and whom He will bring close." Moses stared directly at Korah, continuing, "Do this: you and all your band, take fire pans, and tomorrow put fire in them and lay incense on them before GOD. Then the candidate whom GOD chooses, he shall be the holy one. For you have gone too far, sons of Levi!"

Then Moses had more to say to Korah. "Hear me, sons of Levi. Is it not enough for you that the god of Israel has set you apart from the community and given you direct access to perform the duties of GOD's

Ground opens under Korah near Hazeroth

118   ASENET

Tabernacle and to minister to the community and serve them? Now that GOD has advanced you and all your fellow Levites with you, do you seek the priesthood too? Truly, it is against GOD that you have all banded together. For who is Aaron that you should rail against him?"

The next morning Pua and Shifra came with me to watch as Korah and the two hundred and fifty men of his family each took a fire pan; Moses and Aaron also brought their fire pans. Korah's men each put fire in their pan, laid incense on it, and took a place at the entrance of the Tabernacle, along with Moses and Aaron. By this time the entire community had gathered to watch, but Moses urged us to stay well back from the Tabernacle.

Suddenly a fire went forth from GOD and consumed the men's offerings and incense. Before anyone could react, there was a rumbling from below as the earth opened its mouth and swallowed up Korah's men with their households and all their possessions. Then the earth closed over them and, shrieking, they vanished.

Everyone around them fled, screaming, "The earth might swallow us next!"

But Moses called them back and asked each tribe to choose a chief and take one staff for him—twelve staffs in all. Each man inscribed his name on his staff, as did Aaron who inscribed his name on the staff of Levi, and they left the staffs in the Tabernacle. The next day Moses brought the staffs out before all the people, and each chief identified and recovered his own. There was no doubt whom GOD had chosen as high priest, for Aaron's staff had sprouted, produced blossoms, and borne almonds.

My eyes filled with tears of joy and amazement at the sight. The non-Levite Hebrews, as well as outsiders like the Egyptians, Hittites, Nubians, and others who had left Egypt with them—myself included—gave a collective sigh of relief. Elohim had not only found a unique sign to publicly designate Aaron and his descendants for the priesthood, but he had also used a beautiful and peaceful demonstration.

THE MIDWIVES' ESCAPE

While everyone in and outside the camp was relieved that Aaron would be leading the priesthood, it wasn't long before we heard people weeping at the entrance of their tents—and not just the Hebrews, although it was their chieftains who had beseeched Moses for help.

"Take us away from this place," they begged him. "All night we hear Korah, Dathan, and Abiram and their households crying out from Sheol."

We too were distressed at the nightly howls and wails that emanated from below and were grateful when Moses took pity on all of us and replied, "Pack your belongings so you are ready to move in the morning."

He then instructed the Levites to take down the Tabernacle and prepare it for travel. The next morning the cloud began to move and we set out for Hazeroth.

CHAPTER FOURTEEN

SHIFRA

Miriam and Aaron spoke against Moses because of the Cushite woman he had taken (into his household as his wife): "He married a Cushite woman!"

—Numbers 12:1

BY THIS TIME, everyone was so experienced at moving that we arrived at Hazeroth in less than a week and after a few hours had the camp set up in a small sandy valley surrounded by low red rock hills. As usual, as soon as our tents were livable, Gitlam and I hurried off to survey our new surroundings. We could see that water wouldn't be a problem; several streams ran down from the hills. There appeared to be sufficient forage for the goats too, but we wanted to see the view from higher up. There was a gently sloped dry creek bed that looked easy to climb, so we headed up it.

To our disappointment, the view from the top of the hill showed more of the same sandy creek beds surrounded by barren red rock cliffs and hills. Each direction had minimal vegetation. There were some caves in the cliffs, so we headed back down to explore them. We were approaching a small one when we heard an animal growling. We stopped in our tracks and, after a short whispered conversation, decided to cautiously approach.

THE MIDWIVES' ESCAPE   121

We stopped again when we saw a hyena crouching over its victim, a smaller sand-colored furry mammal with pointed ears. Gitlam immediately picked up some rocks and threw them at the hyena. Although his aim was excellent, the hyena merely moved back a little instead of fleeing. We could hear more yipping howls nearby and exchanged worried glances. We both knew we couldn't just turn around and continue down the cliff; the hyenas would attack as soon as our backs were turned.

I could see the Nubians' tents not far below us and had an idea. "I'm going to slip down and ask the Nubian archers to help us. Keep throwing rocks until I return with them."

"I can keep this one at bay." Gitlam looked at me anxiously. "But not more than two."

I scrambled down the rocks as quickly and quietly as I could. Thankfully two of the Nubians were sitting down whittling new arrows, and I recognized them as Amaros and Bahiti. They looked bored.

When I explained the situation, they eagerly grabbed their bows and quivers and mounted their horses. Amaros threw me a hand to climb up behind her. "Show us where to go and we're with you."

Part of me wished our flight would last longer, but mainly I was relieved when we arrived in time to reinforce Gitlam. Other hyenas were approaching, and it was clear he couldn't hold out much longer against so many. But before I could call out that we were coming, arrows were flying and hitting their targets, generating yelps of pain from the hyenas as they fled. I joined Gitlam, and the Nubian archers followed the hyenas until we heard only silence.

When they returned, they praised Gitlam for his excellent throwing prowess. "You should definitely take up the javelin or maybe the sling," they encouraged him. Then Bahiti's expression turned serious. "That hyena caught a sand cat," she said sadly. "A nursing mother."

Amaros nodded. "So her litter should be hidden nearby."

"Help us find it." I couldn't stand the thought of those kittens starving to death.

122 SHIFRA

Gitlam was as softhearted as me. "Surely we'll be able to hear her kittens mewling," he suggested.

The two Nubians looked at each other and shrugged. "It's not as if we have anything better to do right now," Amaros said.

We searched the nearest caves first, without success. But just as the sun began to fall, Bahati stood still and put her finger to her lips. We immediately quieted and listened carefully. Sure enough, we heard feeble cries coming from the back of the cave we'd just entered. Gitlam was younger than me, but my hand was smaller, so I was the one who reached down into their hidey-hole. The two kittens, miniature versions of their mother, weren't strong enough to scratch me badly, but my hands were still bloody when I pulled the kittens out.

Gitlam and I, each cradling a terrified kitten, were soon mounted behind the Nubians as they galloped to our tents. Mother took one look at what we carried, then smiled and rushed off. She returned with two rags and a small bowl of goat milk. She twisted the rags, submerged them in the goat milk, and held them up to the kittens' noses. To my delight, and great relief, the kittens took hold and began to suck. Tears filled my eyes and tenderhearted Gitlam actually began to cry.

Mother gave us a serious look. "I know you think they're adorable, but if you two want to keep these creatures, then you will be responsible for them: feeding them, making a bed for them that they can't escape, cleaning up after them, and protecting them from Tantana." She paused and shook her head before continuing. "You don't need to worry about this yet, but Grandfather will be furious if they get into his workshop when they're older."

"Don't worry," Gitlam said. "I'll make sure they stay out of it."

Then Mother smiled. "On the other hand, it will be good to be able to store grain without rodents spoiling it."

I remembered a torn reed basket that I hadn't gotten around to repairing. When lined with a worn blanket, it was large enough to contain the kittens and keep them comfortable. Gitlam wanted them to

THE MIDWIVES' ESCAPE   123

sleep in bed with him, but Mother insisted on waiting until they were bigger. However she did allow us to keep the kittens' basket in the children's tent, as long as it was placed out of my baby sister's reach.

Two weeks later I got up from bed to discover blood running down my legs. I couldn't find any wound and nothing hurt, so I ran excitedly to tell Mother. She'd obviously been expecting this because she brought me a sinar, something like a loincloth, stuffed with the same soft and absorbent kid's wool swaddling that Tantana wore. "You are a woman now," Mother whispered as she gave me a long hug. "You will need to take care around men when they are in our family's tents, because tradition limits contact between men and menstruating women."

She hugged me tighter, and I could see tears on her cheeks. "It is your responsibility to rinse the blood from your sinar with cold water, hang the wool in the sun to dry, and replace it with clean dry wool. You should also note the phase of the moon when your menses start, for that is when it will come each month."

"But there is no moon out tonight," I said.

"That's because it was a new moon, the start of a new month, an auspicious time for beginnings," Mother explained. "You will probably see a small crescent moon tonight."

"What phase of the moon is it when your menses starts?"

She smiled. "I'm still nursing Tantana, so I don't have any. When I start again, we'll likely bleed at the same time since we live together."

I'd gotten up to go put on the sinar and its swaddling, when she stopped me.

"Wait," she said. "I have something for you." Mother opened a box that Grandfather had made and removed two bronze anklets. "These anklets symbolize your transformation from girl to young woman; they mark you as marriageable in our community," she said as she slid them over my feet. "Now we can plan your wedding to Eshkar."

124 SHIFRA

There was nothing else to do but go back to bed. But along with feelings of pride and excitement, there were now cramps in my belly. When I complained to Mother, she sighed and said that I'd probably have them every month until I married.

She must have shared the news with the rest of the family because the topic of conversation at our midday meal was how soon to announce my betrothal to Eshkar, after which we could start planning the wedding. Arrangements would be simplified because I wasn't actually leaving home. True I would move out of the children's tent and sleep with Eshkar in our own marital tent, but I wouldn't require a dowry, and he didn't need to pay a bride price. Best of all, I wouldn't be marrying a stranger.

There was one complication—something I must keep secret from anyone not in our immediate family. Grandfather explained it to me. "You know that the Hebrews, like most peoples, permit a man to marry two women; that is, to have two wives, as long as he can support both of them." He waited until I nodded my understanding; then he sighed. "Well, the Lagash custom is for a woman to marry two men—provided that they are brothers."

My jaw dropped in astonishment as I looked from Eshkar to Gitlam and back again; then I quickly closed my mouth. "So their father and uncle were actually both married to their mother?" Eshkar appeared unfazed, but Gitlam was blushing furiously.

"True," Grandfather answered. "The elder is called 'father' and the younger 'uncle,' but either one could be the father of the mother's children."

"But why have such a custom?" I asked. I understood that in a place where armies regularly fought each other, women might outnumber men, like with the Hebrews and Hittites today. I shivered as I thought of poor Haggith, second wife to an old wealthy Danite whose first wife hated her.

Eshkar replied, "The Lagash land was poor and infertile. If a father had many sons and wanted to divide his land equally among them when he died, none of them would inherit enough to support a family."

Grandfather grinned. "Marrying brothers means the wife only has one mother-in-law."

"Take as much time as you need to consider this," Mother said.

There was nothing for me to consider. I'd understood for years that I would marry Eshkar. If he didn't object to my also marrying Gitlam, I didn't either. I liked them both well enough, and I would have several years to get used to the idea of having two husbands before Gitlam was old enough to marry me. I didn't want to reject their Lagash customs, but I especially didn't want to hurt either of their feelings.

So I told Mother, and the rest of my family, "I would be happy to marry Eshkar and Gitlam." Then I gave Gitlam a smile. "Once Gitlam is a bit older, of course."

During the following month, the sand cat kittens began eating manna mixed with goat milk. Gitlam and I were astonished when the manna abruptly appeared inside their basket one morning, but we decided to keep giving them goat milk as well. They were now playing with each other, although it looked more like fighting to me. Gitlam used some wood scraps to make a barrier to the woodshop's entryway, but the kittens merely crawled in under the tent's lower edges. Grandfather tried to discourage them by throwing dowels at them, although he didn't use enough force to hurt them. The kittens considered this an excellent game and batted the dowels around relentlessly.

Our Nubian friends, Amaros and Bahiti, stopped by a few times a week to visit, once bringing a string toy woven from strands of horsetail. The kittens chased it so vigorously and wholeheartedly that sometimes they just fell over asleep where they were.

One time Gudit came with Amaros and Bahiti, although she spent most of her time with Mother. I quietly sat and enjoyed the kittens while I listened to Gudit and Mother talk.

Sand kittens eating manna near Kadesh

THE MIDWIVES' ESCAPE   127

"I'm so tired all the time," Gudit complained. "And though I don't vomit every morning like I used to, I still feel ill most afternoons."

"It looks like your belly is distended. Have your breasts gotten larger or more sensitive?" Mother asked.

I'd been an apprentice midwife long enough to understand what Mother suspected, and my hunch was bolstered when Gudit admitted how her breasts had changed. It took a great effort on my part to remain calm and appear uninterested.

"When was your last monthly menses?"

"I don't recall exactly, maybe two or three months ago." Gudit shrugged. "I've never been regular."

Mother confirmed my diagnosis with her next sentence. "It appears that you are with child, probably for about twelve weeks."

Amaros and Bahiti perked up and stared wide-eyed at Gudit, who sighed with resignation. "Do you have any herbs to lessen the nausea?" she asked Mother.

Mother turned to me. "Shifra, can you see how much silphium we have?"

Gudit shook her head. "Not that. I want to have the child."

"We have a lot of ginger," I said. "Shall I make her some ginger tea?"

Mother nodded, and I went to boil the water.

Amaros couldn't restrain herself. "So who's the father?"

When Gudit remained silent, Bahiti asked, "Do you even know who he is?"

Gudit scowled. "Of course I know, but I'd rather other people didn't . . . at least not until after I tell him myself."

My eyes widened as I realized whom she meant. There was only one man she spent nights with—Moses! Mother saw my expression and put her finger to her lips.

By the time we were preparing to leave Hazeroth, Gudit's condition was no longer a secret—especially when Miriam and Aaron spoke publicly against Moses about the Cushite woman he had taken into his household as his wife: "He took a Cushite woman!" they accused him, "not an Israelite."

Elohim heard this and called to Moses, Aaron, and Miriam, "You three, come out to the Tabernacle." The words were clear, though I heard them only in my head.

The three of them went, and when some of the Hebrews followed without any interference, I did too. Awestruck, I stopped at the entrance and watched as Elohim came down in a pillar of cloud and called out, "Aaron and Miriam!" The two of them came forward and Elohim said, "When prophets of GOD arise among you, I make Myself known to them in a vision; I speak with them in a dream."

Mother and I knew this was true for Miriam.

"Not so with My servant Moses," Elohim continued. "With him I speak mouth to mouth, plainly and not in riddles, and he beholds My likeness. How then did you dare to speak against My servant Moses?" Still incensed with them, Elohim said nothing more and the cloud began to depart.

When the cloud had completely withdrawn, I began to shake with fear, for there was Miriam stricken with milk-white leprous scales!

Aaron fell to his knees and begged Moses, "Let her not be like a stillbirth which emerges from its mother's womb with half its flesh eaten away!"

So Moses cried out to GOD, "O GOD, pray heal her!"

But Elohim told Moses, "Let her be shut out of camp for seven days, and when she is healed, then she may be readmitted."

The immediate question for us outsiders was where Miriam should stay for those seven days. There were already tents outside the camp for women impure by menstruation or childbirth, but it appeared improper that one with leprosy should live with healthy women and

THE MIDWIVES' ESCAPE   129

children. Yet Miriam wasn't contagious, so she should certainly keep her distance from the actual lepers. It was also unseemly that Miriam stay near the harlots' tents. So Mother finally convinced the outsiders that Miriam should have her own individual tent.

But she was not alone. Each day different women brought her some special food to supplement her daily manna, and others sat with her while they spun thread or wove it. Mother and I felt sympathy for Miriam for two reasons. First, it was greatly unfair that she should be so severely punished while Aaron avoided blame entirely. Second, Miriam was right to chastise Moses for secretly marrying the Cushite. If he was going to marry again, especially a Nubian princess, it should have been done openly.

But I saw that opinions changed once word spread that Gudit had been studying Elohim's laws and regulations for the purpose of bringing them back to Nubia so her people could also worship the One GOD. I heard women praising Moses for marrying Gudit rather than being secluded with a woman he wasn't related to. Eventually I stopped hearing disapproval of their relationship. Gudit told us that after Elohim decreed that Hebrew men would die before entering the Promised Land, Elohim ceased speaking with Moses directly, face-to-face. Then she and Moses could live in the same tent.

Those of us who dwelt outside the camp permanently felt honored to host the prophetess, even if only for a week. On the morning of the sixth day, Miriam's skin was perfectly healed. Indeed, her skin was now as smooth and soft as little Tantana's. That evening Miriam came to our tent with a white-haired woman I didn't recognize. Mother did though, and the woman recognized Mother as well.

Mother hurried to embrace the woman. "Serach, you are still with us! I have been wanting to thank you for helping me across the Reed Sea."

"I've been staying in Miriam's tent," the woman, now identified as Serach, said. "Trying to maintain my privacy."

Miriam turned to Mother. "Now that I know your ancestry from Joseph, I thought you and Serach bat Asher should meet." Miriam proceeded to explain how both women were related, albeit distant cousins.

I examined Serach's face carefully, but her skin was unlined and she appeared to have all her teeth. How could she possibly be so old that her father, Jacob, was my more-than-fourth-great-grandfather? I couldn't even count that many generations back.

Serach recognized my skepticism and sighed. "When my uncles returned from meeting Joseph in Egypt, they were afraid that informing their aged father, Jacob, that Joseph lived would shock him into the next world. So I sat before Jacob and played my lyre, singing 'Joseph my uncle did not die; he lives and rules all the land of Egypt.' Jacob blessed me, saying, 'My daughter, because you revived my spirit, death shall never rule you.' And here I am, still living after all these years."

I was stunned into silence for a few moments until I felt brave enough to reach out to touch Serach's hand, whose skin felt as smooth as my own. Serach's laugh was like tinkling bells. "I'm quite real, dear," she said.

"Are there any more like you?" I asked, and she laughed again. "You mean women who have lived so long?"

I blushed at my rudeness, for it was inexcusable to ask a woman's age. And I nodded.

Serach chuckled; then her expression turned serious. "Not that I know of."

Elohim had shut Miriam outside the camp for seven days, but the people did not march on until she was officially readmitted, after which the cloud over the Tabernacle started to move out from Hazeroth and into the wilderness of Paran. Like before, we had no idea where the cloud was going and when it would get there.

Thankfully, I was allowed to rest on the Sabbath.

I surmised that frustration over Elohim's decree that it would be almost forty years before we entered the Promised Land was what had made everyone testy. One morning I was at Eshkar's mother's big loom weaving what would eventually be the roof of our marital tent, when Maratti raced in, a scowl on his face.

"Where's my sword?" he demanded. He turned on Eshkar. "Have you been practicing with it again?"

Before my intimidated betrothed could find his voice, Mother stepped between them. "Your sword is on the top shelf of the new cabinet Father made for us," she told him. "I didn't want Tantana playing with it."

Maratti sprinted into their tent and appeared moments later with his sheathed sword belted around his waist. He must have known Mother would ask questions because he paused to explain his urgency. "There's trouble in the camp of Dan."

"What kind of trouble?" she asked.

"Shelomith's son is fighting with Aran, and the others are egging them on." He shook his head in annoyance. "I need to break them up before anyone is badly hurt."

"Shall I come with you?" Eshkar asked. "Maybe I can help calm them down."

"Very well," Maratti replied. "But take a club with you, just in case."

CHAPTER FIFTEEN

ASENET

*The Israelites arrived in a body at the Wilderness of Zin on the first
new moon, and the people stayed at Kadesh.*

—Numbers 20:1

I WASN'T HAPPY ABOUT Maratti and Eshkar's getting involved in a
situation that only affected Hebrews, but Eshkar was eighteen now, a
grown man, so I had no power over him. And nobody would challenge
Maratti. The camp of Dan was on the opposite side of the Tabernacle
from the camp of Reuben, where the Simeonites and Gadites also
pitched their tents. So we rarely saw them.

But Pua had told me about Shelomith's son, Hushim. Shelomith
was a Danite, but Hushim's father was an Egyptian taskmaster. Apparently Hushim had developed a lust for the slave girl and lay with her
regularly despite her protests. Knowing it would infuriate the jealous
taskmaster, no Hebrew dared marry the girl. Mother had dosed Shelomith with silphium repeatedly, but eventually Shelomith gave birth
to a son. In a strange coincidence, Hushim's father was the very taskmaster Moses killed before fleeing to Midian. But afterward, Shelomith
never married. She and Hushim lived with her parents in Egypt, and
now in her father Dibri's tent in the camp of Dan.

THE MIDWIVES' ESCAPE   133

Maratti and Eshkar didn't return until sunset. Maratti wolfed down what would have been his midday meal, but Eshkar shook his head and went back outside. I immediately followed him, and we walked a lengthy distance from the camp before he spoke. He could barely get the words out.

"The fight started when Hushim wanted to pitch a tent next to Dibri's rather than continue sharing a tent with his mother. The Danites asked him why he wanted to have his tent there, and he replied that he was from a daughter of Dan. But they retorted, 'Israelites shall camp each with his standard, under the banners *of his father's house*. Although your mother is a daughter of Dan, your father is not a son of Dan, and the encampment follows the father's line, and not the mother's.'"

"I suppose that is so, but other mixed families aren't treated that way," I said.

"Immediately a fight broke out between Hushim and some of the Danites. When Hushim became so angry that he reviled Elohim's holy name in blasphemy, he was brought to Moses and put under guard until Elohim's decision would be made clear."

I was filled with trepidation. "And that was?" I didn't want to know what blasphemy Hushim had said.

"Elohim told Moses to take the blasphemer outside the camp, have all who heard his words come, and"—Eshkar gulped before he continued—"and let the community leadership stone him."

"Oh no!" I cried out. Zelophehad had been an old man and a Hebrew, but Hushim was partly an outsider and younger than Eshkar.

"Moses declared that anyone who blasphemes Elohim shall bear the guilt, and one who blasphemes the name GOD shall be put to death. Moses also said that GOD would have one standard for foreigner and citizen alike."

"And then?" I whispered.

"The Hebrew leadership did as Moses commanded; they took Hushim outside the camp and pelted him with stones." Eshkar sighed heavily. "I didn't have to watch, but I heard his screams and his mother's wails."

Though this case would have ended the same had the blasphemer been a Hebrew, tension rose between families like my sister Pua's, where a Hebrew was married to an outsider, and those where both spouses were Hebrews. Father tsked and pointed out that there was less prejudice against couples where a Hebrew woman, due to the shortage of Hebrew men, had married an outsider than vice versa. I was thankful that nobody seemed to object when two outsiders wed each other. But I knew that nearly everyone would object when one outsider woman married two outsider men, even if that was the men's custom.

The cloud slowed ten days after we left Hazeroth. We had been following a caravan route for two days when the land began to rise. It was a gentle slope, but people were tired and frustrated when the sun set and the cloud had not stopped. There was nothing to do but quickly set up our tents while there was still light. At daybreak the cloud had moved just a little, so with much grumbling, we packed and climbed the short distance to the trail's peak.

Complaints abruptly ceased as we beheld a verdant oasis below with caravan tracks running through it. A river to the north snaked down and emptied into a lake, beyond which were lush grazing fields. The lake was surrounded by date palms, and olive trees grew on the hills above it. Below were olive presses and plastered cisterns. There was more than enough space for everyone, Hebrews and outsiders, to camp.

What there was not were any signs of habitation.

To my surprise, the cloud did not move toward the oasis but veered to the side, so we remained high on a ridge above the lake when it halted. People were looking around in confusion when Miriam called out loudly, "Don't be concerned. This is where we are supposed to

Kadesh Barnea oasis

camp." She pointed to a line of pale rocks that ringed the ridge. "I had a frightening dream where I saw a flash flood fill this valley with water up to there. The people who lived below, with all their belongings, were swept away."

"I dreamed that too." Caleb's booming voice supported her. "It woke me up."

Others confirmed that they too had had similar dreams, but I was thankful I hadn't. We waited until the cloud halted above a mostly flat area large enough to fit the Tabernacle and the enclosure surrounding it. Then the Levites set to work leveling the land, and when that was done, they erected the Tabernacle.

At the same time, the Hebrews began terracing the hillside for family campsites. Father and Maratti waited until Shaul and Pua had chosen their spot at the edge of the Simeonite camp, then immediately claimed the adjacent one. Leveling the land was hot and dirty work, and I did my part by filling the waterskins down at the lake and then lugging them up to our site. Even Shifra and Eshkar got some work done while Gitlam kept Tantana out of the way. I wasn't the only one who gazed at her with envy when she finally curled up for a nap with the sand cats.

When the sliver of a new moon rose, all the Hebrews' tents were in place, settled according to tribes around and slightly below the Tabernacle. Outsiders were less organized; some tents were on the same ridge as the Hebrews' while some were on the other side of the oasis. The Nubians, who needed more room for their horses and more privacy for their princess, camped on the ridge opposite the Hebrews.

By Shabbat, men had constructed broad switchbacks that made it less onerous to cart things up the hills. And by the next new moon, when Shifra's menses returned, several shallow immersion ponds, surrounded by reeds for privacy, had been dug near the lake's outlet. I was particularly relieved when Joshua and Maratti established outlooks atop both ridges so that anyone approaching our camp from either direction, whether traders or warriors, would be visible at a distance. Each watcher had his own goat shofar to announce any strangers' imminent arrival, or—heaven forbid—a flash flood.

When everyone was settled in, Moses announced that there would be three community assemblies. The tribes in the camps of Dan and Ephraim would meet with Caleb, the camps of Judah and Reuben with Joshua, and those outside the camp with Maratti. Both men and women were encouraged to attend, but there was no penalty if they didn't. The topics to be discussed would be the same.

Father, Eshkar, and I attended Maratti's assembly, along with hundreds of other outsiders. "Now that we are settled here for the foreseeable future, we need to discuss some issues," Maratti began. "First, people need to have trades. Our valley has many olive trees and date palms, so I hope we have people skilled in producing olive oil and date beer..." He grinned and added, "Especially the latter." When the laughter died down, his expression became serious. "Previous inhabitants left us olive presses and a cistern with a large cylindrical stone in it, so we need people who know what to do with them and can instruct others. We want to produce enough oil and beer that we can trade the excess for things we can't make here, like tin and linen cloth."

"Who will we trade with?" a voice called out. "Nobody lives near here."

"I have learned that this oasis is on a caravan route between ports on the western sea and cities in the east and between eastern ports and western cities," Maratti replied. "During the summer especially, there is a great deal of traffic."

An older woman raised her hand to speak. "Oil and beer need large jars to store and ship them. My children and I were potters in Egypt, but we'll need more than the three of us." She looked around at the crowd. "I am willing to teach the craft to others."

I had an idea. "Many of us have goats," I said. "We can trade our cheese and wool cloth."

"My two donkeys have multiplied," a man added. "I would gladly trade the extras."

"I am a wainwright," Father spoke up. "I can repair the caravans' carts and wagons."

Others began offering their skills and items they produced until Maratti interrupted. "Once caravans come, word will spread of our community and how prosperous we are . . . and all the extra women we have. We have a small army, but we need to train a larger force for protection."

A man raised his hand. "I volunteer." His shoulder-length hair, headband, and full beard made him look like a Hebrew, but his accent was Hyksos.

A good many others volunteered, and Maratti asked them to meet with him an hour before sunset. He also instructed that anyone with weapons should bring them.

Within a month, there were more than enough people for all the jobs. The potters started immediately, for we would require a great many large jars to hold all the olive oil and beer we hoped to produce. Thankfully it would be months until all the olives and dates were ripe.

After a few months the young sand cats no longer confined themselves to their basket, or to our tents either. Gitlam almost panicked the first time they were gone when he woke in the early morning, but they quickly returned when their manna appeared. Sometimes they brought us gifts of dead rodents or small birds and reptiles, which I immediately buried. The goats grew sleek and fat from all the grass, while olive branches and date palms hung heavy with fruit. I had already seen a good many potters at work, some more skilled than others.

THE MIDWIVES' ESCAPE

One day an expert in brewing examined the palm trees and declared that some of the dates were ready to pick. Thus I had my first lesson in making date beer. I learned that dates don't ripen all at the same time, and that harvest season begins in early summer and ends in midautumn. I watched with trepidation as fearless young men, climbing barefoot, picked the ripe dates and tossed them down. I had learned that eating six dates daily in the last four weeks of pregnancy helps with dilation and shortens labor, so I had brought a large bowl to take home a supply of ripe ones.

Below, on the ground, children ran around picking up the dates, then squishing them between their fingers to expel the pits. Pits were supposed to be collected in baskets for the goats and donkeys to eat, but the children had to throw them at each other first. The sand cats couldn't resist chasing the errant pits, much to the children's delight.

One of my tasks was to scold the boys—for it was mainly boys— who did too much throwing and make them pick up the pits on the ground. Only then were they allowed to pitch the pitted dates into a waiting cart. When a cart was full, a strong man wheeled it to the cistern, emptied it inside, and returned it to the children to refill.

An Egyptian woman, clearly an expert brewer, stood by and observed closely until the cistern held what she considered the right amount of dates. Then she held up her hand to stop the carts.

Instead of adding any water, the woman beckoned five well-muscled men to climb down into the cistern, where they began pushing the stone cylinder. Judging by the men's grunts and red faces, that huge rock must have been very heavy, and it took some time before they began to move it. Slowly at first, but faster as the crushed dates provided lubrication, the men rolled the cylinder back and forth over the dates. Soon only three men were necessary to do the pushing, and two shifted to the task of raking whole dates into the stone's path and moving the crushed fruit away. It was still a strenuous, messy exercise, so much so that the men wore only loincloths on this hot day. It was also

Dates in a cart

dangerous, as wayward feet could be crushed as easily as the dates. But the men must have been experienced brewers; they moved in tandem and were careful to keep their feet away from the stone.

"How long will it take to crush all the dates?" I asked the woman. "Pardon my poor manners; I'm Asenet the midwife."

"My name is Jomana," she replied. "It should only take a day. Just before sunset they'll fill the troughs with water and stir the contents to start the fermentation."

"And then?"

"Men will keep stirring the dates and water all week, until fermentation stops and the first batch of beer is ready."

My curious expression must have encouraged Jomana to elaborate. "Then we siphon off the beer into jars, add fresh water to the dates, and the brewing process begins again." She paused and sighed. "Back in Egypt, we sometimes got as many as six batches of beer from a single trough of dates."

The children, now bored, looked longingly at the dates left in the carts.

"When your mothers have taken a jarful each," Jomana told them, "you may eat as many each as they will allow." She smiled as the children raced off to find their mothers; then she turned to the men in the trough, a stern look in her eyes. "You aren't slaves any longer, men. We will keep the proceeds from selling this beer or drink it ourselves. So no pissing in the trough like you did in Egypt."

Several of the men wore sheepish looks and the others burst out laughing.

"You will get water and latrine breaks every hour," Jomana announced. "Plus time for a midday meal."

Thankful that I hadn't drunk much beer back in Egypt, I collected my dates, and the sand cats followed me back to our tent.

142 ASENET

I grew anxious waiting for the first caravan to arrive. Shifra would marry Eshkar in the winter—there was much giggling and jokes that the nights were longest then—and I needed some fine linen cloth for her wedding gown. I understood that I wouldn't know what was a good price for linen until I'd bargained with more merchants, but at least I'd be able to buy some. As the Greeks say, "a bird in the hand is worth two in the bush."

Many of us women noticed that our family's clothing and shoes were not wearing out. When children outgrew their clothes and sandals, mothers traded them around for a larger size. True, people's clothes needed washing or small repairs, but that was less onerous than sewing new ones. We still needed to prevent moth worms from eating our woolens, but since nobody slept in their clothes, it was simple enough to shake them out at night along with the bedding. Rugs and wall hangings were another matter; each spring Maratti and Eshkar hung them up outside, following which Shifra and Gitlam beat them vigorously until nothing more came out. Sometimes I wondered whether Elohim kept the moths and worms away, for I never saw any. Even so, we shook out and beat our woolens yearly.

But the strangest thing was that no one, except for Hushim, had died since we'd left Sinai. Being a midwife, I was well aware of the many women and infants who did not survive childbirth, yet since we'd received Elohim's words at Sinai, it had been as Moses had told us, "No woman in your land shall miscarry or be barren. I will let you enjoy the full count of your days."

Thus I wasn't worried that Gudit didn't go into labor until a week or so past when I'd figured she was due because she'd been diligently eating her six dates a day. So I packed my midwife basket and gratefully shared Bahiti's horse to cross to the Nubian's camp. I was not surprised to see Amaros outside waiting for us, a very relieved expression on her face.

I was astonished to find Miriam inside, however.

THE MIDWIVES' ESCAPE 143

Before I could say anything, she turned to me and said, "I asked my sister-in-law to forgive my harsh accusation, and she has done so, after which she asked me to forgive her—and my brother—for hiding her relationship from us, which I was glad to do."

Miriam squeezed Gudit's hand. "She has been kind enough to permit me to be present for my niece's birth."

"Do you think Elohim would have forgiven Hushim for his blasphemy if the boy had asked for forgiveness?" I asked.

Miriam sighed. "True that Elohim is a compassionate and gracious god, slow to anger, abounding in kindness and faithfulness, forgiving iniquity, transgression, and sin," she began. "But the sinner must entreat for it, which Hushim did not."

I crouched down to examine Gudit and sighed. The breech baby was far enough along for me to see that it was indeed a girl, her rump aimed at the vaginal canal. There was a jar of water and another of olive oil nearby. As I rinsed my hands, I asked Gudit, "Is this your first child? Breech deliveries are more dangerous if so."

She shook her head and tears filled her eyes. "I had a son a few years ago, but he died with the other firstborns during the tenth plague."

I was impressed that Elohim's power reached all the way to Nubia. But all I said was, "My own son succumbed in the same way."

Gudit turned to Miriam. "Would you object if I hold a Taweret amulet?"

Of course I had brought several, but I didn't dare offer one if Miriam demurred.

To my amazement, Miriam reached into her purse and held out a beautiful little blue hippopotamus carved with large human breasts and a crocodile's tail. I gulped as I recognized the ancient Egyptian goddess of childbirth and fertility. I'd never assisted at a birth where the laboring woman didn't hold one of the protective amulets, but Miriam was a Hebrew prophetess. Elohim spoke to her in her dreams.

"What happens in this tent does not leave it," she warned us.

When we all nodded, Miriam continued. "My mother held this stone when she gave birth to Moses, as did I when I birthed Caleb. I know that Elohim had not revealed Himself to us back then, but I also know that we must live by His laws, not die by them. We all know how deadly a breech birth can be, so if holding the amulet helps Gudit overcome her fear and relax, I have no objections."

Before anyone could say more, Gudit's membranes ruptured, spilling out greenish amniotic fluid. "Hurry," she wailed. "I have to push."

I promptly dipped my hands in the olive oil to facilitate a vaginal examination. Gudit's cervix was fully dilated, allowing me to confirm the baby's legs sticking straight up in front of the body with feet near the head. "Help her onto all fours," I directed Miriam. That accomplished, I instructed Gudit to push during each contraction.

I gave thanks as the birth progressed well, albeit slowly; eventually the baby's buttocks, thighs, and trunk passed gently through the birth canal. When both legs were born, I gave thanks again, this time that the cord was clearly visible between them and thus not wrapped around the girl's neck. Keeping the legs pointing toward the head, I carefully put both hands around the baby's trunk and waited for the next contraction.

Gudit moaned with each cramp, but I encouraged her. "Don't give up. You're the strongest woman I've ever seen, a warrior."

When she pushed with the next contraction, both arms came out.

Now there was only the head to be born, but this was when things were the riskiest. If the head was large, but not too large, I would need to cut the birth canal sufficiently for it to pass. *But if it were*—no, I told myself. Don't think about this.

So I patiently and gently massaged Gudit's opening wider and, at the same time, slowly pulled the baby's torso downward until I could see the head. Abruptly the rest of the body and the head slid out. Between the amniotic fluid and the olive oil on my hands, the baby was so slippery I almost dropped her, but I managed to hold her up for Gudit and the others to admire. She had a full head of dark curls, but her skin was shades lighter than the Nubians'. I gave her rump a good slap and was rewarded with a vigorous cry, which was joined by cheers from the Nubians and sobs of joy from Miriam.

After I cut the cord, bandaged it, and cleaned up the baby, Gudit held her up to be admired. "She shall be called Dara."

Later, Gudit asked me, "Do you think Dara was born breech because that was the position Moses and I used to beget her?"

I'd heard many strange questions from pregnant women and new mothers, but I'd never heard that one. It took an enormous effort to turn my laughter into a coughing fit, but I was finally able to regain my composure sufficiently to answer, "I don't know."

Moses didn't see his daughter for eight weeks, the time Gudit was proscribed from going back into the camp after birthing a female. During that summer, we hosted, in order of their arrival, Moabite and Edomite caravans. Maratti and Joshua arranged for the marketplace to be set up near the lake at a distance from where the community camped. They insisted that in addition to the Moabite sentries, our swordsmen and spearmen, their weapons and armor conspicuous, would patrol the market. Maratti was particularly proud, and relieved, when the Moabites recognized that our men wore the Egyptian armor that marked them as ex-palace guards.

He and Joshua kept the Moabites back as the harlots pitched their tents at the far side of the lake; then they assigned a rotating number of our troops to guard the area. They tried to discourage other women from even approaching the stalls where the merchants set up their goods, but quickly realized how impossible it was to thwart women eager to shop after almost three years in the wilderness. Joshua did insist that nobody mention the gold and bronze articles in the Tabernacle. Eventually, when we reestablished the copper mines and traded for enough tin to smelt bronze and produce our own metal items, we would trade such luxury pieces.

146 ASENET

Father had Eshkar set up his finest wagon and cart to display the goat cheese and fine woolens we were selling. Thus we brandished our best products. It turned out that I didn't need to leave my place near our cheese to see what the Moabites were selling. Anyone who wanted our merchandise offered us something of theirs in trade. A Moabite with a wagon wheel damaged beyond repair gladly offered me enough lengths of fine linen to make wedding clothes for both Shifra and Eshkar in exchange for a new wheel that fit his wagon exactly. When we asked if he happened to have any cucumber, leek, or melon seeds, mentioning that people missed what they'd eaten in Egypt, he gave us some for free. Gitlam and I planted them immediately, and after they sprouted, diligently fertilized the seedlings with goat manure.

While the date beer sold well, goat cheese became our most popular product. Apparently the manna the goats ate gave their milk, and hence their cheese, a uniquely savory flavor. I traded quite a few pieces, carefully wrapped in palm leaves, for a selection of dyestuffs. Linen didn't take up dye, but wool did. Soon Shifra would have thread to weave blankets, rugs, and wall panels in a multitude of bright colors for her marital tent. By the time the Moabite caravan left, we'd traded away all the cheese we'd stockpiled. Those of us with extra donkeys and he-goats traded them away too, but we kept every she-goat.

We needed to make more cheese right away, before the next caravan arrived.

The Moabites had been gone for a week when we awoke to cries of alarm from the tents where Haggith lived—or used to live. The last time anyone had seen her was ten days before, when she'd gone outside the camp to stay in one of the tents for menstruating women. But she'd never arrived in any of them.

After a thorough search, we all came to the same conclusion.

Haggith had to have been taken by the Moabites.

CHAPTER SIXTEEN

SHIFRA

If he [a man] takes another (into the household as his wife), he must not withhold from this one her food, her clothing, or her conjugal rights. If he fails her in these three ways, she shall go free.

—Exodus 21:10–11

I WAS DEVASTATED BY Haggith's abduction, although Mother and Maratti insisted on my calling it her disappearance. After all, we had no evidence that she'd been taken. When I complained that nobody had gone after the Moabites to rescue her, I was told that even if it were certain that they'd carried her off, their caravan was so far away that it was impossible to catch up with it. I was further frustrated, and grew more infuriated every day, that her husband's family did nothing to reclaim her. Indeed, they refused to even mention her name. Her natal family, even her mother, Helah, were so fearful of offending Haggith's wealthy husband that they also remained silent. In desperation, I turned to the Nubians. They had horses, some surely fast enough to catch up with the caravan.

Gudit was still in seclusion with Dara, so I searched out Amaros and Bahiti, who were watering their mares at the lake. Before I could ask them anything, Amaros put her finger to her lips and beckoned me to walk with them up a stream that fed the lake. When we reached a small riparian grove of trees sufficiently dense to shield us from the camp's view, they halted and waited for me to catch up.

Amaros spoke first. "I understand your concern for your friend, but there is nothing you can do to retrieve her."

"Not even with your horses?" My voice must have sounded pitiful because they both looked at me sympathetically.

Bahiti shook her head. "You must never reveal what we tell you."

Amaros gave her a stern look and warned, "A secret held by three is no secret."

Bursting with curiosity, I swore to say nothing.

"She was not abducted; nor was she in any way taken away against her will," Bahiti began. "She absconded *with* the Moabites."

My jaw dropped as Amaros explained. "One of the younger merchants seduced her and she ran off with him."

"It was more likely she seduced him and they ran off together," Bahiti said.

I stared at them in disbelief. "How do you know this?"

Bahati smiled at me. "Because I waited until two days after the Moabites had gone, then picked her up with my horse at this very spot. She rode behind me until we approached the caravan and her lover ran out to meet her." She sighed and added, "Their reunion was quite enthusiastic."

"I knew that her husband was too old for her and that his first wife hated her," I admitted. "She complained bitterly about how poorly she was treated, but I never imagined she'd . . ."

"Leave him for a younger man," Amaros finished for me.

"He offered to send me back with a virgin's bride price to give her father," Bahiti said. "Very honorable fellow, but that would have revealed her secret."

"She was a virgin." I couldn't help but blush. "She told me her husband was unable to even begin the marital act, never mind complete it."

Amaros spat with disgust. "Then it was fortunate she was able to escape."

The Edomite caravan showed up in late summer. By that time we'd brewed and stored all the beer our first batch of dates could produce. Mother tried to conceal it, but her pregnancy was apparent in that she found it too onerous to walk from our tent down to the marketplace and back up more than twice a day.

I volunteered to sit with Grandfather and trade our cheese, but my family's response was unanimous. "Absolutely not—not after what happened to Haggith!"

Considering how my heart beat faster whenever I caught Eshkar gazing at me, which he did often, the last thing I wanted to do was run off with a stranger. But I was sworn to silence.

So Mother and I had plenty of time to dye wool, spin it into various colored threads, and weave it into beautiful multihued items. Actually I was the one to dye the wool and then spin it into thread. Pointing out that she was a far more experienced weaver than I was, which was true, Mother insisted on weaving all the items I'd need when I was married. When I complained that I'd never become a competent weaver that way, she gave in and watched me weave new blankets for her upcoming child and Tantana from the softest kids' wool. She'd saved red thread left over from making the Tabernacle curtains for this very purpose, to protect the children from demons.

A month after the Edomites left, it was time to harvest olives and, for most of us, learn how to make olive oil. The priests, who required olive oil for their rituals, had complained vigorously about the exorbitant price they had to pay the Moabites for a small amount. Now that our olives were ripening, the priests were most eager for us to begin producing our own. Once we were successful, this would be our most lucrative commodity. And just as there were expert brewers among

Olive press

THE MIDWIVES' ESCAPE

the former slaves, so too were there some experienced in olive oil preparation.

The man that our Egyptians considered the most expert was named Omari. He was a small, skinny fellow with skin the color of ripe olives. He could climb an olive tree by hand faster than most men could climb a ladder, causing the children to call him "monkey man."

Before anyone picked olives, he told us we needed to make baskets to hold them. Thankfully this was a task I'd excelled at since I was seven, and these baskets needed only to be sturdy, not decorative. The baskets had to be large enough to hold as many olives as a man could carry, with a cover to keep the olives inside. Omari surveyed our trees and then announced how many baskets we should make to begin.

"It doesn't matter if you make them from date palm leaves or from reeds that grow around the lake," he told us. "Or if you coil them or braid them. Use whichever source or technique you are most proficient with, as long as they are this big." He held his arms out to make a large circle.

While I and other women worked on making baskets, Omari had the families that raised goats herd the kids and he-goats to eat all the olives left on the ground from previous seasons. I didn't yet know how terrible uncured olives tasted or how foul-tasting milk from she-goats that ate them would be. Since goats eat anything, even old rotting olives, this saved us the work of keeping the old olives from mixing with the new ripe ones we would soon be harvesting.

Once we had enough of what Omari deemed sufficiently large baskets, he had us weaving mats to lay under the trees and catch the ripe olives. "The black or dark purple ones," he warned us, "not the green ones."

I watched the boys and men set to work; boys climbed into the trees, picked the ripe fruit by hand, and tossed it down onto the mats while men used long paddles to beat the fruit off the trees. The experienced workers laughed heartily when Gitlam and other novices bit into a ripe olive, made a disgusted face, and immediately spat it out.

Omari grinned. "At the end of work today, each of you whose mother or wife knows how to cure olives may take some green ones home to her."

I held up my hand, but before I could ask, he added, "Bring a container back with you after your midday meal."

Then he dismissed us, though our baskets were not yet full. "You are no longer slaves," he reminded us. "You are entitled to one hour to eat before work resumes."

When Gitlam and I got to our tent, Mother was outside picking the ripe melons and cucumbers. She stood when she saw us, an alarmed expression on her face. "What did you do wrong that Omari sent you home?"

"Nothing, Mother," I replied. "He gave us time to eat."

"He told everyone to be back to work in an hour," Gitlam said. "He asked me to bring along our donkey."

"And me to bring a container if we want some green olives to cure," I added.

Mother was so astonished at our being given time to eat that she didn't say anything as she waved us inside our tent. She did give us each a jar to fill when we went back to work. "You can bring home any green olives that fell off the tree, but only select olives that aren't bruised or damaged by pests, in particular, the olive fly, whose larvae burrow into the fruits. Then cover them with clean water," she said. "Green olives are useless for making oil, so we may as well cure them."

Gitlam, leading the donkey, and I returned to the olive grove to find some workers already there, filling the baskets with ripe olives. A few well-muscled men were carrying full baskets to an enormous cylindrical stone basin with a large stone wheel standing on its side in the center. Omari explained that this was a crushing stone and pointed out how it was held upright by a vertical post connected to a long handle

THE MIDWIVES' ESCAPE   153

that extended beyond the basin's edge. The men emptied their baskets into the basin, stopping when it was full. At that time, Omari beckoned Gitlam to lead our donkey to where the handle rested on the side of the basin.

When he noticed me standing behind Gitlam, Omari addressed me. "You may remain and watch the oil-making process. We have enough baskets for the time being. But be careful to stay out of the workers' way."

I thanked him and moved closer for a better view. There were already ropes attached around the end of the handle, which Omari instructed Gitlam to tie to our donkey's collar. Then, at Omari's signal, Gitlam urged the donkey forward. Of course she could only circle the basin, and as she did, the crushing wheel rolled over the olives inside.

When Gitlam passed by me, he said, "Seeing all those water reeds around the lake reminded me that Maratti, Eshkar, and I need to make new ropes. Help me remember to tell them when we get home."

"If I remember," I teased him. I liked collecting water reeds. The fluffy cattails at the top made excellent stuffing for pillows.

I knew when Omari was satisfied that the olives were sufficiently crushed, because he had the men scoop them back into the baskets, secure the covers, and carry the now-covered baskets to another stone basin, this one with round grooves along the basin's edge and an opening on the side.

"This is the olive press," he told me and Gitlam. We watched as the men carefully placed the baskets in the center, then together lifted a large, undoubtedly heavy stone and lowered it gently on top of the baskets. Two of the heaviest men climbed up to stand on the rock, and soon after I could see liquid oozing into the grooves and dripping through the opening into a vat below. I also saw that Gitlam and I were not the only ones watching.

"This," Omari informed his audience, "is the first pressing oil, the finest and most expensive oil. In the morning, after it has settled to allow the oil to rise above any water, we will ladle it off into the storage jars."

He pointed to a row of neck-handled amphoras, whose wide bellies narrowed to a pointed base pushed down into the ground. For extra security, ropes attached to the two neck handles were tied to trees. "Then we pour hot water over the pressed baskets to wash out any remaining oil, wait until that has settled, and ladle it off. That is the second pressing oil, not as fine as the first pressing, but adequate for lighting home lamps and cooking."

We repeated this process each day, except the Sabbath, for four months. After the first week, nobody watched the workers anymore. We didn't need so many baskets, but there was a lot of amorge left after all the oil had been collected. I'd known nothing about olive oil production, so I was unaware of what the Greeks called "amorge," the smelly liquid residue remaining in the vats. I soon learned that it had many uses. When spread on surfaces, amorge formed a hard finish useful for sealing olive jars, and when boiled it was used to grease axles—the latter of great value to wainwrights like Grandfather and Eshkar. Amorge also made a plaster, which was applied to floors and cisterns, where it hardened and kept out mud and pests.

I found that I enjoyed spreading amorge on the amphora jars to make them shine. But as Mother entered her last months of pregnancy, I left the olive groves behind to take over more of her tasks. Thankfully this was the goats' mating season, so milk production lessened and finally ceased as the she-goats' bellies swelled, relieving me of cheese making. Instead, now that all the cucumbers and melons had been eaten, I carefully dried their seeds and saved them for planting in the spring.

I also continued Mother's work curing the green olives. She'd already shown me how to select olives that hadn't been bruised or succumbed to pests. After that, she watched as I washed the olives thoroughly and then sliced or cracked them to allow the brine to penetrate the fruit. I tried not to be distracted by thinking of how soon we'd be eating these olives at my wedding.

"Be careful not to cut the pit," Mother warned me. "And not to cut your hand."

I placed these prepared olives in a pan and covered them with cold water. Now they would sit in the pan for a week while I changed the water twice a day. Mother taught me that water removes the bitter taste of raw fruit, leaving it with a fresh, nutty flavor and a firm texture. Every week I sampled a few, waiting for the bitterness to disappear. Then it was time to put them in pickling brine, a salt and water solution.

When Gitlam and I first began bringing home green olives, Mother had stopped us after we'd filled a few jars. "We're going to need more salt for the brine, and we can only cure as many olives as we have salt for," she explained.

"Maybe I could go around to all the women whose babies we'd help birth and ask each for a small amount of salt," I suggested.

"It can't hurt," she replied. "But I expect we'll obtain the most salt from the Moabites; their land includes the southwest shore of the Salt Sea."

"I remember." Maratti said that the sea was so salty a man could float in it, and when I and the other children laughed, he told us that we'd see for ourselves when we continued our journey to the Promised Land. I also remembered how wistful his voice sounded, and I sobered when I realized that he'd likely not live to make that journey.

I prepared the brine by mixing one part salt to ten parts water. When the salt had dissolved completely, I filled a pot with olives and poured in the brine to cover them. Mother taught me that the longer the olives fermented in brine, the less bitter their flavor. So I would leave our olives in the brine for six weeks, changing the brine every week and shaking the pot once a day. After that the olives would last up to a year if stored in their brine, although I thought it was likely there wouldn't be many left after my wedding. So I started curing another batch.

While I was curing and brining more green olives, Gitlam was collecting water reeds and grassland sedges for new ropes. Now that he'd cut enough and soaked the stems to make the fibers pliable, he, Grandfather, Maratti, and Eshkar could start making the ropes—right outside where I could observe them without their seeing me in the relatively dark kitchen. Rope making was strenuous work, especially since they were twisting a long three-ply strand and not a thin string; they'd already made enough string for what Mother would need to tie newborns' umbilical cords for months.

It was warm in the sun, so the men wore only kilts. I confess that I spent more time comparing, and admiring, their half-naked bodies than I did on the olives. All three men were well muscled and their sweaty skin glistened in the sunlight. Grandfather, who must have been at least fifty, was a grizzled elder with leathery, weathered skin. Like other Egyptians, his head was clean-shaven, both on top and on his face. Maratti, whom I estimated to be around forty, also removed his beard, but he wore his straight dark hair to at least shoulder length, either loose or tied back like a horse's tail. Today it was tied back. Eshkar and Gitlam had dark curly hair that came to their shoulders. Eshkar grew a beard like the Hebrews did, but while the Hebrews had short, pointed beards, my betrothed let his grow even longer than the hair on his head. Gitlam, of course, had no beard—yet.

My betrothed—I sighed—was so handsome, and I was so lucky. In just over a month, I would be his bride. He must have sensed my gazing at him, for he turned to stare in my direction, whereupon I modestly resumed mixing a new batch of brine.

When I looked back outside, Grandfather was standing up holding out two strands of fibers to keep them from tangling and in a position to feed them to Maratti, who was holding the rope's finished end. Maratti then used a special tool to twist Grandfather's fibers into his and lengthen the rope. Eshkar stood behind Maratti and, muscles bulging, held the rope taut as it was produced to ensure the strands were tightly twisted together. When Grandfather paused for Gitlam to bring him more fibers, Maratti and Eshkar switched places. Eventually, when Grandfather or Maratti decided the rope was long enough, Gitlam cut the ends and bound them together.

Then they began a new rope.

I found the process fascinating, and entertaining.

Two weeks later than we'd thought the baby would come, Mother went into labor at dawn. At first I wasn't worried that the baby was coming late; after all, this would be her fourth child and the other three had come easily. I found her Taweret amulet in her midwife's basket and placed it in her hand, but she didn't want it.

"This birth is going to be hard," she whispered in between pains. "If any god is going to help me, it will be Elohim, not Taweret."

Now I was worried. I brought her some leather strips to grip when the pains hit. The hours seemed to drag on interminably, and no matter how Maratti tried to comfort Tantana, the toddler only cried louder. Even the sand cats didn't distract her. Maratti refused to leave Mother, so finally Grandfather put Tantana in a small cart and pushed it on a path away from us. When the sun began to set, Mother was whimpering that she needed to push.

It had been over twelve hours, longer than labor should be for a mother who'd already birthed so many children. I was so worried that I sent Eshkar to bring Aunt Pua back with him. Maybe it was the fear in my voice, but he left with alacrity.

When they returned, Pua shooed out all the men. Then we helped Mother onto a table so Pua could examine her without bending too much. Something had to be wrong, but I didn't know what. Without saying a word, Pua took my hand and moved it along Mother's lower belly.

"The baby's head is engaged," I said, "but it doesn't feel right."

Pua nodded. "Usually a baby is born looking down. That way the narrowest part of the head is directed down the birth canal." She must have seen my confused look because she quickly added, "True, it doesn't seem like the head's circumference can be different enough to impede delivery, but if the baby is looking up, it's sufficiently wider to delay things."

I'd never witnessed a birth like that. "What can we do to help?"

"Your hands are small. You might be able to turn the baby to face down."

But the baby was wedged too tightly for me to get my hands in.

Mother, who'd obviously heard what Pua said, groaned and whispered, "Use the spoons."

"There's a special technique we learned back in Egypt," Pua said. "But it's risky."

She reached into her midwife's bag and pulled out what looked like two elongated bronze spoons with even longer handles, but the bowl was only a rim. Its center was empty.

I immediately understood what they were for. "You're going to try to slide them around the head and pull the baby out." I was so frightened I could barely get the words out. "But what do you need me for?"

"This requires two people. One to cut my sister's opening to make it wider, and the other to slide in a spoon to cradle the baby's head and start pulling with each push." She looked at me intently. "You will make a small cut first, but be prepared to enlarge it if necessary. Use the same knife as for cutting the cord."

I gulped hard, as if I could swallow my fear, but I had to do it.

CHAPTER SEVENTEEN

ASENET

Enjoy happiness with a woman you love all the fleeting days of life that have been granted to you under the sun—all your fleeting days. For that alone is what you can get out of life and out of the means you acquire under the sun.

—Ecclesiastes 9:9

THANKFULLY PUA WAS NOW an expert midwife, so Shifra only had to make one cut for her to slip a spoon through the now larger opening. I was in agony, but I choked back my screams. I don't know where I found the strength, but with each contraction I pushed even harder.

Please, Elohim, no women have died in childbirth since we left Egypt. Save me from being the first.

Still it seemed like hours of slow but steady pulling before Pua drew the head out far enough that it continued moving without her help. She gently removed the spoon and encouraged me to keep pushing, that the child was almost born. That must have given me the fortitude to keep going until the head was fully out, after which the rest of the body followed quickly.

"A boy," Pua and Shifra shouted as they hugged each other, ignoring the blood. Exhausted, I let out a long breath. How I longed to sleep.

Pua reached back into her bag and handed Shifra a needle threaded with fine linen yarn. "You may have the honor of sewing up the cut after I've cleaned it, Shifra." She leaned down and inspected the area. "An excellent job, no tearing at all. I only needed to use one spoon, not both of them."

With my newborn son at my breast, I gave thanks to Elohim. And I was relieved that I had refused the Taweret amulet.

It was almost a month after my son was born before I was finally able to sit without pain, but I was hesitant to resume marital relations. I adored Maratti, who was a considerate, and passionate, lover, so the last thing I wanted was for his lovemaking to hurt. Pua insisted that where Shifra cut me had healed as good as new, and with a lecherous grin, she added that Maratti would find my passage as tight as a virgin's. But Pua was referring to how tightly Shifra had sewed the cut at the entrance to my womb. Surely the spoon had bruised the passage itself as it slowly dragged my baby out, and there was no other way to know how healed it was.

Then there was the question of the child's name. Traditionally the mother chose her baby's name, often to memorialize an ancestor or deceased family member. I didn't want to name my new son Hantilt; the less I remembered my first husband the better. Our son Ziwini, however, had been named for his paternal grandfather, who was, of course, also Maratti's father. Both Hantilt and Ziwini were firstborns, and thus died in the tenth plague. I didn't want to recall that night either.

So I asked Maratti if he had any name he preferred for his first son. To my surprise, and relief, he did, saying, "Hantilt and I had a younger brother, Utti, who was a delightful child. He brought love and joy wherever he went, but he was also too curious for his own good." Maratti's chin quivered as he fought back tears. "Utti fell into a fissure while exploring a cave, and he was dead by the time we found him."

"Won't naming our son Utti bring back those sad memories?" I asked.

Maratti shook his head. "I will always remember him with fondness."

So our boy became Utti at his thirty-day naming ceremony. Like his namesake, he was a delightful child, one who already slept through the night. However, after what Maratti had told me, I was determined to not let his curious nature lead him into danger. His naming was not a large celebration; we were saving that for Eshkar and Shifra's wedding the following month.

But Maratti and I had our own small celebration that night, during which my bliss when he entered me far outweighed the minimal pain I felt. He was exceedingly gentle, and early in the morning, before Utti woke, I encouraged him to pleasure me again, this time with a bit more vigor.

I was not surprised that Tantana was unhappy with Utti's sudden arrival. Thank goodness for Gitlam, who showed her how to play with the cats with lengths of string and, when the cats tired, encouraged her to help him with the goats. He carved small blocks out of Grandfather's unused wood and together they stacked them until the pile collapsed. He could even get her to nap during the day and go to bed at night by pretending to be so tired that he needed to lie down himself.

Assuming that Eshkar would become a father in the upcoming year, I asked him to help care for Utti. Not that he'd change swaddling, but he was willing to carry the crying baby around interminably when he wasn't working with Father or practicing swordplay with Maratti. Most people who'd wanted new wagons and carts had acquired them, so he and Father were mainly occupied repairing old and damaged ones. I saw no enmity or jealousy between Eshkar and Gitlam, but I still couldn't imagine how the two of them would get along once they were both married to Shifra.

162   ASENET

As that day drew near, I realized that I wouldn't have to imagine how the two of them got along once Shifra was Eshkar's wife. We would all be living together. But I was soon too busy with wedding preparations and a new baby to be distracted by potential worries, and less than a week before the wedding, there were real problems to worry about.

We all knew winter was the rainy season, but other than posting some men with shofars on the ridges—who had primarily been used to alert us to approaching caravans—nobody considered what to do if the river through our valley actually did rise significantly. Thus when the shofars blared before dawn, I panicked. I confess that my second thought— the first was to run to see how high the water had risen—was to bring enough beer up to our tents before it was all swept away and left us nothing for the wedding. Once reassured that the water was unlikely to reach our camp before we could move to higher ground, I directed Shifra and Gitlam to watch Utti and Tantana while the rest of our family focused on filling Father and Shaul's wagons with all the beer we would need.

I wasn't concerned about the olive oil. Their amphoras were tied to trees and tightly sealed, and besides, the Levites were already rushing to take the first pressing to safety. Omari calmly directed his workers to load amphoras containing the second pressing into wagons and carts and then to tie the others to both sides of donkeys and he-goats. A few of the workers tried to do this so quickly that they fumbled and dropped an amphora, only to see it float away. If Omari was angry, he didn't show it. He merely urged them to continue working; people could retrieve them later when they came to rest downstream.

Still, it was impossible not to look down at the roiling brown water, still rising, and not feel my anxiety rising as well. The outsiders' camp

THE MIDWIVES' ESCAPE 163

on the opposite side of the lake was now inaccessible from our side, and it looked to me like the cistern would soon be underwater. The olive presses were higher up, so they might not be flooded. But, as Father reminded us regularly, there was nothing we could do about it, so best to leave the future to Elohim. Perhaps we would be fortunate and the muddy waters would be like the Nile flooding its banks, bringing fertile soil to our small oasis.

That advice didn't make me sleep easier, although I did manage to get some sleep snuggled in Maratti's arms in between nursing our baby. If the moon had been closer to full, I would have gone out during the night to look at the water, but it is more propitious to hold weddings when the moon is waxing, and now it was waning. So I was one of many people outside at sunrise, all of whom were smiling at each other with relief to see the water level was now below the cistern. It would still need to be cleaned out before making beer, but that could wait until summer.

What couldn't wait now were Shifra's wedding preparations. The first thing for me to do was to cut her hymen so the wound would heal in time to prevent her from feeling pain on her wedding night, like I'd had on mine. When Maratti explained to Eshkar what he should do to give Shifra the most pleasure, he would casually mention why Shifra wouldn't bleed despite being a maiden. Shifra didn't need any tutoring on what would happen on her wedding night; she was an apprentice midwife and understood that it took the joining of a man's white seed and a woman's red seed to make a baby. This act happened inside the woman's womb, into which the man released his seed through the same passage that the baby would be born from nine months later. If done correctly, it would be pleasurable for both man and woman.

Needless to say, I never intimated that it had been anything but pleasurable for me with Shifra's father.

Then there was the matter of food. Of course the nuptial feast for a virgin would be finer than that served at my wedding to Maratti. Father and I had carefully planned it so no one would think we'd stinted on

164   ASENET

the menu or that we'd been excessively lavish. There would be manna bread with herbed olive oil for dipping along with pickled green olives and cucumbers. Then lentil stew and goat stew with leeks, salted fish and grilled fish with goat cheese, and finally, two roasted yearling kids with baked onions. My mouth watered just thinking about it. For afterward, sweet melons and nut cakes with honey.

But we'd also arranged special entertainment. Despite their father's ignominious end, Korah's sons had begged, and received, Elohim's forgiveness. They had devoted themselves to bringing beautiful music to the Tabernacle to make sacrifices more pleasing to Elohim. I was beyond delighted when Maratti surprised me with news that he'd prevailed on Joshua to persuade these musicians to provide melodies and songs at the wedding.

Finally the day arrived. Father must have already put the young he-goats on the spits because I woke to the savory smell of roasting meat. I put on my finest outfit, a pleated white linen shift with a wide gold collar, gold bracelets on my wrists, and gold hoops in my ears. Pua braided my hair, tying each braid off with a small gold bead. Then the two of us dressed Shifra similarly, although her gold collar was smaller. Also, instead of braiding her hair, we followed the Hebrew tradition of a bride's wearing her hair loose, covered by a sheer white headscarf held in place by a gold diadem.

She looked so lovely that Pua and I both sighed with delight.

By the time Shifra and I were both dressed, the musicians were already playing. I peeked through an opening where the tent walls met and saw a great many people milling around chatting, most of them holding jars of beer. I could hardly believe my eyes to see seven musicians off to the side with their instruments—a lyre, harp, lute, pipe, drum, and two timbrels.

THE MIDWIVES' ESCAPE   165

I signaled to Maratti, who signaled to the musicians, who switched to a new melody. It was time for the guests to help themselves from the platters, bowls, trays, and dishes on the serving tables and take their seats on the large number of rugs and cushions on the floor. Then Eshkar, also dressed in a pleated white linen tunic, took his food, followed by Maratti, Gitlam, and Father, who sat to Eshkar's left.

It was my last chance to speak to Shifra before she wed, but I couldn't think of the right things to say. Suddenly I remembered how Father had blessed me, only he had asked that Hathor, the Egyptian goddess of love and fertility, bless me, not Elohim. So I changed his words to "May you know nothing but happiness from this day forward, may Elohim be with you and bless you, may you see your children's children, and may your life be filled with laughter, endless joy, and good fortune."

Tears welled in her eyes, and I kissed her forehead.

Finally everyone was sitting except me and Shifra. The musicians started a slow, stately tune, the crowd quieted, and we walked to our spots—mine next to Maratti and Shifra's beside Eshkar. Pua, who had already chosen food for Shifra, handed it to her.

Shifra gulped and turned to me. "I can't eat all this, Mother. I'm too nervous."

I smiled and patted her hand. "Eat only as much now as you feel comfortable with. We will bring the leftovers to your nuptial tent," I said. "Once you two have closed the tent flaps behind you, you won't be coming out until morning."

"What about when we need the latrines?" Her whisper was full of anxiety.

"Don't worry. We'll make sure the guests are gone by then—or at least not looking in that direction. But make sure to use them first."

About halfway through the meal, Father stood up and gestured to Shaul. As Shaul approached, the musicians burst into a lively tune. The crowd broke out in cheers, for Shaul was pulling a cart holding a keg of wine. People lined up to fill their cups, but instead of sitting down, men and women formed separate circles and began to dance. Slowly at first, then faster, the dancers circled one another, men on the outside facing in, women on the inside facing the men, bride and groom clapping and watching on the side. When it appeared that the dancers were tiring, especially the men, the musicians slowed their pace.

The men refilled their plates with sweets while the women beckoned me and Shifra to the center of their circle. We danced sedately while the women danced around us; I was so tired I couldn't wait to sit down, but Shifra was full of energy—jumping, spinning, and twirling with one woman after another. However, the men began to mock Eshkar with taunts such as, "You're eating so much; how will you do your bride justice tonight?" or "With all the beer and wine you're drinking, you'll be asleep before your bride is satisfied."

Shifra ignored the teasing and modestly kept her eyes downward. When the dance came to an end, she remained standing while Eshkar stood up and, without the slightest stagger in his walk, took his place beside her. Tears filled my eyes as he gently lifted her headscarf so her face was visible. Then he placed a gold ring in her hand, which she promptly put on her finger.

"Behold"—he turned to the attendees—"in the presence of these witnesses, this woman is consecrated to me as my wife."

Maratti rose and beckoned to the newlyweds. "Now, away to your tent that you may consummate the marriage we have all celebrated."

Not only did Eshkar and Shifra follow him there, but so did our families and a good many of the male guests, all yelling out advice and guidance so bawdy and indecent that my ears burned. Once inside their tent, Eshkar tied the flaps closed, but this encouraged even more ribald and lewd comments. Thankfully the musicians started playing a series of loud and lively tunes, encouraging the guests to clap and sing along.

THE MIDWIVES' ESCAPE 167

And thus my daughter and her new husband began their married life with a modicum of seclusion.

The last guests didn't leave until shortly after midnight, when the half moon set. Exhausted as I was, I couldn't allow myself to go to bed until all the leftover food was stored away; otherwise the sand cats, and who knows what other creatures, would eat it. We could wash the tableware and pots in the morning. All was quiet in the nuptial tent as I nursed Utti, but Maratti assured me that the newlyweds would resume relations soon after the sun rose.

"I hope their nighttime relations please Shifra sufficiently so that will be the case," I told him. My first wedding night had done the very opposite of pleasing me.

Maratti took my hand and gazed into my eyes. It was a look that never failed to kindle my passion. "Speaking of nighttime relations," he whispered, "now that our son has a full stomach and fresh swaddling, he should sleep for at least several hours."

I gently pulled Maratti toward our tent. "Then let's not waste any time talking."

The sun was already up as I put away the clean cups and dishes. Suddenly Shifra, dressed in her usual goat's wool tunic, walked up and put her arms around me. "Oh, Mother," she said softly. "Pleasurable can't begin to describe what Eshkar did to my body. His hands, his mouth, and his lips and tongue brought out feelings I'd never imagined could feel so sweet."

She sighed with happiness, and I sighed with relief. "How did he know what to do?" she asked. "I wouldn't have known what to do if he hadn't shown me."

"I assume Maratti taught him," I replied. I didn't mention that Maratti also had taken Eshkar to visit harlots so he would be prepared and not too nervous.

"I can't thank you enough for cutting my maidenhead in advance." She hugged me tighter. "And Eshkar thanks you as well."

I was getting embarrassed. "Considering how little you ate yesterday, you must be hungry. I saved some roasted meat and grilled fish for you to eat this morning, and I collected your manna. Plus there's still melon and cake. I'll reheat the stews later for our midday meals."

"Did I hear someone say 'roasted meat and grilled fish'?" Eshkar closed the tent flaps behind him and licked his lips, but he was looking at Shifra.

Shifra gazed at him with adoration as she filled their plates and poured them beer. They sat down and were immediately joined by the two sand cats. "Mother, is it all right to give them some fish?" Shifra asked. "There's so much it will spoil before we eat it all."

I waved my hand in acquiescence. What could I say on this happy morning? Especially since my daughter was right. The sun went behind a cloud, and I could hear a cacophony of birds in and above the lake. I sat down next to Maratti and took his hand as the rest of our family slowly joined us. Before everyone else was done eating, the bridal couple excused themselves and returned to their tent. Maratti and Father shot me questioning looks, to which I merely nodded and smiled. Hopefully we would have another baby in the household by this time next year.

Sadly that would not be the case. After no menses the following two months, Shifra bled more than usual the third month, also expelling a great many clots.

A small consolation came when each of our sand cats gave birth to a litter of healthy kittens. It was an embarrassment to me, a midwife, since I was not even aware that they had mated, let alone that they were pregnant. Children both inside and outside the camp begged to see them, but the sand cat mothers would not allow anyone except Gitlam, Tantana, and Shifra to come near. And that was only if they brought an offering of meat or fish. Ultimately, unlike their orphaned mothers who'd been raised by people, the kittens eventually disappeared into the desert.

Sand cats and kittens at Kadesh

170   ASENET

The first summer caravan arrived in the fourth month, this one
from Midian. According to Maratti, Midian had a port at the northern
terminus of the Red Sea, where grain and linen from fertile Babylon
were traded with lands to the east, south, and west. From the east came
Arabian incense along with Indian spices, precious stones, and pearls.
From the Horn of Africa in the south there were frankincense and
gold. Except for grain, linen, and incense, most of these goods were too
pricey for us, although this year we had the benefit of olive oil and beer
to barter with.

I, along with Gudit and Miriam, was curious about what had happened to Moses's family—his father-in-law, his brother-in-law, and his
sons. But all we learned was that his father-in-law, whom some called
Jethro, and others Reuel, had died.

On the subject of death, a very strange thing happened in the second week of the fifth month. Up until this time, almost nobody innocent of sin had died—other than in accidents or in battle. Normally
most deaths would be among the elderly, but I couldn't think of an old
person who'd died a natural death.

Until the night of the half moon.

Everybody went to sleep as usual, but in the morning, the air
echoed with women's cries and screams. Hundreds of men were dead,
all of them Hebrews over the age of forty, including Haggith's elderly
husband. Almost none had shown any signs of illness or injury the day
before. More strangely, nobody else died the next day—or the next. I
didn't know what to make of it; none of the women or children had
died or shown any sign of illness or poison. But after the dead were
buried, our family was soon distracted by the Moabite caravan's arrival.

Shifra was particularly distracted when Bahiti came to visit and
took her aside to speak privately. I admit eavesdropping and couldn't
restrain myself from interrupting when I heard that among the merchants was the man Haggith had left with.

THE MIDWIVES' ESCAPE

"Are you certain Haggith left with this Moabite under her own will?" I blurted out.

"Mother!" Shifra protested. "We were sworn to secrecy."

Bahiti shrugged. "Haggith's a widow now, so she's free to remarry her paramour." She continued with a grin. "Who happens to be Prince Eglon, son of King Balak."

"I don't suppose she traveled back here with him," Shifra said. "Helah misses her terribly, and so do I." When Bahiti shook her head, I had to ask, "Is this Eglon on this caravan? Could I see him?"

Thinking how I would feel if Shifra had disappeared under similar circumstances, I could sympathize with Helah. "Shifra should stay secluded at home; she is still a new bride," I said. "But I don't see any reason why Maratti and I shouldn't meet Eglon and confirm from him that Haggith is happy. And if that goes well, perhaps Maratti and I could go back to Moab with the caravan and see Haggith in person."

Shifra beamed. "You could say you're going to fulfill a large order of salt."

"And you could return here with the Edomite caravan that comes at summer's end," Bahiti said. "So you won't be traveling alone."

Initially Maratti was disinclined to go on what he considered a fool's errand. But after meeting Eglon, who was eager for us to bring relief to Haggith and her mother and who also insisted that he would supply us with all the salt we could carry at a very reasonable price, my husband was persuaded. When it was time to leave, Maratti dressed in full armor, his sword and shield at his side. He made no threatening moves and the Moabites recognized him as a Hittite mercenary. So they accepted that he was armed as a precaution to protect me and our son.

Utti was no trouble. I carried him in a sling across my breasts, where he could suckle as needed. Soothed by the gentle swaying of the

172   ASENET

donkeys we rode, he rarely cried. Eglon rode beside us as we traveled and gave us his own tent to sleep in, while he slept with his guards. There were no other women in the caravan, and I wore my veil so it covered my hair completely and all of my face except for my eyes. I ate inside our tent, while Maratti ate with the Moabites at the campfire outside it.

I didn't like hearing the Moabites constantly disparage and belittle the Hebrews, complaining that there were too many of them. "Who can count their dust, number their dust clouds?" They also criticized the Hebrews for being a people that dwelt apart, not reckoned among the nations, who worshipped some strange invisible god. And when Eglon was out of hearing range, they censured their prince for marrying a Hebrew woman. All I could do was tense my fists and say nothing; Maratti and I were their guests.

However when the caravan approached Moab, I couldn't believe my eyes. The people lived in enormous caves carved into the red sandstone cliffs. Winding roads, stairways, and water channels were cut along the natural curves of cliffs and canyons. It was truly spectacular. When we got closer, I could see that the caves were natural but had been enlarged and adapted for human living and storage of goods with stone walls built to subdivide the caves' interiors.

I couldn't wait to explore them.

We received an enthusiastic welcome. At first I assumed it was because their caravan had returned safely from a successful trading journey, but while that had been the case, it was my appearance that was so opportune.

Haggith was in labor.

I was surprised that my arrival was so appreciated; surely the Moabites had experienced midwives among them. But the most expert one was suffering from a fever, and once Haggith learned that I had come in on the caravan, she insisted that I attend her. Not wanting to insult the local women, I suggested that a Moabite midwife assist me,

THE MIDWIVES' ESCAPE   173

which was just as well because I hadn't brought my birthing bag. Considering that this baby would be King Balak's first grandchild, I was in no position to decline, not only because I wanted Haggith to labor with a familiar presence, but also because if things went badly without me, I would surely be blamed for neglecting her. Of course, I would also be blamed if things went badly while I was attending her.

Fortunately, Haggith's labor progressed slowly, although not slower than normal for a first child. I encouraged her to scream all she wanted. It would reassure those outside that she was still alive and well. After she'd pushed for several hours, a healthy baby boy made his appearance with a lusty cry. Once he'd been cleaned and swaddled, he fell asleep, which gave Haggith, and me, the opportunity to sleep as well.

The next morning, Haggith took advantage of her son's sleep time to show me the city she was so proud of. We wandered past intricate temples honoring pagan gods, etchings of snakes, lions, and eagles, and some of the more than six hundred massive burial chambers, all hewed from the soaring rock faces that glowed in swirling hues of terracotta, red, and blush pink. The Moabites' agricultural abundance was demonstrated by the many storage facilities both inside the houses and outside in courtyards. I could see by the way these storage pits were arranged within households that large families lived in each quarter of the city.

As impressive as the site appeared, after a while it all looked the same. I was relieved when Haggith began to yawn and we returned to her rooms, where Maratti was outside walking back and forth impatiently. I hurriedly examined Haggith and was reassured that all was well. I was so exhausted I couldn't wait for her guard to escort me and Maratti to our quarters so I could rest.

When the Edomite caravan heading west arrived a few weeks later, Haggith and her baby were thriving. So she and I said our farewells,

174   ASENET

which included permission—indeed encouragement—to inform Helah of her daughter's excellent circumstances. When no one was around, I peeked at the gifts Eglon had given me. There was a lovely embroidered linen gown as well as a collection of gold jewelry: earrings, bracelets, and a necklace set with various colored stones. I'd protested that I didn't deserve such a royal payment, that any reasonably skilled midwife would have sufficed, but Elgon replied that this was a small price for his and Haggith's happiness.

Once we were back in Kadesh Barnea, Maratti proudly revealed that in addition to a large amount of salt, he'd brought back both balsam oil and incense, all of which were gifts from Prince Eglon.

CHAPTER EIGHTEEN

SHIFRA

David put his hand into the bag; he took out a stone and slung it. It struck the Philistine in the forehead; the stone sank into his forehead, and he fell face down on the ground.

—Samuel 17:49–50

I LEARNED HOW TO MAKE slings five years later. Gitlam and I were working with Grandfather on some new storage boxes; most of ours had sold to the earlier caravans, and Grandfather wanted more to be ready when the final Edomite caravan arrived. Gitlam, almost fully grown, was in a foul and unproductive mood. He'd nicked himself twice and mis-sized the lengths of a box's two sides.

He'd just cursed under his breath when Grandfather turned to him and said sternly, "If you can't even measure two pieces of wood accurately, why don't you go outside and practice throwing rocks."

"I can throw rocks accurately," he complained. "But not far enough."

"Have those boys been bothering you again?" Grandfather asked.

I looked up at Gitlam, whose angry frown looked like it could curdle milk. "Just because I'm Lagash doesn't make me ugly and stupid."

I put my knife down and hugged him. "I think Lagash men are very handsome and quite intelligent."

"It doesn't matter what you think. They're the ones who want to beat me up."

Grandfather stroked his chin in thought. "I've heard that you are an expert stone thrower, so maybe you could learn to use a sling to launch rocks and stones across long distances."

This made Gitlam look up with excitement. "Will you teach me?"

"I have no doubt that you can teach yourself to use a sling . . ." Grandfather paused and looked at me. "But first we have to make you one or two. When used correctly, properly positioned between a man's fingers, it acts as an extension of his arm and allows more precision and greater range." Then he turned to Gitlam. "Slings can cause blunt-force trauma that shatters bone, damages organs, and sometimes results in death. Some mercenary warriors, especially archers, think only ignorant barbarian peasants use slings. In truth, the sling has many advantages over the bow."

Both Gitlam and I gave Grandfather our rapt attention as he explained. "A sling is much smaller than a bow, easier to carry and conceal. I have made a few slings and find that when folded and bound up by their own strings, they become a tiny soft bundle. Bows take far more time and skill to make, requiring more materials and rarer materials too. Bows need more maintenance, can break when you fall, and are more cumbersome."

I wondered where and how Grandfather had become such an expert, but he continued before I could ask. "You can carry a sling without ammunition, assured that stones can be found when needed. But bows take very specialized ammunition that needs to be well made in advance and maintained, since they can warp in damp weather. Arrows are expensive, so an archer wants to recover as many as possible after use. They need to be carried in an awkward quiver that flops about as the archer runs. But a pouch of sling stones makes a neat bundle, a more manageable load."

THE MIDWIVES' ESCAPE   177

Grandfather's voice was getting hoarse, and he paused to drink some water before continuing. "Battles have hinged on whether one side, with superior archers, was able to use its bows effectively. Even a light wind blows arrows off course, while rain spoils bow strings and drags arrows down from the air. Slings, while still adversely affected by wind and rain, suffer not nearly so much from bad weather. Slingers are generally more mobile than archers. They find it easier to sling on the move and have the advantage of needing only one hand to sling, which allows them to use a shield in their free hand to protect themselves. Plus your enemy can see arrows coming, but a stone is almost invisible, thus particularly difficult to defend against."

Gitlam's eyes blazed with impatience. "How soon can you start teaching me?" he asked.

To which Grandfather replied, "As soon as Shifra makes your sling, which she should be able to accomplish this afternoon. Keep in mind that it takes much practice to get good range and accuracy with a sling. Fortunately you are young enough to achieve this skill in a short period of time. I've heard there are boys who use slings to herd sheep and goats. They sit in the shade of a tree, and if an animal strays, they sling a stone in front of it to scare it back into the flock."

If Grandfather expected me to make slings today, I needed to start soon. "So how do I make a sling?" I asked him.

He replied immediately. "You will need two pieces of rope made of braided goat's hair thread, each a little longer than a cubit and as wide as your little finger. You will also need some thin leather cut to the length of a man's middle finger and half as wide.

"First, fold the leather over lengthwise and punch a hole in each side to create a pocket for the rock to rest in until released. Next tie a knot that attaches one of the ropes to one end of the leather. Then repeat with the opposite end, and knot a loop at the end of that rope. The loop will fit over the center finger of the throwing hand. Then you pull both of the cords, keeping the leather pocket level. Finally, grasp the nonloop between your thumb and forefinger and tie a knot there."

When we both looked at Grandfather blankly, he stood up and began rummaging in a box on a high shelf. "Wait while I find one of my old ones."

Before I could count to ten, he pulled one out and held it up so we could view the whole sling. Once I saw its entirety, I was confident I could duplicate it.

I located sufficient goat's hair thread thick enough to duplicate the braid in less than an hour, while Grandfather found some leather and cut it to size. I finished it so quickly that Gitlam was still collecting a pouch of good-sized smooth, round rocks when I brought it to him and announced, "Now you are ready to load it and start slinging."

When he took it and turned to thank me, I hugged him again, this time pressing my hips against his suggestively. Tonight was Gitlam's turn to share my bed, and I wanted to take advantage of his excited mood. "Do you know what all this talk of loading and slinging has made me think of?" I whispered.

After checking to see if Grandfather was watching, Gitlam put his hands on my bottom and pulled me close. "Me as well," he murmured, his voice husky with desire.

I couldn't wait for sunset. Lying in bed after what I knew would merely be our first coupling, I contemplated my two husbands' different bed practices. Eshkar had started calm and restrained but had become more vigorous, rough even, when I'd responded with encouragement. Not that he ever hurt me, even when I bit or scratched him. We reached our first climaxes swiftly, then rested briefly before resuming more leisurely.

Like most new husbands, Gitlam had climaxed quickly when we first wed—not that we had a public wedding—but once it was clear that he was sufficiently mature, he and Eshkar worked out a schedule to share my attentions. After we had been married a month, Gitlam

THE MIDWIVES' ESCAPE 179

preferred moving slowly and gently as I grew more excited, teasing me until I impelled him to move so fast and energetically that our climaxes came quickly. At first I had nipped his shoulder or neck on occasion, but stopped once it was clear that he did not enjoy my love bites like Eshkar did.

I didn't know how I could live without either of them.

I'd seen how accurately Gitlam threw stones, but I was still astonished at how rapidly he mastered the sling. Grandfather suggested that Gitlam ask the Nubians if he could practice with his sling at their targets sometimes when they weren't shooting arrows at them. The Nubians were immediately intrigued and soon were challenging him to competitions in which they seemed delighted when they lost. Fortunately for Gitlam, who was shy about showing off his skill while he considered himself a beginner with a sling, only a few people were welcome to visit the Nubians' camp. Thus he could practice in relative privacy.

Eshkar didn't complain about spending extra time in Grandfather's workshop so Gitlam could become more expert with a sling. He didn't like his brother being bullied, but they both knew that Gitlam would receive more abuse if Eshkar interfered. For my part, I knew the day would come when Gitlam had to demonstrate what would happen if the boys ganged up on him again. I had two worries: that Gitlam might lose his temper and use his sling to severely injure or even kill one of them, or that there might be too many boys to keep at bay and thus Gitlam would be overpowered. Gitlam was more afraid of the latter, and he practiced diligently to sling a stone and reload another as quickly as possible so as to leave no time for his adversaries to get close enough to lay hands on him.

But it turned out as Grandfather expected. The boys, like most bullies, were cowards. When they realized how expert Gitlam was with a sling, none of them wanted to be the first to challenge him. Eshkar

180   SHIFRA

acted disappointed that Gitlam didn't get a chance to teach them a lesson, but I knew he was as relieved as I was.

Nobody outside our family cared about Gitlam's sling prowess on the morning of the fifth month's first half moon. This year many more men died during the night than last summer—all of them Hebrews over the age of forty. Again, most hadn't shown any signs of illness or injury the day before. Last year families of the deceased had used carts to remove the bodies to local caves and bury them inside. This year they wanted to do the same, but when it occurred to enough people that this could be an annual occurrence, the quarrels began.

First the Levites demanded that, just as people impure from leprosy and other skin lesions, menstruation and childbirth, and seminal and abnormal genital emissions must remain outside the camp, a corpse must be removed from the camp. This enraged us non-Hebrews who resided outside the camp and who didn't want any dead bodies buried where we lived. As far as Mother and Grandfather were concerned, since the bodies were all Hebrews, they should be the ones to bury them—far away from us. However, considering that there were suddenly thousands of corpses to deal with and this number was likely to increase each year, a solution had to be found quickly.

To complicate matters, the foreign cultures had diverse funeral customs. Moses, wise enough to know that a committee composed of leaders from the different Hebrew tribes plus the various outside peoples would argue interminably without reaching a conclusion, also knew that this was not something he could impose by fiat. So he appointed Aaron, Joshua, Caleb, and Maratti to implement a practice that everyone would follow next year, which the four leaders did, surprisingly, in less than a month.

First of all, no remains could be burned. Funeral pyres were forbidden. Second, bodies must be buried, either in the ground or in a cave, the day they were found. To make this less onerous, here is what every Hebrew man over the age of forty must do: on the eve of the first half moon on the fifth month, he would go at least one thousand cubits beyond where those outside the camp reside, as well as two hundred cubits away from the latrines. There he would dig a grave, and that night, he would sleep in it. If he was too infirm to dig the grave himself, another in his family may help him. If he died during the night, his body would be buried there.

This protocol had to be followed until all the Hebrew men from the generation of the spies were dead. After that time, those remaining alive could enter the Promised Land.

While some Hebrews thought it was unfair that the outsiders were exempt, Joshua and Caleb reminded them that the spies had all been Hebrew men, so only Hebrew men should bear the consequences of the spies' craven actions. Since none of the Levites or women were condemned either, the complaining minority was ignored.

What I'd discerned later, however, was so odd that I had to ask Pua about it. "Don't you think it's strange that twice as many baby boys as girls are being born these days?"

"So you've noticed it, too?"

I nodded. "Do you think Elohim is responsible?"

"Of course. Elohim is responsible for everything in nature."

"I mean, do you think Elohim is giving us more boys to make up for all the men dying? It does make sense."

Pua wrinkled her forehead in thought. "You could be right, but we won't know for sure until several more years pass."

The full moon had just risen when I heard the guards' shofar calls that announced a caravan's imminent arrival. I had spent the day painting designs on the newly fired amphora. All of last year's amphora had gone out with their olive oil contents, and it wouldn't be long before this year's olive harvest was upon us. As the days grew shorter, I'd missed Mother more and more. Surely she and Maratti would return soon, I told myself, which was what Gitlam and I had told Tantana since the day they'd left.

I didn't care that it was getting dark. I could see the caravan approaching, a string of torches moving slowly in our direction. I left my sister in Grandfather's care and raced down the hill, Eshkar right behind me, our eyes peeled for the two donkeys bearing Maratti and Mother. However before I saw them, Mother had seen me.

"Shifra." A man called my name. I couldn't see anyone I recognized, but I ran toward the sound. Then I saw Maratti, his bronze armor glinting in the moonlight, waving at me. And there was Mother, Utti in her arms, alighting from her donkey.

I embraced her, careful not to squeeze my little brother. "Did you see Haggith again? How is she? Is she happy?" I was overflowing with questions.

"If you will quiet down, I will tell you everything."

Eshkar and Maratti led the two donkeys and, as we slowly walked up the hill to our tents, Mother recounted their exploits in Moab. "In the morning I'll show you the gifts we received," she concluded. "After we've spoken with Haggith's family."

I could scarcely contain my joy. "Imagine, Haggith married to a Moabite prince and mother of his first son," I whispered to Eshkar. "And to think I was so worried about her."

"Have you told your mother that you haven't bled since before she left?" he whispered back.

I shook my head. "Let's wait another month or two or until she notices that I'm sick every morning." I was confident that Mother would soon discern my condition without my saying anything.

After breaking our morning fast, Mother and I delivered Prince Eglon's bride price and other gifts to Ziza and Helah. Helah was crying so many joyful tears that Mother couldn't tell Haggith's story without continual interruptions.

Olive oil amphoras tied to an ancient olive tree

184   SHIFRA

Ziza kept repeating, "I can't believe it. Our daughter is not only alive, but she has given us a grandson."

"We must make a thanksgiving offering at the Tabernacle," Helah declared.

"I disagree," he said. "I don't think we should publicize our good fortune so soon."

Helah sighed. "I suppose you're right." Then she turned to Mother. "Tell me everything that happened with Haggith in Moab. I promise not to interrupt."

I was still vomiting every morning while other people were occupied with brewing date beer or producing oil. Most of our goats' milk had dried up, which was just as well since the smell of fermenting cheese only made me feel more nauseated, as did the odor of pickling green olives. But I could still assist Grandfather in the woodshop.

Which is where I was when I looked up and saw Joshua at our tent's entrance. Both Tantana and Utti had miraculously taken their naps at the same time, so Mother took advantage of the quiet to lie down as well. Grandfather saw Joshua just after I did, and he quickly stood up and put a finger to his lips. Joshua gestured for Grandfather to join him outside, so I quietly followed and hoped nobody would stop me.

"Maratti is out training the men," Grandfather said, "but perhaps I can be of service."

"I suspect you can," Joshua replied. "Now that the lake is starting to dry up, Aaron is concerned that the water level has dropped so much that it will soon be impossible to immerse in it."

"I imagine that Aaron is more than merely concerned," Grandfather said.

Joshua grinned and nodded. "Indeed, he is quite distressed."

"So you think I can help?"

THE MIDWIVES' ESCAPE   185

"I hope you, or some of the Egyptians you know, can help." When Grandfather remained silent, Joshua came to the point. "We need to build a dam so the lake's water level will not drop much lower, and I have heard that in the past, Egyptian workers would construct weirs along the Nile."

"I have heard of such things, but I was only marginally involved."

"Can you find men here who are experienced in this kind of work?"

"I don't know, but I will ask among the Egyptians." Grandfather paused before adding, "Assuming I find some, I doubt they will work for free. Aaron will need to pay them a reasonable wage."

"Of course. We're not slaves anymore." There was pride in Joshua's voice. "So our workers not only get paid, but they will receive time for a midday meal."

I wasn't surprised when Grandfather returned the next afternoon with a heavily built Egyptian man he introduced as Gyasi. "Gyasi is an expert at building weirs."

Gyasi shrugged off the compliment and said, "I'm no expert, but I've seen it done."

"What's a weir?" I interrupted. I'd never heard the word before.

Gyasi smiled at me. "A weir is a dam that allows the water behind it to rise to a certain level to maintain a pool. Then once the pool is filled, the weir allows the same amount of water that entered it to continuously flow out over its top. This keeps the pool full and the river running," he explained. "You might think the job only requires strong men, but there are some tasks that are best done by women."

"Please explain," said Grandfather.

"The first task can be done by anyone," Gyasi began. "We look downstream from the lake to find a narrow place with relatively high walls. We want our weir to be just over two cubits tall so the lake will be deep enough to immerse in near the weir but not so deep that people are in danger of drowning."

"And once you have the location?" Grandfather asked.

"Then everyone looks for large rocks nearby, ideally those with at least one flat side. But the best rocks are big and round so they can be rolled to the site and not carried."

"Why flat sides then?"

"The fewer gaps between rocks in the weir, the more water it will hold back and the less likelihood of it collapsing."

"What else can women do besides look for rocks?" I asked.

"It is rare to have sufficient large rocks that fit together well," Gyasi replied. "When we can't find enough, then we use large baskets of smaller rocks."

"Palm fronds make big sturdy baskets," I said, thinking of the baskets we used when extracting oil from olives.

"I assume the best time to build a weir is when the river is at low flow," Grandfather said.

Gyasi nodded. "Which is usually early in autumn, before the rainy season."

I couldn't hold the words back. "But it's already autumn. Are we too late?"

"I suggest that we find the best spot now," Gyasi replied, "while you marshal some of your friends to do the rock hunting. Wait until we've chosen the place, and then start looking nearby so we won't have to move rocks too far later. There's no need to move any rocks to the creek now. Just mark the location so we can find them later."

I raced back to our tents. I knew exactly whom to ask to look for rocks, and both of them were there. Gitlam was always on the lookout for good slinging stones, and Eshkar was tired of leading our donkey in circles around the olive press every day.

The next morning when I couldn't avoid retching where my entire family, including Mother, could hear me, my secret was out. Not that it had been a secret from Eshkar, but now he showed his joy and embraced me publicly.

Mother was delighted of course, but also irked that I hadn't told her immediately when she'd returned from Moab. "How long has this been going on?" she scolded me.

"Three months," I admitted. "Since midsummer."

She insisted on examining me and declared the baby would be born in spring.

Grandfather adroitly changed the subject by bringing up the topic of the weir and asking us to join him at the lake and advise him which location would be best. We passed the cistern, bubbling with fermenting beer, on our way to the far end of the lake.

"We want a place where the creek narrows," he reminded us. "But also where we can dig a side trench to route the water away from the construction."

He took us to three sites, all of which looked much the same to me. Maratti pointed out, however, that the slope of the hill next to one was too steep to easily transport rocks down it. We all agreed so that spot was eliminated. Mother objected to another because there weren't enough reeds around it to provide privacy for the women who'd be immersing just above the weir. The third was private and the hills on both sides weren't too steep, but it wasn't as narrow as the other two.

So the weir would be a little wider. Once Gyasi offered to pay the workers in beer, he rounded up an ample number of men who quickly dug the side trench. Finding enough good-sized rocks turned out to be simpler than moving them into position, but eventually there were enough for the men to lay a large rock base. When it settled, they troweled clay dirt in between gaps and over the top. After it hardened they positioned the flat-sided rocks as close together as possible until the weir was two cubits tall, then applied amorge to seal it. Satisfied with the weir, Gyasi directed the men to pile leftover rocks on its downstream side to further strengthen it. A month later the men filled in the side trench, and a month after that Aaron declared the pool fit for immersion.

CHAPTER NINETEEN

ASENET

Every Erev Tisha B'Av, each individual (over 25) would go out and dig (his grave) . . . and sleep in it, in case they would die . . . and the next day, the living would separate themselves from the dead.

—Rashi on Talmud Ta'anit 30b

"TAKE THAT RUCKUS OUTSIDE, boys," I shouted. "The little ones are sleeping." *And this old one wanted to nap too.*

Father came to my rescue. "Why don't I take the bigger ones down to the lake? Birds are still migrating south for the winter, and Gitlam is bringing them down with his sling. The boys can practice swimming by racing to fetch the fallen birds."

He was immediately surrounded by boys entreating, "Take me, take me," and not a moment too soon, I was left in blissful silence.

It seemed as though I'd spent the last fifteen years yelling at sons and grandsons: three sons of my own and two of Shifra's. Thankfully I was done bearing children, but Shifra was in her twenties, the prime of her fertility. Sometimes I wondered if having two husbands made her more or less likely to conceive. Not that I could tell which of my grandchildren were Eshkar's and which were Gitlam's. But that was probably just as well.

THE MIDWIVES' ESCAPE

I went into my tent and lay down, but thinking of my daughter's unusual conjugal situation kept me awake. We all knew that by becoming betrothed to Eshkar, she had also been promised to Gitlam. That was the Lagash tradition. Their mother had also wed brothers and had lived with both at the same time. I reassured myself that plenty of men had two wives, so why shouldn't a woman have two husbands?

Thus nine years after Shifra's wedding to Eshkar, she'd married Gitlam. Of course they couldn't celebrate their nuptials the same way—with an elaborate banquet, musicians, and dancing. I sighed remembering there had been even less rejoicing than when Maratti married me after I was widowed. At least everyone knew I was Maratti's wife; now only our immediate family knew that Shifra was Gitlam's wife in addition to Eshkar's.

I had to admit that despite the conflicts common between two women married to the same man, Eshkar and Gitlam never seemed to quarrel. They amicably drank from the same cup, although not at the same time. Shifra shared a bed with Gitlam exclusively for the wedding week, during which she reported to me that despite his being tutored in marital skills by both Maratti and Eshkar, his bed practices were quite different from his brother's.

"It's like with my sons," Shifra told me. "They're different, but I love them all and don't prefer one over the other."

She alternated between the brothers, sleeping with Eshkar for two consecutive nights and then spending the next two nights with Gitlam. When she had her menses, she slept with her sister.

This system worked better than I'd expected. The Amalekite copper mine our warriors had captured on the way to Mount Sinai had been reopened by the Egyptians and Akkadians previously enslaved there. To protect the workers and mining equipment, Joshua and Maratti had posted a modest regiment of soldiers. Some of them alternated duty, spending two nights at the mines followed by two nights back home in the camp.

190   ASENET

Eshkar, now an accomplished swordsman, was one of the guards, so for the two nights when Shifra slept with Gitlam, Eshkar was away at the mining camp. Thus he wasn't confronted with Shifra and Gitlam's sleeping together in the tent nearby; plus, he received a share of the smelted copper for his efforts. Gitlam, however, had spent years knowing that his brother was sleeping with Shifra. Apparently it didn't bother him then any more than it did now.

I must have fallen asleep because the next thing I knew Father, Gitlam and the boys were back inside. Shifra was plucking feathers from two large birds as the sand cats wound around her ankles, meowing hungrily. I couldn't tell whether the birds were storks or cranes, but they were going to be our evening meal. So I got up and lit the oven.

As soon as I did, Shifra said, "Aunt Pua came over while you were sleeping. She wanted to remind you that you, Maratti, and Tantana are to join them for the evening meal so you can start making arrangements for Rephaiah and Tantana's wedding."

"I haven't forgotten." I turned and called out to Gitlam, "I hope you got a good-size bird for Pua too."

"I downed a crane for them, Mother," he replied. "I gave it to her on my way back." Not long after he and Eshkar came to live with us, they began calling me Mother. I preferred it rather than their calling me Grandmother like their children did.

"When do the birds migrate back from the south?" I asked Gitlam. "I'd like to have a spring wedding when we can serve both fowl and yearling kids."

"As far as fowl are concerned, make the wedding whenever you want," he replied. "Many birds stay at the lake the whole winter."

"I'm learning to knock down birds with a sling too," Utti piped up. "I'm so good with rocks now that Uncle Gitlam has me practicing on ducks."

THE MIDWIVES' ESCAPE   191

I gave my son a proud look. "That's wonderful. In the spring your brothers and nephews can search for duck eggs too."

Other than sharing unleavened bread and a roasted kid under the full moon of Nisan at the yearly Pesach festival, I couldn't recall the last time I'd dined with my sister's family. Pua and I regularly did our weaving together now as we worked on materials for our children's marital tent. Still, our conversations were awkward; I had borne four sons and two daughters, while Pua had only the two sons. Yet despite our both being midwives, neither of us had found a way to restore her fertility.

"Remember your manners, Tantana," I admonished as I helped her dress and then braided her hair with strings of beads. At home, in her ordinary clothes, I still saw Tantana as a little girl. Now I saw her on the cusp of womanhood.

Tantana was too intimidated to say anything, and the most I could get from her was a nod or shake of her head. She modestly kept her gaze down, except when she exchanged glances with Rephaiah, at which time both would quickly avert their eyes. Maratti had taught Eshkar and Gitlam well; Shifra has had no complaints about either of her wedding nights, and the way her eyes shone and glistened when she and her husband exited their quarters made clear what was unspoken. But Shaul would be the one instructing Rephaiah, and I had never been brave enough to raise the subject with my sister. Thus it would fall to me to edify Tantana about the pleasures of the conjugal bed.

Fortunately our children weren't strangers. Tantana had known Rephaiah all her life, and as far as I could tell, they liked each other well enough. But once they were married, my daughter would go live with Pua's family, and who knows how often I'd see her. True, Shaul and Pua's tents were a short walk from ours, but the Hebrew custom is that a bride leaves her natal family and joins her husband's. After Haggith married, she rarely saw her mother, Helah, and now that she was married to a Moabite, the two women would probably never see each other again.

192   ASENET

Thinking of Haggith reminded me of the winter after we returned from Moab, when everyone—both in the camp and outside—was taken by surprise when a Nabataean caravan arrived from the west. This tribe, established in a tent community on the coast just south of Gaza, plied a trade route up and down the coastal road between Egypt and Phoenicia. Their brother tribe, located near the Edomite capital, traded mostly in the east. The Nabataeans had heard from the Edomites that our oasis would be a good winter trading stop, especially for fresh olive oil and beer, and that we had a good-sized garrison for protection from thieves and bandits.

But the bigger surprise was that even Joshua and Caleb had no idea that the tribe was descended from Ishmael. It was only when the Ishmaelites sought permission to set up a temporary trading camp in our valley did they learn that most of our community were Hebrews, descended from Ishmael's younger brother Isaac. Their patriarch, Ishmael, also had twelve sons. I found their relationships confusing because there were other desert dwellers who called themselves Hagarites, Hagar being Abraham's concubine and the mother of Ishmael. From what I heard, there were many tears and embraces as the tribes of long-lost cousins, both of whom worshipped Elohim, celebrated their reunion.

I was so proud when Gitlam demonstrated his sling skills by bringing down every kind of large bird for the feast: storks, cranes, pelicans, herons, ibis, and marsh harriers. For their part, the Ishmaelites provided lentils and yearling lambs and calves, in addition to freshly baked wheaten loaves. Unsure whether Elohim would furnish enough manna for our guests, we were reluctant to share our manna at first. However, just as Elohim had provided manna for all the outsiders, the Ishmaelites woke their first morning to find the flakey white foodstuff at their thresholds. That evening there was a great celebration with much singing, dancing, and storytelling.

As the days grew longer and hotter, so did our family's anxiety increase as the fifth month approached. It had been several years since older men started dying, and each year more of them died. The oldest man in our family was Father, but he wasn't yet sixty, and he wasn't a Hebrew either. Even so, he'd dug a grave and slept in it on the ninth night every year since Moses made his dire pronouncement that only Hebrew men younger than twenty when we left Egypt would live to enter the Promised Land.

While the rest of our family went to bed with great trepidation, Father was the epitome of calm. "If Osiris decides to take me tonight, I will go without complaint," he said. "I've lived a good long life, long enough to see grandsons and great-grandsons. And from what I've heard, those who die on this night do not suffer; they merely do not wake in the morning."

"That may be true, Father," I told him. "But I do not think you will want to miss your grandson and granddaughter's wedding."

"And I do not want to be grieving for you during their wedding either," Pua added.

Father allowed us to accompany him to the gravesite and kiss him good night, and then he climbed down and settled himself on the sleeping mat below. Other families were doing the same thing, and as if there were a signal, we all left silently at the same time. Nobody wanted to be the last one to leave; it was a bad omen.

When I woke at sunrise, for the first time I could recall, Father wasn't outside in the stable currying the goats. Terrified, I woke Maratti, who looked around and came to the same conclusion. We waited mutely until we began to hear screams coming from the graves, some cries of relief to find their relatives alive and some of mourning to find them not. By that time, all of us except the babies were awake and throwing on clothes.

Eshkar and Shifra were the first out the door, with Eshkar carrying their oldest sons, Anki and Temen, and Shifra holding the baby, Sagar.

Open graves under a half moon at Kadesh

Slightly behind, Gitlam walked with their daughter, Atuwe. I picked up Piruwi, my youngest, and Maratti herded the other children while Shaul and Pua raced past them. In the distance I could see people, many giddy with relief and delight, helping men out of the holes. Others, fewer, were weeping as they filled graves with dirt.

When I finally reached Father's grave, the others were standing around it quietly, looking confused and bewildered.

Father lay below, snoring loudly.

Even with all the noise, he slept on. None of us dared wake him. His spirit might be wandering so far away that it couldn't find its way back.

"You can all stand around waiting if you like," Shifra said. "I'm going back to fry some onions for breakfast. When I have a panful, I'll bring some back here. If that smell doesn't wake Grandfather up, I don't know what will."

"I'll wait here," declared Eshkar. "The rest of you should go gather our manna. If he wakes before Shifra returns, I'll help him up and get him home."

"I'll wait with you," Pua said.

I was nearly home when I smelled fried onions. Shifra was running toward me, a steaming pan in her hand. I waved her to continue and then decided to follow. I wanted to be there to see whether the delicious odor would rouse Father from slumber. I didn't run though, and when I got there, Father was sitting up rubbing his eyes.

"Hand me down that pan of onions," he called out. "I'm starving."

"Absolutely not," Pua replied. "You can eat when you're out of that grave."

Shifra handed me the pan, then assisted Eshkar in getting Father onto the ground. By the time we returned home, Father had eaten the entire panful of fried onions. Thankfully Tantana had several plates of fried onions and manna waiting for us.

196 ASENET

I almost cried with relief that Father would now live at least another year. Not that there was anything I could do to prevent him from dying next summer; when he died was Elohim's decision.

The next winter Shifra and I were surprised to see Ishmaelite women accompanying their traders. Of course our women invited them to stay with us until their caravan returned on its way home. They'd brought us wheat and barley seeds, insisting we must learn how to grow our own grain before entering the Promised Land.

Miriam, who considered herself the Hebrew women's leader, thanked them enthusiastically, agreeing that "while we are more than satisfied with manna, we must be prepared for the day in the future when it ceases. In the meantime, we could bake bread to feed the caravans coming through our valley."

On the subject of the Promised Land, the Ishmaelites were bewildered when we tried to explain that on account of the spies' failure, all the men over twenty who'd been slaves in Egypt would not live to enter it. They were dumbstruck when Miriam recounted how these men would dig graves on the ninth day of the fifth month and then sleep in them. Those destined to die that year would not wake in the morning, but those who climbed out of their graves were assured another year of life.

"You mean that every man fated to die in a certain year does so during the same night?" a skeptical woman asked, shaking her head in disbelief.

Several of us, including me and Pua, assured her that this was the case, although it was usually the elderly men who died.

"What about women? When do they die?" challenged a graybeard.

Miriam paused to think. "I have noticed that out here in the wilderness, women live longer than they did in Egypt. I think it's the manna."

"How old are you, Miriam?" I asked. "Your skin is unlined, your hair is more black than gray, and you aren't stooped over at all."

THE MIDWIVES' ESCAPE   197

"I don't know exactly, but I am older than both my brothers."

I looked at her in awe. "So you could be close to a hundred."

Miriam deftly changed the subject. "You're a midwife, Asenet. Do you think fewer young mothers are dying in childbirth now that they have plenty of manna to eat?"

I nodded. "And it seems that hardly any children die once they're old enough to eat manna."

"We all know that before Elohim provided manna, which must be distributed equally, men and boys received larger portions of whatever food we had." Miriam spoke with equal sadness and anger.

"So of course some young women didn't survive childbirth, and many female babies didn't live past infancy," I added. "But generally once a woman stopped bearing, she lived a long healthy life."

A white-haired beldame chuckled. "You know what they say, 'An old man in the house is a nuisance, but an old woman in the house is a treasure.'"

Many of the women burst out laughing. I said nothing but inwardly I resolved that once we entered the Promised Land and no longer received manna, food in my household would be distributed more evenly between males and females.

One woman sighed. "The ninth day of the fifth month must be a sad one for the people who've lost a husband, father, or grandfather."

"Yet there is a comfort in knowing that once that day dawns, no man will die until the following year." Pua turned to me. "Sister, let's bring out more beer."

It must have been the beer, but when it came to sharing tales of our ancestors, I revealed that my great-grandmother had been the daughter of Jacob, Ishmael's nephew. The women were both astonished and excited. Most didn't know that Jacob had fathered any female offspring, and those who'd heard that Jacob's first wife, Leah, had borne him a daughter, Dinah, thought the girl had died childless. That I was named after Dinah's daughter, who'd married Jacob's son

198 ASENET

Joseph, made the women sigh at how Elohim had arranged everything so beautifully.

Some Ishmaelite women also noticed that we seemed to have more boys than girls. "Do you keep your daughters inside while your sons play outdoors?" one asked.

Pua shook her head. "I am a midwife, as are my sister and niece," she replied. "And we have each noticed that after Moses declared that older men would not live to enter the Promised Land, it seems that twice as many male than female babies have been born."

"Other midwives have observed this as well," I added. "We've speculated that Elohim wants us to have a large army when it comes time to conquer the Promised Land."

"So who are all these warriors going to marry?" one of the women asked with a suggestive smile.

Another was bolder. "Would your Israelites consider Ishmaelites kin?"

"It depends on the men," Pua replied. "Here fathers set up the matches, so yours would have to agree that Israelites are their kin."

Fortunately I hadn't consumed so much beer that I divulged Shifra's two-husband marriages, which would also solve the problem of there being too many men. Instead I deftly changed the subject to the advantage of Shifra's marrying one of my father's orphaned apprentices, thus guaranteeing that at least one daughter continued living with me.

"And since your younger daughter is betrothed to my son, you'll also see her often," Pua added.

Shifra had the final word. "Here, thankfully, most women carry water back from the lake daily, giving them many opportunities to see their relatives."

The following winter was mild with just enough rain to keep the lake full but not flood the valley. Gitlam was right about fowl overwintering in our

THE MIDWIVES' ESCAPE   199

lake. It seemed that every morning and evening the air echoed with their honking and squawking. He and Utti earned a good profit trading birds their slings brought down. This year Gitlam exchanged most of them for copper and bronze pots, bowls, and trays, some of which became part of Tantana's dowry. But a few went for malachite jewelry for Shifra.

The week before Tantana's wedding, she and Shifra immersed in the pool created by the new weir. While I supervised them, Gudit rode up with her two daughters.

"I wanted to say goodbye in private," she said after dismounting.

I blinked back my tears. "So soon? Aren't you staying for Tantana's wedding?

"I wouldn't dream of missing it, but now we have the pool to ourselves."

Something in her voice sounded guarded. "Have you told Moses you're leaving?" I inquired. When she shook her head, I had to ask, "Are you planning to?"

"I am, but I don't know when or how."

"Have you told your daughters?"

"Not yet."

"So what did you want to tell me?"

"I want to thank you for ensuring that I, and Dara, survived her breech birth. I doubt a less experienced midwife would have saved us. Do you think any of your boys would like one of our horses? Especially the good slingers?"

I didn't hide my surprise. "Of course they would, but won't you need your horses to get back to Nubia?"

"We'll be returning by boat," Gudit replied. "Our old horses will just take up room, but I expect they'll still provide you with some use. We'll replace them with young, fresh steeds when we're home."

I gave her a long hug. "I wish you a safe journey."

A wave of sadness washed over me. As I walked up the hill, I realized that, just as I hadn't wanted to leave Egypt, I didn't want to leave

Kadesh Barnea either. My family, and the other foreigners, had worked so hard to turn this place into a good and prosperous home. I didn't want to leave it to others and start all over again in Canaan.

Besides, Elohim had promised Canaan to the Hebrews, not us. Why shouldn't we stay here?

CHAPTER TWENTY

SHIFRA

The sons of Moses: Gershom and Eliezer. The sons of Gershom: Shebuel the chief. And the sons of Eliezer were: Rehabiah the chief. Eliezer had no other sons, but the sons of Rehabiah were very numerous.

—1 Chronicles 23:15–17

Shebuel son of Gershom son of Moses was the chief officer over the treasuries.

—1 Chronicles 26:24

AFTER TWENTY SUMMERS in Barnea, our lives seemed settled. Grandfather was still alive, and my brothers, Maratti's sons Utti, Harli, and Piruwi, were all learning woodworking as his wainwright apprentices, as was Pua's son Rephaiah. Of course they displayed various degrees of enthusiasm and competence. Piruwi, perhaps because of his youth, was more inclined to goat herding, where he could be active outdoors and practice slinging rocks. I had nursed my babies as long as possible, not only because I greatly enjoyed it but also to avoid the agonies of childbirth. Thus my children were spaced four years apart, while most mothers' came every three years.

202   SHIFRA

Thankfully, my first child was a daughter. I named her Atuwe. I would have someone with whom to share my woman's skills and help take care of the boys. I looked forward to the days when my brothers and sons brought wives into our household who would weave us more rugs and blankets, as well as tend the garden and assist with food preparation. But as important, they would provide me with female companionship and friends.

While most men, both Hebrew and outsiders, were proud to have fathered so many boys, the Hebrew women weren't pleased that their sons would likely have to take foreign wives. Not that I had anything against the Ishmaelite girls. From childhood their mothers would have them doing the simple tasks that a woman needed to know: household chores like fetching water, sweeping floors, gathering kindling for the fires, and washing the dishes, pots, and pans. Ideally, the younger girls learned by watching and imitating their mothers and older sisters. Eventually the girls would grow tall enough to lean over the oven and do some baking, sufficiently experienced with fruit to know the difference between ripe ones ready to pick and those that needed more time and adept enough to do their own hair as well as their younger sisters'.

Most importantly, they would be skilled at spinning thread, weaving, and sewing. Until we entered the Promised Land, Elohim would provide us with manna, so women and older girls needn't spend hours grinding grain into flour to prepare bread for our families. While our clothing didn't wear out, and thus an older child's clothes could be passed down to younger ones, they did need repairing sometimes— more often the boys' clothes. And as our families grew, there was a constant need for larger tents, larger rugs, and more blankets.

One day, Pua surprised me by announcing that she had a midwife lesson for me and Tantana, who was also following in our family vocation. We met late in the morning, when Rephaiah was with Grandfather perfecting his box joint technique and Shaul was out with Maratti.

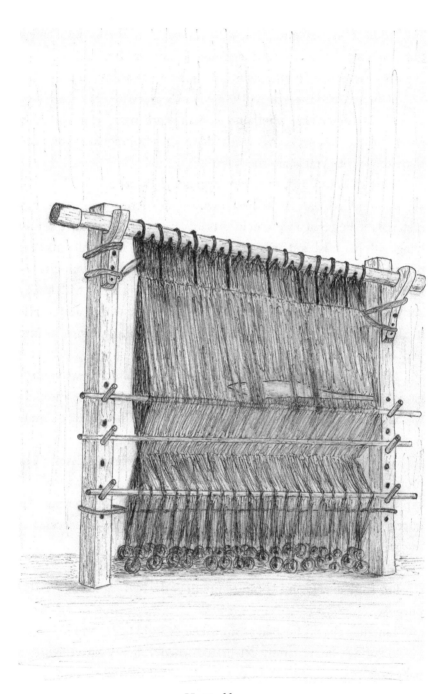

Vertical loom

"Today I am going to share with you some midwives' knowledge that is so secret even Asenet doesn't know about it," Pua said.

My heart started pounding in anticipation of learning such a thing.

"When we're done, you will know some ways to prevent pregnancy as well as to determine whether a woman is pregnant," Pua said. "My sister is the one who knows methods to abort a pregnancy; she can share those with you at another time."

"First show us how to prevent pregnancy," I asked.

Pua nodded. "Most of these involve concocting, out of various materials, a plug that a woman inserts into her womb's entrance before lying with her husband," she said. "The simplest is made of a mixture of gum, honey, and sour milk. If a woman wishes to avoid pregnancy for two or three years, she mixes finely ground acacia leaves with honey and sour milk, then moistens some soft lambswool with it and inserts it. She could also commingle acacia gum, cedar oil, and frankincense with olive oil."

Tantana and I prepared these contraceptives under Pua's vigilant gazes until she was satisfied with our efforts. Then, after we carefully washed our hands and ate our midday meal, Aunt Pua shared a simple test for determining whether a woman was pregnant.

"Starting a month after her last menses, the woman pisses every morning on two small bags containing grains of wheat and barley," she explained. "She also pours the same amount of water on another pair of grain-filled bags. If the woman is pregnant, her urine will accelerate the grains' growth compared to the watered grain."

"But we only have manna," I pointed out.

Pua smiled. "I keep a goodly amount of the two grains for just this purpose."

Tantana's cheeks flushed as she asked, "Could I use some?"

In spring Shaul's family celebrated when Tantana gave birth to a baby boy.

THE MIDWIVES' ESCAPE 205

The summer Midianite caravan brought unexpected newcomers. Word spread quickly that two Midianite shepherds, along with their good-sized flocks, asked if they could set up a tent in the empty high pasture across the lake. The handsome young men seemed harmless, and when manna appeared at their tent's entrance and inside the sheep paddock, it was clear that Elohim welcomed them. So while we didn't need two more unmarried men, nobody wanted to reject Elohim's acceptance—or the opportunity to trade for their sheep's wool. The brothers kept to themselves, and their sheep kept to their high pastures.

It was Pua who discovered their identities.

People had stopped gossiping about them when Pua burst into our tent. "Asenet, Shifra," she called out. "You'll never guess who those shepherds are."

"You're right," Mother replied, peeved because the sand cats had gotten into her latest batch of cheese and it was her fault because she hadn't covered it securely. "I have no idea who they are, and I don't care."

Pua grinned. "I'll give you a hint. Brothers named Gershom and Eliezer, whose deceased mother was Midianite and whose father, who deserted them when they were young, was Egyptian."

Mother's eyes widened. "No. That's impossible. What would they be doing here?"

Pua chuckled. "They came here because their tribe disbanded when it got too small and their uncle said our people included many Egyptians so they'd feel at home."

I couldn't stand the suspense. "So who are they? Why the big secret?"

Pua let Mother answer me. "Gershom and Eliezer are the names of Moses's sons. Don't you remember that they ate with us and played with your brothers when Jethro came to visit Moses?"

I vaguely recalled the memory. "But that was so long ago. Gershom and Eliezer would be grown men now."

"Who don't want to reveal their relationship to Moses," Pua pointed out.

"Or to Miriam or Aaron," Mother added.

"Especially not to Aaron," Pua agreed, "who apparently went to some effort to keep them away from Moses."

Before Mother or Pua would tell me, I had a sudden epiphany. "Aaron is the eldest brother. He resents that Elohim chose Moses instead of him to lead us out of Egypt and that Moses is the only one whom Elohim speaks with face-to-face. If Moses's sons stayed in Midian, then Aaron's sons would be the next high priests."

"They might not know that they're Moses's sons," Mother said.

"We should tell Miriam," Pua insisted. "She'll know what to do."

"Not yet," Mother objected. "I think Maratti should introduce them to Joshua."

When Maratti mentioned that he and Joshua were taking a walk to survey the pasture where Moses's sons were camping, I decided to get there first. I'd already ventured up there once and noted which bushes would both conceal me and give me the best view. The two shepherds were dressed alike in undyed knee-length tunics belted around their waists. They wore twin keffiyeh on their heads for sun protection, but they had tanned skin, and I could see dark wavy hair that matched their beards escaping around the keffiyeh edges.

I gambled that the men would be too interested in Gershom and Eliezer to spot me, so I chose a leafy bush close enough that I could eavesdrop. Thus I clearly heard Joshua and Maratti introduce themselves, remaining unfazed when Gershom and Eliezer calmly shared their names and mixed ancestry. I was impressed when Joshua, under

THE MIDWIVES' ESCAPE 207

the pretext of informing the brothers that the Hebrews needed warriors to defend their camp and would need more when it was time to claim the Promised Land, asked if they were skilled with any weapons.

Gershom consulted Eliezer. "He looks too old to be a warrior. You take him, and I'll fight the younger one."

With that exchange, they raised their staffs into defensive positions as Gershom faced Joshua and Eliezer approached Maratti. No sooner did Joshua pull his sword from its sheath than Gershom's staff knocked it out of his hands. The next moment Gershom's staff was at Joshua's neck.

Maratti started laughing. "Maybe he is too old to fight, but he's a good leader. Why don't you two show me how you fight each other? And don't tell me you don't sometimes fight each other—you're brothers."

The two promptly faced off, and suddenly the air was split with the crashing sounds of staffs pummeling each other. Yet their defenses were so good that neither man could land a blow on the other person. Finally Joshua motioned them to cease.

"I see you carry slings," he said. "How good are you with those?"

Eliezer removed his hat, folded it into a small square, and then carried it a distance away and dropped it. Immediately Gershom slung a stone that landed right on top of it. Then he placed his folded hat at his feet, and Eliezer slung a stone that landed on the hat, right between his brother's feet.

I gasped with wonder while Joshua and Maratti cheered. "We must see how they perform compared to Gitlam," Maratti called out as Joshua started back down.

"Shepherds are always the best slingers," Gershom said. "We not only have to keep our sheep from straying, but we also have to kill any predators that threaten them."

"Sometimes we hunt gazelles for food," Eliezer added. "Gershom once downed an oryx."

208 SHIFRA

"On the subject of food, you two must dine with us," Maratti declared. "My Egyptian wife is an excellent cook, and it will be a change from all that manna."

"You speak Egyptian," Gershom said, "but you're a Hittite."

"I was captain of Pharaoh's palace guards until we left Egypt with the Hebrews."

"So your tents are outside the Hebrews' camp." Gershom's tone was cautious.

"Just outside it. I'll let you know what day my wife prefers."

Eliezer spoke up. "Any day is fine for us."

With that confirmed, Maratti turned to go. But instead of walking directly back, he detoured past the bushes. He paused behind one near me and pissed. When he finished, he whispered, "Don't you have things to do back home, Shifra?"

Then, without waiting for my reply, he continued down the hill. It was just as well he hadn't waited for my reply; I was far too mortified to speak.

Gershom and Eliezer agreed to dine with us the following week, as would Joshua and his two daughters. The way Maratti and Mother whispered about it, I had a feeling that neither couple knew the other would be there, and I couldn't wait to see what would happen. Joshua and his daughters arrived first, not surprising since the Ephraim camp was just to the west of us. They brought gifts of the most striking baskets I'd ever seen, surely woven by the daughters' hands, in an assortment of colors. Joshua introduced them as Bithia, the elder, and Naarah, the younger, both of whom were wearing perfume. I said nothing but thought that their mother didn't have much of an imagination to name them the Hebrew words for "daughter" and "girl." I was about ten years older than them, and it surprised me that they were still unmarried, but I didn't dare ask why.

THE MIDWIVES' ESCAPE   209

Mother, however, boldly broached the subject. "Joshua, how is it that your lovely and talented daughters remain unwed? Their baskets are beautiful."

Both of them blushed as he replied. "My wife died in childbirth along with our third girl when these two were almost grown. I couldn't bear losing another wife, so I never remarried. I became completely occupied with training the Hebrews to be warriors, so I let my daughters keep house for me." He paused and sighed. "I am a selfish father. I did not want to be left alone when they married and moved to their husbands' homes."

Mother and I exchanged looks, and I knew we were thinking the same thing. Gershom and Eliezer had no family. If they married Joshua's daughters, they could all live together with Joshua. Some Hebrew mothers of sons might complain, but it was Joshua's decision.

The two young men arrived somewhat later, apologizing that they had gotten lost. Mother gently chastised them, reminding them that they had been here with their mother when they were little. Eliezer looked around blankly until his gaze stopped on Naarah, while Gershom thought for a few moments and finally admitted that the place did look familiar. Seeing his brother focused on Naarah, he turned his attention to Bithia. The two girls were immediately captivated, so Mother and I exchanged knowing looks.

Afterward, when Maratti complimented Mother on the excellent meal, I couldn't resist saying, "I don't think those two couples even knew what they were eating,"

Maratti grinned. "That's what we hoped would happen."

"Was Joshua in on it too?" I asked.

"It was your mother's idea, but I agreed completely," he replied. "Joshua was skeptical, but he didn't object."

"He must have told his daughters about it," Mother suggested. "I doubt they would have worn perfume for a meal with me."

"Of course, you seated them near each other," I accused her.
She smiled. "Of course."

Joshua waited a month to announce his daughters' betrothals. To my surprise, Gershom and Eliezer had the wherewithal to furnish their intendeds with the traditional gifts of jewelry: gold earrings, nose rings, and bracelets, which likely had been their mother Zipporah's. The wedding would be celebrated in late summer, after the sheep had been sheared and the wool sold. Then most of the male lambs could go to slaughter. Equally important, the first batch of beer would be finished.

The next morning Miriam was at our tent, protesting to Mother, "How could you allow those two Midianite shepherds to woo Joshua's daughters right under your nose when so many Hebrew men can't find a Hebrew bride?"

Mother stayed calm. "Gershom and Eliezer aren't just any Midianite shepherds."

Miriam's eyes narrowed. "What do you mean they aren't just *any* Midianite shepherds? What are they, then?"

"The question is 'who are they,' but I won't tell you unless you swear to keep my answer absolutely confidential, that you won't tell anyone."

I could see that Miriam was curious but didn't like being sworn to secrecy. I wondered which impulse would prevail.

"Very well," she sighed. "I swear not to even mention Gershom and Eliezer."

"These two Midianite shepherds are the sons of Moses." Mother's voice was confident as she described how we'd offered hospitality to them and their mother when they had accompanied Jethro to visit Moses years ago. "I doubt either Moses or Aaron knows they're here now."

Miriam was shocked silent for quite some time before saying, "I agree that Aaron shouldn't know, but why keep them from Moses?"

"It seems cruel, but I don't see how it would stay a secret if Moses knew."

Miriam sighed sadly. "I would very much like to attend the wedding, but I suppose that would draw untoward attention to it. Yet I can't have Moses's sons not provided a groom's feast. They are my nephews."

"The community usually provides for orphan brides' weddings. Shouldn't the same thing be done for orphan bridegrooms?" I asked.

"Eshkar was an orphan," Mother said. "So Maratti and I gave one large feast when you married him."

"I will talk to Joshua." Miriam's voice was firm. "I will donate whatever he needs to make such a feast for his daughters' weddings. I'm sure he'll invite Caleb's family, which includes me."

Mother sighed. There was no diverting Miriam once she was determined in her path. "As long as you can do this clandestinely."

Miriam nodded absent-mindedly. "I'll commission my grandson Bezalel to create something very special for each couple."

Sharing a tent, Bithia and Naarah had their monthly menses at the same time. Thus they could conveniently immerse together and then have a joint wedding.

I thought that choosing their living arrangements would be complicated. But as the bridegrooms were orphans who shared one tent up near their sheeps' pasture, nobody disagreed when Mother suggested that they should live with Joshua and his daughters once they married. Since it was impractical that the men should sleep at Joshua's and the sheep sleep up in the pasture, Joshua hired a watchman to guard the sheep at night, and his daughters began weaving goat's hair into the walls, roofs, and floor coverings of two new tents. When that was complete, they took the thread they had spun from the sheep's wool, dyed it into various colors, and wove themselves cloth for wedding garments. The whitest thread they wove into cloth for their husbands' wedding tunics.

Finally the first batch of beer was finished and the moon was waxing. Women from Joshua's tribe of Ephraim spent days preparing the feasts for the wedding week, while Mother made a lamb stew for our contribution. The tribe's men set up tables and benches in the courtyard, enough for all the Ephraimites. Mother and I arrived at Joshua's in midafternoon, just in case the brides needed assistance dressing. But they'd been helping each other dress and fix their hair ever since their mother died, so we went out to the courtyard to assist with the food.

The musicians arrived shortly before sunset so they could entertain the arriving guests. On a normal wedding night, there would be women singing melancholy songs bidding farewell to the bride before she left her natal home for her husband's. Except Bithia and Naarah weren't leaving home. So all the music was celebratory. Maratti, Eshkar, and Gitlam got there just as the sun was setting, as did many other men.

Right before it was time for the couples to leave for their new tents, I noticed a small commotion at the courtyard's entrance, as Joshua, Maratti, and Miriam rushed to welcome a latecomer. Thankfully the rest of the celebrants were focused on the bridegrooms and brides. First Gershom took Bithia's hand and said, his voice shaking a little, "I, Gershom the Midianite, take you, Bithia bat Joshua, for my wife forever; I take you for my wife in righteousness and in justice, in steadfast love, and in mercy. I take you for my wife in faithfulness." Then Eliezer took Naarah's hand and repeated the vow to her, his voice trembling more than his brother's had as he substituted Eliezer for Gershom and Naarah for Bithia.

That was what the musicians were awaiting, for they broke into a loud, lively ballad that only got more raucous as Joshua and the men followed the fleeing couples. Like at my wedding, the men bellowed such lewd guidance that I thought someone should quiet them. But the women, who'd had their share of beer too, only laughed with encouragement. Eshkar caught my attention and gave me a lecherous grin that I returned with a lascivious smile of my own. Eventually the dancing

THE MIDWIVES' ESCAPE 213

began and nearly everyone stood, either to clap to the music or to dance themselves. Curious, I made my way through the crowd toward the entrance to see the straggler, who was sitting on a bench, shielded by Maratti, Mother, and Miriam.

It was Moses.

I didn't dare interrupt them, and thus I waited until the musicians left, followed gradually by the men, including Moses. Finally, when only a few women remained, packing up leftover food and clearing away the dishes, I found the courage to approach Miriam and Mother to learn how Moses had come to attend his sons' wedding.

"Moses had no idea the bridegrooms were his sons," Miriam explained. "He only knew that the daughters of Joshua, his best friend and most trusted adviser, were getting married. Yet Joshua hadn't said a word to him about the wedding."

"Remember, his Cushite wife and daughters had gone home to Nubia," Mother added. "He's probably still lonely and missing them."

I persisted. "So does Moses know that Joshua's sons-in-law are his own sons?"

Miriam sighed. "He knew as soon as he heard their names in their wedding vows. He asked me if Aaron knew and was relieved when I told him that Aaron didn't. He envied their being shepherds; his happiest days were back in Midian tending sheep."

"I have a feeling he'll be dining with Joshua's family more often now," Mother said.

While I felt relieved that the dual wedding had gone as planned, without encountering any difficulties, my body was insisting that I get back to my tent where Eshkar was waiting, undoubtedly impatiently, as soon as possible. Tomorrow night it would be Gitlam's turn.

CHAPTER TWENTY-ONE

ASENET

Five hundred of the Simeonites attacked the encampments and the Amalekites who were found there, and wiped them out forever and settled in their place, because there was pasture there for their flocks. So they destroyed the last surviving Amalekites, and they live there to this day.

—1 Chronicles 4:42–43

"GRANDMOTHER," MY GRANDDAUGHTER, Atuwe, complained as we washed the dishes, "my belly hurts, but Mother says not to worry; it will go away in a few days."

I reached out and felt her forehead, but there was no fever. Atuwe was a sensitive child with many vague aches and pains but very few actual illnesses. Her body had matured quite a bit recently; her breasts were small but definitely those of a woman. Maybe it was finally her time. She was sixteen, after all.

"Go lie down for a while, child," I suggested.

Atuwe did so, and I returned to my loom.

My weaving was interrupted by Atuwe's excitedly running into what Shifra and I called the women's room and lifting up her skirt. The cloth and her legs were stained with blood. I wasn't surprised at all. Shifra also had her menses at the moment, as did two of Atuwe's friends who regularly teased her for not having attained womanhood as they had. Now my granddaughter was no longer an outsider.

"Mother and the other girls kept telling me it wouldn't be long until I saw my first blood," Atuwe declared. "But I thought it would never happen to me."

I left my loom and took Atuwe to a corner of the room devoted to women's tasks like weaving, making baskets, and midwifery. There, we located the supply of rags saved for this purpose. I helped Atuwe strip off her blood-spotted clothes and put them in a tub of water to soak.

"In the morning you will rinse them out and then hang them up to dry far away from where men's clothes are drying," I told her.

Just as we were selecting some rags to put in Atuwe's special undergarment women wore when they bled, Shifra raced in. Her face broke into a broad smile, and she rushed to embrace Atuwe. "Now you are a woman." Her eyes filled with tears as she stood back to gaze at her daughter.

"We will have a special meal for you this evening," I added, "that the women will eat before the men have theirs. Pua and Tantana will be there too."

Shifra opened the box that Grandfather had made for her and removed two bronze anklets. "These anklets symbolize your transformation from girl to young woman; they mark you to our community as marriageable," she said as she slid them over Atuwe's feet. "Now we can plan your wedding to your uncle Utti."

"You should be grateful that you won't have to leave your family and move to your husband's home like most brides do," I added.

Shifra and I sent Atuwe off to rest while we prepared the meal. Once my sister and daughter, Tantana, sat down to eat, we gleefully recounted our first blood experiences and taught Atuwe the specific customs she had to keep while she was bleeding. While her daily chores were essentially the same as always, she must take care not to handle

Bronze anklets

the men's clothing or bedding. She ought to stay closer to home than usual and only collect manna for herself or another woman, never for a man.

Pua presented her with a small bottle of special perfume prepared by one of the community's herbalists to wear during her menses. "Be careful to apply this sparingly," she advised.

Finally, after their five days of menses had ended, Atuwe and Shifra walked together to the end of the lake where women immersed. Atuwe was so delighted at the opportunity to wash herself completely, including her hair, that she stayed to splash in the water with her friends when they arrived. Shifra had to tell her three times that they needed to return home before Atuwe could be coaxed out of the water.

By our twenty-fifth year in Barnea, my oldest son, Utti, was married to Shifra's daughter, Atuwe, and they had a six-month-old son. The other boys were betrothed, although it wasn't as easy to find a bride for Piruwi as it had been for his older brothers. I kept hoping that Shifra would have another girl, but with Pua's assistance, she hadn't borne any more children. Shifra wasn't worried; she figured that enough girls would be available by the time her sons needed wives. I understood her optimism. Whereas five years before there were twice as many male babies as females, now the ratio was more like three boys to two girls.

I was more distressed that Father, Shaul, and Pua had died. None of us were surprised when Father died four years ago. His vision and hearing had been declining for some time, and during his final year he'd needed a stick's help to walk any distance. During winter he hadn't refused the blanket I'd woven him from some of Gershom's softest wool, but he forbade me to bury it with him. He seemed to know his end was near because he hugged and kissed all his progeny, something he'd never done previously, before slowly climbing down into his grave at sunset on the ninth of Av, the name the Hebrews gave to the fifth month.

But Pua and I were shocked, my sister so much so that she collapsed with a shriek, when we checked her husband Shaul's grave and discovered him cold and motionless. Maratti, Rephaiah, and Eshkar filled the graves while I comforted Pua as we walked back to our tents. I'd never thought she was that fond of him, but maybe she was just reticent. Or maybe her distress was not only about losing a husband, but that as a widow, her son became the head of the household, while his wife, my daughter Tantana, took over as matriarch. I wish there were a way to turn managing our household over to Shifra without Maratti or me dying first. Pua still went out when a midwife was needed, but it seemed to me that she was merely going through the motions. She perked up when Tantana gave birth to a son, her and my first grandchild. Tantana named him Shaul after his grandfather, but the baby was small and survived only a few months. The infant's death was too much for Pua, who took to her bed and never got up again.

I still missed Father: his devotion to me and the children, his patience and kindness, and that he so seldom lost his temper. Now I missed my only sister too.

I had a continuous feeling of dread that our household was cursed. We had Levites render guilt offerings to Elohim on our family's behalf. I hired an Egyptian sorceress to make protective amulets for all the children, while the adults fasted two days a week. But it was too late; the demons weren't quite done with us. The worst was yet to come.

We were still eating our usual morning meal of manna and cheese when Maratti rode up in a cloud of dust. "Quickly, men, prepare yourselves for battle," he shouted between breaths, "Amalekites attacked our mines at dawn. Gitlam, call up Simeon's and Gad's best fighters, then Joshua, Gershom, and Eliezer. Their hireling can watch the sheep longer."

I had never seen our young men move so fast. Gitlam jumped on his horse and rode off in the direction of Joshua's tent as I approached my husband. "Should I get my healer's bag and come back with you?" I asked.

THE MIDWIVES' ESCAPE   219

"Yes," he said quietly, "but Shifra shouldn't come with us."

"Eshkar?"

He nodded. "You'll see when we get there."

I held on tight as we rode at full speed to the copper mine. Maratti lifted me off to where Eshkar had fallen, and my hopes sank. There was so much blood. I forced myself to assume my healer role and directed men to carry him gently away from the mines so I could examine his wounds and staunch the bleeding. I did my best, but one gash was mortal. Just as I closed his eyes, Gitlam rode up with Gershom seated behind him, followed by Joshua and Eliezer.

Gitlam took one look at his brother's body and went berserk. He pulled out his sling and began sending rocks flying so quickly that I couldn't see him reload, only that he seemed to have an unending supply of stones. Every time I looked up from the injured I was tending I saw Gitlam in action. One by one an Amalekite went down and our soldiers rushed to finish him off. Gershom and Eliezer did fine work with their slings, but their fury couldn't compare to Gitlam's.

Maratti blew his horn and our men halted. "Don't waste time following the stragglers," he yelled. "It's almost sunset, and we must bury our dead. Tomorrow we will enlist more Simeonites and Gadites to take our battle to the Amalekite camp."

I rode slowly with Maratti as Gitlam brought Eshkar's corpse back. I could see Shifra waiting outside our tents, her expression anxious. When she saw us, she ran toward Gitlam, who jumped off his horse and embraced her as they both broke into sobs. According to both Hebrew and Egyptian traditions, we needed to bury Eshkar before it was dark, so I maintained my supervisor role and held back my tears. Since it was too late to build a coffin, I found Father's most beautiful storage box and collected Eshkar's grave goods to put inside: his bronze armor and helmet, sword, shield, and his best leather sandals and belts. Shifra and Gitlam washed and oiled his body and dressed him in his white wedding clothes, while Joshua procured a length of fabric woven from the finest white

220   ASENET

sheep's wool for Eshkar's shroud. Lastly, Shifra and Gitlam placed some of Eshkar's gold jewelry—earrings, nose ring, neck collar, and matching armbands—where he would have worn them. Then we buried Eshkar in the cave where Shifra and Gitlam had found the sand kittens.

That was when I could no longer hold back my tears.

Just after the sun set, the wives of Eshkar's fellow soldiers brought out and served the funerary meal. Nobody except the sand cats had much of an appetite. But Eshkar's comrades praised his bravery, boldness, and fearlessness and his encouragement to the younger men. Some eulogized him as a great warrior brought down in battle in his prime, not even forty. In closing, Maratti told us that Eshkar had died at the front line, protecting the weaker men behind him.

It was a dreadful night for our family. Even the youngest children knew something was wrong, but I told only Atuwe and Shifra's oldest son, Anki, that their father had died and that Uncle Gitlam would be their father now. We all quickly retired to our beds, yet I doubted anyone slept well. At first I heard weeping in Shifra and Gitlam's tent, but after a brief silence, I discerned the unmistakable sounds of lovemaking. The principal mourners were finding what solace they could in each other's arms.

I could no longer restrain my tears and buried my head against Maratti's chest, but I kept seeing Eshkar's bloody wound when I closed my eyes.

In the morning I made everyone eat all their manna, no matter how little appetite they had. I packed some cheese and dried dates along with my healing kit and insisted Shifra do the same if she was going to join me. I left the children with Helah and the other Simeonite women whose men were riding with Maratti to attack the Amalekite camp. The Gadites were close behind, with Joshua, Gershom, and Eliezer. I had no idea how many fighters the Amalekites would muster, but I

THE MIDWIVES' ESCAPE 221

told myself that our five hundred Simeonites and almost four hundred Gadites could defeat them.

I hadn't realized how many horses we had until I saw them all together now. I knew that the Hittite cavalry, assisted by the tribes of Simeon and Gad, had rescued many of Pharaoh's mounts from the Sea of Reeds. Plus we'd captured some from the Amalekites in the battle on our way to Sinai. Then the Nubians left us theirs. In all the years we'd been wandering together, the mares and stallions had been fruitful and multiplied too.

I sighed as I watched my son, Utti, collect stones. Some of our fighters were so young; he was barely twenty.

Everyone made as little noise as possible as we slowly crept up a hill overlooking the enemy's camp. All appeared quiet below. A few women tended cooking fires, but apparently the survivors of yesterday's battle were still abed. Their horses were tied to trees not too far away, and at Joshua's signal, several of our men stealthily approached and freed them. The horses didn't walk away, but they would surely run when our army charged down the hill yelling battle cries.

The field between the two forces was bare, flat, and so remarkably even and smooth that it would have made a good pasture. Gitlam, Gershom, and Eliezer helped me and Shifra set up our healing tent behind some bushes partway down the hill. The ground wasn't as smooth as it had looked. I stumbled and nearly tripped, but Gershom steadied me.

I watched as Maratti gave one last address to our troops.

"Did you all piss before we formed ranks?"

There were a few embarrassed excuses. "I didn't have time—"

"Go now."

"Here, Captain?"

"If you don't, you'll have it running down your leg in battle; distracting you, maybe killing you. Do it!"

He waited until the last man had tucked his prong back under his leather tunic. "Most of our opponents will break and charge." Maratti's voice and stance exuded confidence. "Amalekite commanders aren't good enough to keep their men in formation." He turned and directed his remarks to the slingers in the back. "Aim for where the enemy's men are most crowded, where you have the greatest chance of hitting someone."

I could see the veneration in his troops' eyes and shared it. Indeed, I was overwhelmed with feelings of admiration and love for this man who was my husband.

Finally the Amalekite men began coming out of their tents. When Joshua raised his hand and let it fall, our men ran toward them, causing the now-untied horses to scatter. First, a wave of stones flew into the air. I watched as they arced and fell, dropping down on the Amalekites. Their soldiers screamed in pain as stones crashed against shields. Most ran awkwardly, shields angled up. That slowed them enough that they risked getting trampled by the men behind them.

Joshua, Maratti, and our other swordsmen wielded their weapons as the slingers paused to reload their pouches with stones. When the second volley flew, our men rushed the Amalekites, stabbing those who'd been felled. The charging enemy seemed to have no careful formation; they all just ran forward, yelling in a frenzy, seemingly determined to make up for their lack of cohesion with passion as they bellowed in fury. The two forces met with a crash of metal on wood, shields slamming together. The battlefield was chaotic, but our men held their ground, our slingers hurling stones at our adversary while the rest of our men engaged the Amalekites only when they came too close.

It was over quickly. The enemy pulled back, leaving their dead and injured on the field. I could scarcely believe it, but it appeared that we hadn't lost anyone. Seeing our opponent break ranks and scatter made us bold. Our soldiers rushed forward while our slingers targeted their men in the front, forcing the ones behind to stumble over their fallen comrades in their desperation to get away. The retreat turned into a rout.

THE MIDWIVES' ESCAPE   223

Joshua lifted his bloody blade high. "First get our injured men to the healers, and then put all Amalekite males to the sword, even the youngest. Take the females captive to be sold as slaves to the Ishmaelites. Then collect all the enemy's weapons and horses." He paused before shouting, "We will need them when we fight to enter the Promised Land."

Our men, many of whom were already retrieving booty from the fallen, cheered. A few left the field to retrieve the Amalekite horses; we would get the donkeys later.

I gazed in horrified awe at the battlefield covered with dead and wounded men and our men plundering them. My blood, previously so hot with vengeance, cooled, and my strength left me; I leaned over and vomited.

No amount of spoils would bring my son-in-law Eshkar back.

"I'm such a coward, Mother." Utti was quaking with fear. "This isn't like training out in the fields, slinging rocks at targets. It's actually happening, and men are dying. *This is real!*"

I could feel Utti's heart pounding as I examined him further, but except for a gash in his left leg, his wounds weren't severe. I cleaned and bandaged them, then helped him stand on his unsteady legs.

His tears trickled down, leaving trails on his dirty face. "Father will be so ashamed of me. I panicked."

"This is your first battle, Utti. You did the right thing to come to the healing tent when you were injured." I helped him stand, but his bad leg didn't support him. "Sit here. You can help me prepare more bandages. Heaven knows we'll need them."

"I'm a terrible soldier." Utti wept harder. "I should have stayed home with the goats."

Shifra brought over a wet cloth. "You're a fine soldier." She cleaned his face and tousled his hair. "I tried to count all the men your stones brought down, but I lost track."

I felt sorry for our inexperienced soldiers who were assigned the difficult task of having to exterminate all the Amalekite males, even

224 ASENET

the youngest. They had no qualms about slaughtering their foes on the battlefield, and though they knew that any Amalekite left alive would continue to seek vengeance, it was another thing to murder innocent children. But Elohim had vowed to blot Amalek out from under heaven after they attacked the Hebrews on the way to Mount Sinai, and our army would be His instrument.

Joshua was sympathetic to the fathers with young sons at home such as Utti, Eliezer, and Gershom, and assigned them to dispatch the adult males. The hardened warriors herded the boys, the older carrying the younger, behind the bushes so no one could see the innocents put to the sword. Particularly their mothers.

Regarding the women, those who had known a man were separated from the maidens. Joshua had been so confident of victory at the beginning of the battle that he'd sent an emissary to the Ishmaelites by horseback, offering to give them the captured women. Now the emissary had returned with the traders and some donkeys to carry the women. Before the women were taken away, Joshua offered our unmarried men their choice of the older maidens. Those fathers who, due to the excess births of boys compared to girls, had been unable to find their sons a bride were encouraged to select girls for them now.

Gershom and Eliezer huddled together and then consulted me and Joshua. "We do not wish to privilege any Hebrew men by choosing their daughters for our sons," Gershom began.

"But if we choose two infants, not necessarily sisters," Eliezer continued, "our wives can raise them together to become familiar with our laws and customs."

I turned to Joshua. "The girls would only need to be told that they are orphans, like their fathers."

"I have no objections, but first let us see these children," Joshua said. "There may not be any who appeal to you."

I sighed as he and his two sons-in-law tried to make a choice between the equally adorable babes in arms. "See their mothers and older sisters," I suggested. "That will give you an idea of what they'll look like when they're grown."

After that it didn't take long for Gershom to pick out a plump toddler with dark curls for his son, Shebuel, after which Eliezer chose a younger one with hardly any hair for his son, Rehavia.

Joshua assured them that his daughters would be delighted with their selections. I was relieved, and thankful, that these children would have no memories of any parents other than Gershom and Bithia or Eliezer and Naarah. I was also glad to have saved some innocent infants from death.

The older maidens, however, were another matter. None would forget that their new husband had killed their parents. Thankfully our warriors didn't desire any of them. There would be other battles when it came time to enter the Promised Land; it was the Amalekite horses they wanted now.

Maratti left it to the officers of his Hittite cavalry to select the new troopers, match them with appropriate steeds, and train them as horsemen. Ideally, these would have been archers, but he could make do with slingers.

He would have to.

CHAPTER TWENTY-TWO

ASENET

On the first new moon (of the final month) the people stayed at Kadesh. Miriam died and was buried there. The community was without water, and they joined against Moses and Aaron, saying, "Why did you make us leave Egypt to bring us to this wretched place ... ? There is not even water to drink!"

—Numbers 20:1–5

IT CERTAINLY SEEMED THAT it had been a long time since we'd come to Kadesh Barnea. But had it been the forty years that Elohim intended to pass before the Hebrews could enter the Promised Land? I didn't know anybody who had actually counted the years. Moses said nothing of how much longer our punishment would last. Myself, I had no desire to leave Kadesh for some unknown land in Canaan, especially since it would be my sons and grandsons fighting the Canaanites and my husband at the head of our army. I was pleased to stay at Kadesh; it had everything my family needed to thrive—permanent stone and brick houses, olive trees and date palms, good pastures for goats and sheep, a copper mine—and regular caravans coming through in the summer.

As happened every summer, I grew anxious as the days drew closer to the fifth month. Who would die on its ninth day this year? To our

226

dismay, this year death came early. On the night of the new moon of the fifth month, it was Miriam who didn't wake in the morning. However, she died in her bed, not in a grave in the desert, and she was buried that same afternoon.

All the women, Hebrews and outsiders, mourned her passing. Our prophetess—the one whose messages from Elohim came in her dreams, who was not intimidated by her brothers, who found no shame in being confined outside the camp, who could always find water—was no longer with us to guide us.

Three days after her burial, two of my grandsons, or maybe great-grandsons—forgive me, but after all these years I had trouble remembering all their names—ran in yelling that there was no water coming down into the lake.

"All the wadis are dry. All of them!"

"Don't worry," I assured them. "It's the middle of summer. They'll come back when it starts raining again in the mountains."

On the ninth day, like in previous years, the older men slept in their graves. Yet in the morning, to everyone's astonishment, they were all still alive. Naturally thinking they'd somehow miscalculated the date, they slept in the graves again that night, and the next, and the next. Finally, when the full moon rose, we could all see that it was well past the ninth day of Av.

All the men cursed to die in the wilderness and never enter the Promised Land had died. That meant those still alive would be the generation to enter it.

Our many years of waiting were over.

We should all have been thrilled, except that there had been no rain in the mountains, so the dry wadis remained dry. Without its source of water, the lake shrank smaller and smaller. And while there remained a small amount of water sufficient to drink, it tasted foul and smelled worse. But the foremost problem for the Hebrews was that there was no longer enough water collecting above the weir for people to immerse. And if a woman couldn't immerse after her menses finished, then she couldn't lie with her husband. That wasn't a problem for me and Maratti; I hadn't bled for years and could lie with him whenever we wanted.

But younger couples with their stronger urges were horror-struck. They weren't even permitted to touch each other.

Once again complaints arose against Moses and Aaron. "Why have you brought our congregation into this wilderness for us and our animals to die here? Why did you make us leave Egypt to bring us to this wretched place, a place with no grain or figs or vines or pomegranates? There is not even water to drink!"

I was so appalled by the criticism that I had to vent my frustration. "I don't understand these Hebrews," I fumed to Shifra. "Just as we are finally on the brink of leaving for the Promised Land, they are complaining again. Haven't they seen enough of Elohim's miracles to trust Moses to find water for us?"

"You would think so," she agreed with me. "But Hebrews are stubborn people."

I was not surprised when Elohim told Moses to take his staff and assemble the community in front of a large rock. But I was shocked when Moses lifted his staff and yelled, "Listen, you rebels, shall we get water for you out of this rock?" before striking the rock twice.

Shifra and I exchanged "I told you so" looks when out came copious water, enough for the community and its animals.

But GOD was angry with Moses and Aaron and chastised them. "Because you did not trust Me enough to affirm My sanctity in the sight of the Israelite people, therefore you shall not lead this congregation into the land that I have given them."

Of the Hebrews' three leaders, only Miriam had died and been buried in what would be part of the Promised Land. The other two, both men, would not even enter it, let alone be buried there.

Moses strikes a rock to get water outside Kadesh

Not that anyone could leave immediately. First the Hebrews needed thirty days to mourn Miriam's death. Then Moses, Joshua, Caleb and Maratti had to decide when would be the best time to begin the campaign.

Maratti explained to me that a major consideration was the season. "Summer is too hot," he told me, "and winter days are too short." He thought for a moment and then smiled. "However, a big advantage for us is that, because we receive manna, we won't be planting or harvesting cereal grains as our enemies do."

I returned his smile. "So our army should attack the Canaanites in the spring, forcing them to divert men from those necessary labors."

Thus it was decided; the following spring it would be.

During autumn we brewed date beer and produced olive oil so that by winter we had enough for our own use and more to trade. Then there began a great deal of discussion, and arguments, over who would be first to enter the Promised Land.

Eli, Aaron's grandson, was vehement. "No foreigners should accompany our holy army," he insisted. "It is bad enough that they have intermarried with Israelites, and now they want a share of the land too."

Eli was supported by the other Levites until Caleb repudiated him. "You Levites aren't trained as soldiers and would be useless—or worse, a hindrance on the battlefield." This was greeted with loud shouts of agreement by the Gadites and Simeonites. "In addition, it is undisputed that foreigners, especially Hittites, are the finest warriors. Without their defense, the Amalekites would have murdered us all."

Maratti struggled to calm his warriors, and I was afraid that mayhem would break out, until Joshua stood and blew his shofar. "Everyone at Sinai heard Moses repeat the commands and rules of GOD to the people. And all the people"—Joshua emphasized the word *all*—"all answered with one voice, saying, 'Everything that GOD has commanded, we will do!'"

"So even foreigners are entitled to enter the Promised Land," Caleb declared. "Do they not bring offerings and sacrifices to the Tabernacle as Israelites do? Perhaps more than Israelites do? Does Elohim not give them manna too?"

I didn't recognize the man's face or voice, but he yelled at the top of his lungs, "I don't care who offers sacrifices or not. We must field the best warriors against our enemies if we expect to defeat them."

"And the most experienced physicians and healers," another voice rang out.

With that, the shouting was reduced to mere grumbling as it was further agreed that most of the women with children would remain in Kadesh with a small contingent of soldiers for protection.

Despite my age, my healing skills would be needed on the battlefield. I exchanged looks with Shifra and could see we were thinking alike. If either of our husbands, or any of our sons, fell in battle, we would be there—either to heal them or to hear their last words and bury them.

As springtime approached, gossip spread that Moses had sent messengers from Kadesh to the king of Edom: "Thus says your brother Israel: You know all the hardships that have befallen us; that our ancestors went down to Egypt, that we dwelt in Egypt a long time, and that the Egyptians dealt harshly with us and our ancestors. We cried to our god GOD, who, upon hearing our plea, freed us from Egypt. Now we are in Kadesh, on the border of your territory. Allow us, then, to cross your country. We will not pass through fields or vineyards, and we will not drink water from wells. We will follow the king's highway, turning off neither to the right nor to the left until we have crossed your territory."

But Edom repudiated them. "You shall not pass through us, else we will go out against you with the sword."

Moses's envoys replied, "We will keep to the beaten track, and if we or our herds drink your water, we will pay for it. We ask only for passage on foot."

To our dismay, the Edomites replied, "You shall not pass through!" And Edom came out against us in force, heavily armed.

So we turned away from them and headed toward Mount Hor. There, at the boundary of the land of Moab and Edom, GOD said to Moses and Aaron, "Let Aaron be gathered to his kin: he is not to enter the land that I have assigned to the Israelite people, because you disobeyed my command about the waters of Meribah."

I turned in shock to Maratti and Shifra. Did they hear the words of GOD as clearly as I had? Though they said nothing, the awestruck expressions on their faces verified that they had.

GOD continued. "Take Aaron and his son Eleazar and bring them up on Mount Hor. Strip Aaron of his vestments and put them on his son Eleazar. There Aaron shall be gathered unto the dead."

Moses did as Elohim had commanded. The three men ascended Mount Hor in the sight of all of us below. There Moses took off Aaron's vestments and put them on Aaron's son Eleazar. Then, with all the Israelites watching, Aaron collapsed and died. Thus when Moses and Eleazar came down alone from the mountain, carrying a body wrapped in a white shroud through the astonishingly beautiful red and orange rock canyons that Haggith and I had wandered through when I visited her so many years ago in Moab, we all knew that Aaron had breathed his last.

Once Moses received permission from the Moabites, Aaron's body was interred in one of the many caves among the variegated rock formations. The land was so spectacular that we set up camp there and remained to bewail Aaron for thirty days. We then moved on, avoiding Seir where the descendants of Esau, another of the Hebrews' kin, lived.

THE MIDWIVES' ESCAPE

As we sat around our fires at night, Serach bat Asher—who looked just as young as when she and I crossed the Sea of Reeds together—enlightened us with tales of her ancestors. "Esau was Jacob's twin brother, who also had twelve sons. Esau was the firstborn, but crafty Jacob had tricked their blind father, Isaac, into bestowing the birthright on him instead of Esau. In fear of Esau's justifiable rage, Jacob ran off to his uncle Laban in Haran. That's where he fell in love with Laban's beautiful younger daughter, Rachel, but was tricked into marrying Rachel's older sister, Leah, first. Poor Jacob had to work for Laban for seven years, during which time Leah gave birth to Reuben, Simeon, Levi, and Judah, before he could marry Rachel, mother of Joseph and Benjamin."

The Hebrews knew these stories well, but they always wanted to hear Serach tell them again. Thus we foreigners eventually learned them too.

We continued away from the Arabah Road and encamped beyond the Arnon River. Moses now sent messengers to Sihon, king of the Amorites, saying, "Let us pass through your country. We will not turn off into fields or vineyards, and we will not drink water from wells. We will follow the king's highway until we have crossed your territory."

However, like Edom, Sihon would not let us pass through his territory. Instead, Sihon gathered all his troops and went out against us in battle. But our warriors, enraged at being refused even this minimal hospitality, defeated them, put them to the sword, and took possession of their land from the Arnon to the Az River.

Sihon's land was mostly desert, nothing like the beautiful red-rock country of Moab, so we were pleased to camp in the steppes of Moab. We knew not to harass the Moabites or Ammonites or provoke them to war, for their land had been designated to the descendants of Lot, Abraham's nephew.

234 ASENET

Serach explained that Lot had joined Abraham and Sarah in leaving for the new land of Canaan. But the two men's herds were too large, so they separated there, Abraham to Hebron and Lot to Sodom, an evil and depraved city. Elohim sent angels to warn them to leave Sodom before Elohim destroyed it, so Lot and his two daughters fled to a cave while the city was obliterated. The elder, fearing there were no men left to marry, told the younger that they should lie with their father to continue their lineage. To this end, they plied Lot with wine until he was too drunk to know what he was doing, enabling the daughters to lie with their father without his knowing. The elder bore Moab, father of the Moabites. The younger bore Ben-Ammi, father of the Ammonites.

Naturally, the Hebrews considered themselves superior to the Moabites and Ammonites, whose ancestors had been conceived in incest, but Elohim had forbidden them to harass or provoke these peoples.

Shifra and I hoped to see Haggith again, so Maratti arranged to escort us to her quarters in Moab. Haggith must have been advised that she had visitors because she was waiting just outside her tent, which was even more lavishly furnished than when I had seen her previously. Shifra ran up and embraced her, generating sobs of happiness from them both that were so loud the baby in a basket near the bed began to bawl.

Haggith put the infant to her breast, and soon all was quiet. "This is my daughter Ruth. Isn't she a beauty?"

"Indeed she is," I said, admiring the girl's plump fair cheeks and dark curls. "Your husband isn't disappointed that you didn't give him another son?"

Haggith's eyes brimmed with tears. "I am a widow now, one who already has five boys." Then she lowered her voice to a whisper. "I've been praying to Elohim for a daughter for over ten years, even when I thought I was too old to conceive again." Then she turned to Shifra. "So tell me what has happened to you and your family since I ran off with Eglon. Surely you too are a mother."

Shifra nodded. "And a grandmother."

Shifra and I spent that evening around their fire, sharing what had happened to us, and the Hebrews, during those long years in Kadesh. We deliberately avoided mentioning Eshkar's demise and Shifra's "remarriage" to his brother.

"Finally," Shifra concluded, "all the men who'd been older than twenty when we left Egypt were dead, and we knew it was time for us to come into the Promised Land."

Haggith was silent for a little while and then sighed. "Now I want to tell you what has been happening here." She let out another sigh. "It is a very strange tale, but you'll appreciate it." She motioned for a maidservant to serve us all some wine, and then she began. "After the Israelites defeated the Amorites, my father-in-law, King Balak, grew alarmed because my people were so numerous."

I interrupted her. "But Elohim specifically warned us to travel peaceably past Moab. And Moses intends for us to do so."

"Even so, Balak feared the Israelites so much that he sent messengers to Balaam, the sorcerer, saying that there were a people who came out from Egypt who were settling next to him. Since these people were too numerous, he wanted Balaam to put a curse on them for him. Balak thought that perhaps he could thus defeat them and drive them out of the land, for he knew that whomever Balaam blesses is blessed indeed, and whomever Balaam curses is cursed."

Shifra harrumphed. "Balaam cannot curse the Hebrews. Elohim will not allow it."

"That is what Balaam told our king's messengers," Haggith said. "But Balak sent more dignitaries to tell Balaam that he would reward him richly if only he would come and damn this people." She paused to take a deep breath. "Balaam replied that even if Balak were to give him a house full of silver and gold, he could not do anything, big or little, contrary to the command of Elohim."

"Then what happened?" I asked. For this was surely not where things ended.

"That night Elohim came to Balaam and told him that he may go to Moab, but that he shall do whatever Elohim commands. So the next morning, Balaam saddled his she-ass and departed with Balak's men." Haggith shook her head in disapproval. "But Elohim was angry and sent an angel holding a drawn sword to stand in the ass's way. Balaam couldn't see the angel and was so enraged when the ass swerved from the road that he beat her. The angel then stationed himself in a lane with fences on either side, and when the ass saw him, she pressed herself against the wall and squeezed Balaam's foot against it, so he beat her again."

Both Shifra and I were mesmerized, so I waved for Haggith to continue.

"When the angel moved forward to a spot so narrow that there was no room to swerve right or left, the she-ass lay down under Balaam, who beat her furiously." Haggith started to smile. "Then Elohim opened the ass's mouth, and she asked Balaam what she had done to him that he should have beaten her these three times. Not even realizing the strangeness that his donkey had actually spoken to him, Balaam told her that he was so angry at how she'd mocked him that he wanted to kill her. Yet when she pointed out that he'd been riding her for a long time and asked if she'd ever behaved like this before, he conceded that she had not."

Haggith's voice rose so we knew the climax was coming. "Then Elohim uncovered Balaam's eyes, and when he saw the angel standing in the way, drawn sword in hand, he bowed right down to the ground and told the angel that he would turn back. To that, the angel told Balaam to go to Balak but to say nothing except what the angel tells him.

"In the morning, when Balaam looked up and saw Israel encamped tribe by tribe, the spirit of Elohim came upon him and he intoned: 'How fair are your tents, O Jacob, Your dwellings, O Israel! Like palm groves that stretch out, like gardens beside a river, like aloes planted by GOD, like cedars beside the water. Blessed are they who bless you, accursed they who curse you!'"

Shifra and I were so awestruck at how beautifully Haggith sang Balaam's blessing that we couldn't say a word until we were back in our own tents.

Before we left Moab, Haggith gave us a warning. "King Og is a giant, a cruel tyrant who rules Bashan with an iron fist. He is so big that his iron bedstead is nine cubits long and four cubits wide! He taxes his people mercilessly, leaving them barely enough foodstuffs to survive. When his servants die of starvation or after being beaten, he conscripts more from the villages, and when they die, he conscripts more. The women of Bashan live in dread of the king's lust, especially the maidens. Any baby he conceives will be so enormous that only the largest women can survive childbirth." She paused and then encouraged us. "Og's warriors are ferocious, but should you defeat them—and with Elohim's help, I think you will—the villagers will not oppose you."

As we approached the steppes of Moab on the Jordan near Jericho, Moses and Eleazar the priest took a census of all Hebrew males able to bear arms. There were two things about this counting that amazed me. First, the number of male fighters now was exactly the same as were counted on the far side of the Sea of Reeds after we left Egypt. Second, among all these males, there was one female, Serach bat Asher, who was named in both censuses.

Not surprising, however, none of the men seemed to notice this oddity. Not only was a woman named among the potential warriors, but if she had also been named in the first census, then she would have to be well over a hundred years old now. I supposed the men were so focused on the approaching battles that they hadn't paid much attention to the census once their own names were read.

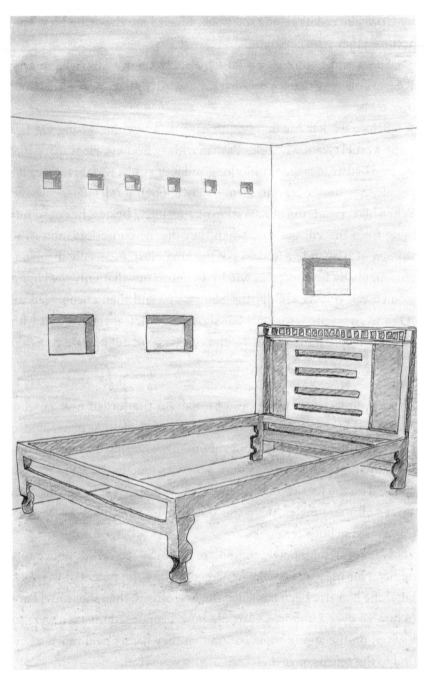

King Og's giant bed in Bashan

THE MIDWIVES' ESCAPE

239

Apparently the purpose of this second census was to distribute different portions of the Promised Land evenly among the Hebrew tribes. But once this was completed, the daughters of Zelophehad, of the Manassite family, came forward and introduced themselves. They stood before Moses, Eleazar the priest, the chieftains, and the whole assembly, and they said, "Our father died in the wilderness. He was not one of the factions, like Korah's faction, who banded together against GOD, but he died for his own sin, and he has left no sons."

Surely Moses remembered, as many of us also did, that Zelophehad had died a martyr to prove that Elohim's commandments regarding the Sabbath must be followed even before we entered the Promised Land. They would have sympathized with his daughter's plea, "Let not our father's name be lost to his clan because he had no son! Give us a holding among our father's kinsmen!"

Moses brought their case before GOD, who replied to Moses, "The plea of Zelophehad's daughters is just. You should give them a hereditary holding among their father's kinsmen and transfer their father's share to them. Further, speak to the Israelite people as follows: 'If a householder dies without leaving a son, you shall transfer his property to his daughter. If he has no daughter, you shall assign his property to his brothers.' Then GOD concluded: 'This shall be the law of procedure for the Israelites, in accordance with My command to Moses.'"

Later Maratti and I learned from Joshua that GOD had told Moses to climb to the heights and view the land given to the Israelite people. Then, after Moses had seen it, he too would be gathered to his kin, just as his brother, Aaron, had been.

As Elohim commanded, we did not encroach on the Ammonites' land as we started up the road toward Bashan, where the giant King Og ruled over sixty walled cities and numerous towns and villages. Og was the only survivor of the Rephaim, an ancient race of Canaanite giants.

240   ASENET

But Elohim told Moses that we should not fear Og, for Elohim would deliver him, his troops, and his country into our power, and we would do to Og as we had done to Sihon king of the Amorites, who had lived in Heshbon.

First, however, we set up a central camp outside Heshbon with the Tabernacle in the center surrounded by the twelve tribes' tents, as we'd done since Sinai. From here our troops would make forays into Canaanite territory and conquer it in stages. Not everyone moved from Kadesh though, for otherwise there would be no one to tend our date and olive trees. Those men disabled or otherwise not competent to fight remained with their families, along with outsiders who had no desire to take up residence in the north. Apparently the Simeonites had persuaded Joshua to allot the land around Kadesh, including the copper mine, to their tribe, so some of them stayed to secure it. To my relief, this included my sons and cousins who had married into the Simeon tribe.

Mother and I intended to settle there as well; it was where Grandfather and Eshkar were buried. But we were healers, needed wherever our soldiers were fighting, so we wouldn't return until the conquest was complete. And from what I overheard Maratti telling Mother, that wouldn't be until after we'd taken Jericho.

CHAPTER TWENTY-THREE

SHIFRA

Moses went up from the steppes of Moab to Mount Nebo, to the summit of Pisgah, opposite Jericho, and GOD showed him the whole land: Gilead as far as Dan; all Naphtali; the land of Ephraim and Manasseh; the whole land of Judah as far as the Western Sea; the Negev; and the Plain—the Valley of Jericho, city of palm trees—as far as Zoar. GOD said to him, "This is the land of which I swore to Abraham, Isaac, and Jacob, 'I will assign it to your offspring.' I have let you see it with your own eyes, but you shall not cross there." So Moses the servant of GOD died there, in the land of Moab, at the command of GOD.

—Deuteronomy 34:1–5

WHEN WE REACHED the outskirts of Bashan, Joshua decided that we would bivouac in the forest between the road and the large field that surrounded Og's walled capital city. Moses assured us that Elohim had begun to put dread and fear of us upon the Canaanite peoples so they would tremble and quake when they heard us mentioned. Mother, Tantana, and I, all midwife-healers, occupied a tent hidden deep in the forest that doubled as the healing tent. Maratti and his sons and Gitlam and our sons stayed closer to the field, near our Hittites and the horses.

242   SHIFRA

For Moses's and Joshua's protection, nobody knew exactly where they lodged.

Maratti reported that he and Gitlam met with some Hittites who lived in Bashan. "At first they were surprised to see obvious foreigners like us among the Hebrews," he told us. "But I found a few eager to spy for us against Og when I offered them a share of the captured Heshbon cattle."

"What else did you learn?" Mother asked him.

He paused and scratched his head. "The local Hittites said that the people of Bashan were frightened. They'd heard how the Hebrews worshipped a powerful god, one so strong that this god enabled them to defeat Pharaoh's army and escape Egypt."

"So are they going to fight us?" I asked. I tried not to sound afraid.

"I'm not sure. Now that they know the Hebrews overcame King Sihon's troops and captured all of Heshbon as well, many are fleeing Bashan to the north."

Gitlam shook his head. "Yet others were complacent, confident that no foreigners would dare attack them as long as King Og rules." He continued. "Like other subject peoples, they complained about high taxes and their young men being conscripted into the king's army, but our spies thought it unlikely conscripts would fight well."

"They assured me that Og was an impatient king who'd only grow increasingly exasperated by our inaction," Maratti said. "Therefore we should wait until his men take the field against us before attacking his fortified city."

Gitlam interrupted. "The narrow city gate, intended to slow down attackers, will be to our advantage, allowing our slingers to pick off their men as they emerge." He sounded enthusiastic at the prospect. "In addition, there are secret underground passages leading out of the city into the forest that the Hittites could open for us."

"Joshua and I don't entirely trust the local spies," Maratti told us later. "We've decided that once Og's soldiers leave the city and bivouac

Bashan's city gate

outside, ours will wait until the moon is waxing close to full to attack them while they sleep."

"How?" Gitlam asked eagerly.

"Shield men with swords and javelins go first, with slingers and archers in the rear." Maratti turned to Gitlam. "You're in charge of making sure our men collect plenty of stones for the slingers."

"When do the chariots come in?"

"Chariots?" I asked. I knew we had horses, but I hadn't seen any chariots.

Gitlam grinned. "See, Maratti, even my wife doesn't know."

I gave Gitlam a peeved look despite feeling proud of our men's training in secret.

"After we fled Egypt and reached the far side of the Reed Sea, we pulled three perfect chariots out of the mud," Maratti explained. "We cleaned them and hid them with the Nubians. In addition to me, two of my Hittite colleagues have been practicing with the chariots, only instead of archers standing in the basket with us, we will have slingers. Gitlam rides with me, Gershom and Eliezer with our two other Hittites."

"This way we don't worry about retrieving arrows," Gitlam said. "We're never going to run out of stones."

Mother gave Maratti a sharp look. "I hope you'll be wearing armor."

"Made from the finest Egyptian bronze," he replied. "Not that any of those Bashanites could get close enough to do us any damage."

"Pride goes before destruction, and a haughty spirit before a fall," Mother chided him. "And don't tell me not to worry. The day I stop worrying about you, you'll know I've taken a lover."

The next day shortly before dawn, nobody had to tell me that the battle had begun. I could hear men shouting in surprise, "Where did those slaves get horses and chariots?" and "How did they learn to drive them?" This was swiftly followed by curses and screams of pain.

THE MIDWIVES' ESCAPE   245

Mother and I waited for the injured to start coming in. Few injuries usually meant more dead, yet fewer than twenty men dribbled in, and only one with a serious wound. We stitched up cuts and gashes, set broken limbs, and bandaged other bruises. But Og, the giant, had not yet appeared.

Suddenly my son Anki ran in, yelling at the top of his lungs, "Og is on the field. He's hefting a massive boulder that he intends to use to crush our men." Anki was a soldier now, like Eshkar had been. He so resembled his father that it brought tears to my eyes to see him wearing armor.

Og's arrival was what Maratti was waiting for. He mounted our fastest horse and rode confidently toward Og, followed by two mounted Hittites and another of our cavalry whom I didn't know. We, and the wounded men who could walk, couldn't resist heading to the edge of the field, where we peered out from behind the trees.

Og was indeed a giant; he appeared to be twice as tall as an average man. I'd never seen a man with such a broad chest or such enormous biceps. He wore neither body armor nor a helmet, but his head and face were covered with long bushy dark hair. Focusing on the horsemen, he held up the boulder and eyed them warily. Maratti rode a quarter of the way around him; then our second Hittite rider followed, and when Maratti was halfway around, our third entered the ring.

Frustrated, Og raised the boulder high and took a few steps toward them, at which time Maratti picked up the pace. This caused Og to turn to keep him in view, but Maratti rode faster, as did the others. Og couldn't seem to decide which one he should crush, so he started turning to keep them in view. At the same time, our slingers pelted his legs with stones from a safe distance while our shock troops began sneaking through the still-open city gate.

246   SHIFRA

That's when I realized what Maratti intended. The faster the horses ran, the faster Og would need to spin to keep watching them and the sooner he'd get dizzy. Indeed, it wasn't long before Og was swaying as he struggled to stay on his feet. His warriors watched in horrified dismay as Og's steps got slower and slower until he dropped the boulder and collapsed.

Immediately our swordsmen ran toward him while Og's defenders raced to protect their king. It was a short battle.

I couldn't see which man or men were responsible, but it soon was apparent that Og's throat had been slit and his hands and feet cut off, at which point our men turned on Og's defenders. Having seen enough slaughter, Mother walked back to the healing tent to check on the injured. Chariots couldn't maneuver well in the forest, but our cavalry rode through the trees, wielding swords and javelins at those foes attempting to escape the carnage. Some Bashan stalwarts remained on the field, but our charioteers made short work of them.

Meanwhile, battles raged inside the city. Our troops had barricaded the gate and I could hear them attacking the Bashan men inside while those on the field were locked outside. They didn't need the Hittites' help to find the city's underground exits; it was obvious where the fleeing inhabitants were coming from. I knew they were our enemies and would gladly kill us if our places were reversed, but I still felt sorry for the women who were trying in vain to herd their children to safety.

We spent the next weeks traveling from one of Og's sixty so-called walled cities to the next, but even the biggest were more like large villages. The small ones barely housed ten families; most of their dwellings sat abandoned. Our men couldn't bring themselves to put any of the poor inhabitants to the sword, never mind the women and children. Looting anyplace was out of the question. We shared some of our provisions with them and learned that, compared to how Og and his men helped

THE MIDWIVES' ESCAPE 247

themselves to whatever they wanted under the guise of collecting taxes, his people would have been better off in Egypt. Yet they refused to leave. The land had housed their ancestors for generations; it was fertile and if it weren't for Og's soldiers, they would be able to feed themselves.

Two of the men pointed to the nearby hillsides, lush with orchards, olive trees, and overgrown grapevines. "If only we had more people to harvest the fruit," one complained. Another sighed. "It's all we can do to grow enough grain for our daily bread."

Upon hearing some of these inhabitants speaking Hittite, the three Hittites who'd help defeat Og declared that this was the land they wanted. If Joshua granted it to them, they would bring more of their cohorts back with them, along with their families.

"I'll talk to Joshua about it as soon as I see him," Maratti encouraged them. "You won't even have to build houses. You can move in and start picking fruit right away."

Mother and I wouldn't leave without examining the children and tending their sores and injuries. We hoped not to see too many villages as bleak as this, but as the days passed, more and more of the towns were empty when we arrived. Perhaps Elohim designated this land for Manasseh's tribe, which numbered less than the others, so they would have the most room in which to be fruitful and multiply.

In the city of Kamon, however, our warriors were met by a formidable force. Maybe we were tired from all the fighting, or maybe we were too discouraged by the pathetic condition of the townspeople we'd seen, but we couldn't bring ourselves to press them, and they refused to yield.

I had stayed to gather those women and children who needed treatment into the town square. This way I could hear Maratti negotiate Kamon's surrender.

"These are grievous losses for one day's fighting," the town chief said. "At this rate we could not hold out for more than two weeks."

"Statistics mean nothing on the first day," Maratti answered. "The wheat is being separated from the chaff."

"What does that mean?" the chieftain asked angrily.

"No disrespect intended to the dead," Maratti replied quickly. "It is a reality in warfare that men with the least skill fall first, making losses greater at the onset. The men fight well, but many of the dead lack skill—that is why they die. The losses will diminish with time, but they will still be high."

I was impressed with Maratti's calm and informative answer.

"If we believe that your men will prevail eventually, what is the point of our increased resistance?"

"Are you suggesting Kamon surrender?"

"No, but we must be careful not to put pride before reality."

"What are your alternatives?" Maratti asked. "Either you fight and win, or you fight and lose."

"If we believe Kamon can hold out, we must fight on by all means. But if not, then we must pursue an honorable peace, as other nations have done."

"An honorable peace?" Maratti sounded skeptical.

"It is where enemies become allies and quarrels are forgotten so each nation may prosper. Ultimately all wars between evenly matched armies are so concluded, sometimes by the marriage between the son of one king and the daughter of the other."

We all knew the two armies were not remotely evenly matched. But Maratti countered, "Or by sharing an underpopulated land. For example, by one people who settle on the plains and another in the hills, so the plainsmen can trade their grain and culled animals for the hillmen's wine, figs, and olive oil."

The chief nodded slowly. "Thus foodstuffs are distributed in a manner equitable to both."

I held my breath in suspense, waiting and hoping that peace was coming.

"Or by fighting jointly against a foe that threatens both of them," Maratti said. Both men then looked to the west, where the Philistines held the seacoast.

So GOD gave Og, all his troops, and all his lands into our hands. The Hebrews took possession of his country, and then we leisurely traveled south along the Jordan River toward Mount Nebo. The river was lined by tall trees and shrubs, but there were dirt pathways on both sides that periodically led down to shallow crossways. We stayed on the east side until we stopped to make camp near Mount Nebo.

Here Moses addressed the people. "Take to heart all the words with which I have warned you this day. Enjoin them upon your children, that they may observe faithfully all the terms of this Torah. For this is not a trifling thing for you. It is your very life; through it you shall long endure on the land that you are to possess upon crossing the Jordan."

Then Elohim spoke to Moses in a voice we could all hear. "Ascend these heights to Mount Nebo, which is in the land of Moab facing Jericho, and view the land of Canaan, which I am giving your people as their holding. Then you shall die on the mountain you are about to ascend and shall be gathered to your kin, as your brother Aaron died on Mount Hor and was gathered to his kin. Thus you may view the land from a distance, but you shall not enter it."

Tears streamed down my cheeks, and many others', as Moses, together with Joshua and Joshua's two sons-in-law, began to climb the mountain. The next day, when only Joshua and his two sons-in-law came down, the Hebrews bewailed Moses in the steppes of Moab for thirty days. We all knew that never again would there arise in Israel a prophet like Moses—whom GOD singled out, face-to-face.

Joshua waited until the remaining twenty-nine days of mourning were completed before telling Maratti and our family what had happened on Mount Nebo. "I knew Moses had recognized that Gershom and Eliezer were his sons back at my daughters' wedding," he began, "but it was only on the mountain that they admitted knowing from the beginning that he was their father."

Mother's jaw dropped in surprise, and it was some time before she could speak. "You mean both sons kept that secret from Moses for all those years?"

Joshua nodded. "They've kept that secret from everyone," he said. "They may have suspected that some of us knew, but they never admitted it."

"So Moses knew that he has grandsons from them?" I asked. The boys, Eliezer's Rehavia, and Gershom's Shebuel and Jonathan, used to come play with my sons when they were little.

"I'm sure he did," Joshua replied. "He knew my daughters gave me three grandsons."

I couldn't restrain my curiosity. "So what was it like on Mount Nebo? Tell us everything you're allowed to share."

"There isn't much to share." Joshua's chin began to quiver. "As soon as we were out of the Hebrews' sight, Moses stopped and embraced Gershom, saying 'Gershom, my son, the first fruit of my loins. Please forgive me.' Then he turned and embraced Eliezer. They held each other a long time until Moses finally pulled away and asked Eliezer to forgive him also."

"But why didn't any of them tell each other?" I asked. "Why all the secrecy?"

"Before Zipporah died, she warned the boys that they would be in danger if Aaron learned who they were," Joshua replied. "And I think that Moses agreed with her. After all, Aaron always resented that GOD had chosen Moses to lead the Hebrews instead of himself, the older son."

Maratti's eyes narrowed. "Aaron was power hungry for himself and his sons to be high priests. I wouldn't put it past them to do anything to keep Moses's sons from challenging their authority."

"Do you think they'd really . . . ?" Mother left her question unfinished, and none of us answered with a denial.

THE MIDWIVES' ESCAPE

251

I had mixed feelings about Moses's reconciliation with his sons. I felt great sorrow for their having to spend much of their lives unable to publicly acknowledge their relationship, yet I was also happy that they were finally able to do so.

After the death of Moses, Maratti told our family that GOD had instructed Joshua, "Prepare to cross the Jordan, together with all this people, into the land that I am giving to the Israelites. Every spot on which your foot treads I give to you, as I promised Moses. As I was with Moses, so I will be with you; I will not fail you or forsake you. Be strong and resolute, for you shall apportion to this people the land that I swore to their fathers to assign to them."

Then Joshua ordered the Hebrew officials, "Go through the camp and tell the people thus: 'Get provisions ready, for in three days' time you are to cross the Jordan, to enter and possess the land that GOD your god is giving you as a possession.'"

They answered Joshua, "We will do everything you have commanded us, and we will go wherever you send us. We will obey you just as we obeyed Moses!"

Three days later I was consumed with anxiety and impatience as officials went through the camp and charged all the troops as follows: "When you see the Ark of the Covenant of GOD being borne by the Levitical priests, you shall move forward. Follow it—but keep a distance of some two thousand cubits from it, never coming any closer to it—so that you may know by what route to march."

Gitlam and I were so excited. Finally, we would be entering the Promised Land.

First Joshua ordered the priests, "Take up the Ark and advance to the head of the people. When you reach the edge of the waters of the Jordan, halt in the middle."

Then he addressed the rest of us. "Purify yourselves, for tomorrow GOD will perform wonders in your midst."

Normally the Jordan keeps flowing over its entire bed throughout the harvest season, like other rivers. But as soon as the priests bearing the Ark reached the Jordan and their feet stepped into the water, the ground began to tremble, causing the waters coming down from upstream to pile up in a heap a great way off. Mother and I clung to our children and grandchildren in terror, but the priests holding the Ark stood calmly on the dry land exactly in the middle of the Jordan. When the quaking subsided, we cautiously began crossing over on the dry land until everyone finished crossing the Jordan. Then, as soon as the priests carrying the Ark stepped out of the water, the Jordan resumed its course, flowing over its entire bed as before.

It wasn't until later that I realized the extent of this miracle. Usually when a river is blocked, there are still puddles or at least some mud left in the streambed that doesn't entirely dry for some time. But the Jordan had dried completely almost immediately.

CHAPTER TWENTY-FOUR

ASENET/SHIFRA

Joshua conquered the whole of this region: the hill country [of Judah], the Negeb, the whole land of Goshen, the Shephelah, the Arabah, and the hill country and coastal plain of Israel—[everything] from Mount Halak, which ascends to Seir, all the way to Baal-gad in the Valley of the Lebanon at the foot of Mount Hermon.

—Joshua 11:16–17

THE NEXT DAY, after we set up camp on the west bank of the Jordan, GOD told Joshua to make flint knives and circumcise as Israelites all those men who had been born during our wilderness wanderings— none of whom had been circumcised in Egypt. I was astonished at how few of the men objected, but Shifra laughed and said that no self-respecting man would refuse to submit to some painful procedure that the other men are proudly enduring.

After all the males were circumcised, we remained with them in the camp until they recovered. At first I was mortified to be inspecting and handling so many men's prongs, but Shifra acted so unaffected one would have thought she did this daily. But then, she'd had two husbands at the same time. I considered it a second miracle that none of the men's wounds became infected.

Joshua reminded us that if a male foreigner who dwells with us wants to offer the Passover sacrifice to GOD, all his males must be circumcised. "Then the man shall be a citizen of the land, an Israelite, and he shall be admitted to offer it," Joshua said solemnly. "But no uncircumcised man may eat of it."

"What about a woman?" I discreetly questioned Serach.

Serach thought about it awhile before replying, "If circumcision admits a foreign man into the covenant, then surely it admits his wife and daughters as well, especially if they immerse after their menses. But that does not admit them to a particular tribe; he enters as an Israelite, a descendant of Jacob, who became Israel after he wrestled with an angel the night before his fateful meeting with Esau."

Encamped at Gilgal, in the steppes of Jericho, the Israelites— now including our family—offered the Passover sacrifice on the fourteenth day of the month, toward evening. The day after, when we ate of the produce of the land, unleavened bread, and parched grain, the manna ceased. From then on we would have to grow our own food or trade for it.

Then Elohim gave Joshua specific instructions on conquering Jericho, and Joshua shared them with us. The Israelites were to march quietly around the city once a day for six days, with seven priests blowing seven shofars and the Ark following them.

I could only imagine how nervous and panicky the people in Jericho would feel each day, waiting for something to happen.

But on the seventh day, Joshua's orders to the rest of the troops were "Do not shout; do not let your voices be heard; do not let a sound issue from your lips until the moment I command you to shout. Then you shall shout as loudly as you can."

On that day the women, children, and injured men who'd stayed behind in the camp crept to the ridgetop to watch. All was quiet, but my impatience heightened as we waited for Joshua to give his command. The men silently marched around the city seven times, the vanguard

THE MIDWIVES' ESCAPE

marching in front of the priests blowing the horns and the rear guard marching behind the Ark, with the horns sounding all the time.

Finally it came to the crucial seventh round. As the priests blew their horns, Joshua ordered the troops, "Shout! For GOD has given you the city."

When our troops heard the horns' blasts, they raised a mighty cry. Those of us on the hill could not restrain ourselves from shouting with them. We stamped our feet so hard the ground trembled beneath us, and the troops began stamping their feet as well until, one by one, stones atop the wall began falling. The priests' piercing horns were ear-splitting and the yelling deafening as more and more stones fell until, with a thunderous rumble, an entire section of the wall collapsed. Our troops rushed through the breach into the city and fought hard to capture it.

It was close to dawn when Maratti woke me. "One of our men says there is a woman in Jericho in hard labor, but none of the Hebrew midwives are willing to enter the crumbling city to help a Canaanite," he whispered. "Gitlam said Shifra was out all night and just returned. He begged me not to disturb her."

I didn't try to stifle a yawn. "Help me up," I said, reaching out to him. "I'll go."

He sighed with relief. "The man is waiting outside."

I used the chamber pot, threw on a cloak, and grabbed my midwife's bag. Maratti gave me a quick kiss and returned to our bed.

"Does the woman have any family?" I asked the man as he led me toward an opening in what was left of the city wall. The air, which had reverberated with sounds of men in the camp snoring, was suddenly silent as we entered what was left of Jericho.

The man shook his head. "She appears to be a harlot." He paused before adding, "A very young harlot."

We walked a distance on a road covered with stones and other debris. He didn't need to tell me to watch my step. It had drizzled

Jericho's collapsed city wall

THE MIDWIVES' ESCAPE   257

enough during the night that the road was slippery. I was about to ask how much farther when the air was split with a woman's cry of pain, just as the man turned to enter a corridor that led to a staircase, which terminated right into the wall.

Maratti had described how the walls of Jericho were so thick that people actually lived inside them. For hundreds of years various armies had attacked the wealthy city, leaving much of the inside in disrepair. The man knocked and a door opened to admit us into a large room with curtained windows that provided light from the outdoors.

A well-dressed woman with kohl-rimmed eyes rose from one of several couches. "Welcome to my inn. Thank you for coming so promptly. Can I bring you anything to eat or drink?" she asked. "Surely you didn't have time to break your fast this morning."

I heard moaning from a curtained doorway. "Take me to the patient first," I said.

The girl on the bed couldn't have been older than eleven. The inn-keeper must have seen my look of antipathy because she explained sadly, "There are men who will pay extra for a virgin."

The younger the better, I thought with disgust. But I needed to know this child's condition. "How long has she been in labor?" I asked as I pulled back the covers to examine her.

"Her water broke yesterday, and she has been pushing since sunset."

The girl cried out in pain but could manage only a feeble push. I put my hand on her sweaty forehead and was not surprised to find it hot. Then I checked the opening to her womb. "This baby is not coming," I told the woman after a long sigh. "After an entire day, I can only get my little finger into her womb. Normally I can fit my entire hand in."

"I'll pay you well if you stay until the end," she replied.

"I always stay until the end. Don't worry about my fee," I said. "What I would like now is some food."

She exited through a different curtain and returned with grapes, cooked eggs, and, to my surprise, fresh bread. "I must leave you now. Get me if anything changes."

However, nothing changed except the girl's contractions weakened and eventually ceased, as did her cries. When I felt no pulse in her neck, I called for the innkeeper.

"The girl is dead, but her child is not," I declared. "At least not yet. I would like to try to save it."

She nodded slowly. "What do you need?"

I grimaced. "Your kitchen's sharpest knife, some bowls to catch the blood, and sufficient cloth to wrap the body in."

"I assume you have performed this procedure before," she whispered when she returned with several women carrying the needed supplies.

"Many times," I replied sadly. "Assuming I am successful, I will need a large bowl to wash the baby in, then some salt and oil to rub his skin with, plus some cloth strips to swaddle him."

The women had brought those as well.

I took a deep breath and put aside my horror. Then, in one smooth motion, I picked up the knife, cut into the girl's belly, and pulled the child out.

"It's a boy!" I held the baby up for the women to see and gave his buttocks a solid slap.

They cheered when he responded with a resounding cry. I cut the cord and then pulled out the afterbirth. One of the older women gathered up the dust the mother's blood had dripped onto and took it, along with the afterbirth, outside to bury. I made a point of noticing which door she'd used, in case I needed to leave quickly.

No sooner was the girl wrapped in her shroud than I felt the earth move. It was a gentle trembling, but the building creaked as the ceiling cracked and some pieces fell. Immediately the women jumped up and ran screaming through the outside door. I was left holding the crying baby, his dead mother still on the bed.

Another tremor, stronger, sent me rushing to the door, but the wall had shifted just enough that the door was stuck fast. Refusing to abandon the infant, I found my way to the entrance I'd come through earlier. If I hadn't been holding him, I would have had my hands free to balance myself against the walls. But the stone floor was more slippery than before. All it took was one sharp aftershock; I lost my balance and fell.

The last thing I remembered was a terrible pain when my hip hit the floor.

"Asenet." It was Maratti's voice, but coming from far away. "Asenet, can you hear me? Try to move your hand if you can hear me." He sounded louder.

I was able to open my eyes a crack, and Maratti's face came into view. "The baby . . ." I managed to whisper.

"Don't worry. The boy is uninjured. Shifra took him to a wet nurse."

I tried to sit up, but it was so painful to move that I let out a moan.

"Where does it hurt most?" Maratti asked. "Your head, your shoulder, your leg?"

"All of me hurts . . . but my right leg and hip . . . the most."

I must have fainted because the next thing I remembered was a small group of people crowding around me while a woman healer carefully prodded different parts of my lower body. When she got to my right thigh, the pain was excruciating. "It feels like she has some broken bones," the healer said. "We need a mat or rug to get her off this cold, wet floor and back to her bed."

It seemed an eternity until a dry rug was procured, and despite everyone's desire to move me gently onto it, the agony made me faint again.

I awakened inside my tent, where Shifra held a cup to my lips. "Drink this," she ordered. "It will taste bitter but don't spit it out. It will make you sleep."

I woke later to the sweet sounds of a lyre. Had I died and gone to Gan Eden already?

Apparently not, because I felt a cool hand on my forehead and heard my daughter's voice saying, "I think Mother's awake now, Serach, but it feels like her fever is worse."

I managed to open my eyes and mumble, "Water, water." Almost immediately a cup was pressed to my lips. The water was cool and refreshing. I opened my eyes wider and saw that it was indeed Serach strumming the lyre. "You play so beautifully," I said.

"Thank you. I've been playing lyres since I was a child, when I sang to Grandfather Jacob to calm him after Joseph disappeared and was presumed dead."

I had heard stories that Joseph's brothers were so jealous of Jacob's preference for the boy that they sold him to Midianite traders who sold him again to Potiphar in Egypt—which is where he met, and later married, Potiphar's adopted daughter, Asenet, for whom I was named. But I'd never heard any stories that mentioned Serach before.

"What did you sing to Jacob?"

Serach smiled and took up her lyre to tune it. "When Joseph was reunited with his brothers and sent them back to Canaan to bring their father, Jacob, to him in Egypt, he ordered them not to alarm the aged man. The brothers summoned me and asked me to sit before Jacob and play the lyre, in this manner revealing to him that Joseph was still alive. So I sang softly, 'Joseph my uncle did not die; he lives and rules all the land of Egypt.' I had to repeat the song many times until Jacob my grandfather understood."

Serach played until I fell asleep.

Mother was sleeping fitfully the next day when I arrived to relieve Maratti. Though he'd spent the night sitting by her, he refused to leave. I lifted her shift to examine her leg and hip, which were now so inflamed and swollen that Maratti and I both understood that unless there was a miracle, Mother was unlikely to recover. Yet I couldn't stop praying to

Elohim to heal her as he had healed Miriam's white scales after Moses had cried out, "Heal her now, O GOD, I beseech you."

The healer returned in the afternoon and, shaking her head, gave Mother another dose of the bitter sleeping draft. Maratti and I continued to pray for Mother's healing, but she was feverish all night, murmuring incoherently to Grandfather. I tried to make her more comfortable with soothing sounds and cool, damp cloths. Maratti dozed off first, lying on the bedding next to Mother, and I struggled to keep my eyes open.

Gitlam was crying when I awakened. I opened my eyes to see that both he and Maratti had cut the edge of their cloaks and trimmed their beards. There was a bowl of ashes from the hearth next to me, and I smeared some on my face and clothes before handing the bowl to Maratti, who did the same. Then I wrapped my arms around myself and sank back down onto the bed.

Mother was dead, which meant that it was my duty to begin keening the loud laments that would bring other people to join our mourning. But duty or not, I would still have been wailing my grief.

When we had ten women, Maratti and Gitlam would leave, accompanied by the other men, as it was traditional that women were responsible for preparing the body for burial. We removed Mother's clothes and jewelry, except for the bronze anklet she'd received when she became a woman. Then we washed her body, rubbed it with olive oil, and dressed her in the colorful tunic that she wore on feast days and at family celebrations. After wrapping her body in a thin linen shroud, I went outside to join the women preparing the meal we would consume after her burial at dusk. But I was impure from contact with a corpse, so I sat on a bench a distance from the others.

I was surprised when Maratti sat down next to me a little later. Of course he was just as impure as I was, but I was still surprised when he leaned close and began speaking in a low voice. "We are not far from the Cave of Machpelah—"

"You mean where Sarah and Abraham are buried?" I interrupted him. "Where Jacob's body was buried after the Egyptians embalmed him?"

"Keep your voice down," he whispered. "The land originally belonged to the local Hittites, and when Joshua told them about me, that I was the Hittite warrior who had killed King Og, Joshua asked if we could bury my wife in the patriarchs' tomb. They agreed immediately—as long as I consented to be buried there as well."

I began to weep. "But you're not in ill health. It could be years," I protested. "Your children and grandchildren won't be able to visit your grave."

"I am not in such good health as you think. There is a growth in my throat that has prevented me from eating solid food for some time, and soon it will prevent me from breathing." Maratti took my hand. "Please, Shifra, I want to be buried with my beloved Asenet."

Soon we were both crying. I squeezed his hand in return and said, "I will do what I can to facilitate it."

We spent the next several weeks near Shiloh waiting out the winter rains. First Joshua had Joseph's coffin buried in nearby Shechem, in the portion of land that was allotted to the tribe of Joseph's son, Manasseh. A month later Gitlam found Maratti's body lying peaceably in the bed where Mother had died. On the floor was an empty bottle. It looked like a flask that had once held Mother's favorite fragrance, but I knew when I smelled it that this flask had not contained perfume. The smell was unmistakable; it had last held the healer's bitter sleeping draft. Gitlam and I cried together until we were cried out, and then he went to inform Joshua. While he was gone I leaned over and sniffed Maratti's lips. My

THE MIDWIVES' ESCAPE 263

suspicion confirmed, I rinsed out the flask until no odor remained.

So many of Maratti's warriors attended his funeral at the Cave of Machpelah that some were forced to stand on the stairs leading down to Maratti's tomb. I stood at the entrance where I could still hear the many eulogies and words of praise for their captain. Despite the distance, a good number of his male descendants—my sons and nephews—made the journey from Kadesh Barnea to honor Maratti, but I was too numb with grief from my dual losses to appreciate the magnitude of esteem given him.

Elohim apparently honored him as well; when we came up out of the tomb when the funeral was finished, we were greeted by a magnificent rainbow.

CHAPTER TWENTY-FIVE

SHIFRA

And they shall beat their swords into plowshares and their spears into pruning hooks. Nation shall not take up sword against nation; they shall never again know war. But every family shall sit under its own vine and fig tree with no one to disturb them.

—Micah 4:3–4

THE ISRAELITES, CERTAIN that the rain was a sign of blessing from Elohim, quickly got to work plowing the soil to prepare it for planting wheat and barley. Having grown up eating manna, Gitlam and I—like most of the Israelites—had never seen how cereal grains were cultivated, but thankfully some of the local people who had begun worshipping Elohim showed us. I hoped that the Ishmaelites had done the same for our people back in Kadesh.

In case they hadn't, Gitlam paid close attention to the process and tools the locals used, while I made my midwife and healing skills available to help the women. Plowing in the heavy, damp soil was a labor-intensive activity best left to the men. Women would have their turn to work hard when it came time to grind the wheat and barley into flour.

THE MIDWIVES' ESCAPE   265

Each day Gitlam shared what he'd learned with me. "If I hadn't seen a plow up close," he told me, "I wouldn't know that the most efficient ones have bronze points instead of plain wood like the rest of the plow."

"What else did they teach you?"

"That the men plow each field twice. The first time, soon after the rain starts, to loosen the damp soil, with women and children following behind, sowing the seeds. The second plowing covers the seeds with soil and pulls out any weeds."

"How soon before they're harvested?"

"Barley ripens first, before Pesach," Gitlam replied. "When the barley comes out, then they plant lentils. Wheat takes longer to ripen, so that gets harvested before Shavuot."

"We won't be here to see a grain harvest, so we might have to go watch the Ishmaelites do theirs," I said.

"From what the men told me, harvesting and threshing are far more complicated and time-consuming than sowing and plowing," he replied. "So everyone in the village has to participate."

The ground was still damp when I recognized the ridge where Gitlam and I had rescued the sand kittens years before. It had been forty years since I fled Egypt with my family, leaving me and Gitlam among the very few who remembered crossing the Sea of Reeds.

At first I thought we'd come to the wrong place. The Kadesh lake was as I remembered it, but there were only a few tents on the low hills around it. Instead there were various permanent residences up on the hillside terraces, many sharing adjacent walls. The villages located closer to the lake had olive trees on their terrace level to facilitate moving the harvest to the oil presses, while those higher up the hill had vineyards. Some structures were made of stone, others from mud and straw bricks like the Hebrews had slaved to make in Egypt. Gitlam and I stood still in confusion. Some of these must house our adult children

Kadesh Barnea village

THE MIDWIVES' ESCAPE   267

and grandchildren who'd remained in Kadesh while their fathers bat-
tled the Canaanites, but I didn't recognize anyone. Our donkey-drawn
wagons were almost overflowing with our belongings, including tents
we probably wouldn't be needing.

Suddenly we were surrounded by children yelling, "Grandfather,
Grandmother." Two of the younger girls grabbed my hands and began
pulling me up a path leading to where the tribe of Simeon had been
located before the Tabernacle moved to Shiloh. Two boys took hold of
Gitlam, who placidly accompanied them.

The girls, either sisters or cousins, couldn't stop talking. "All the
adults and big boys worked from dawn to dusk to get enough houses
built for everyone—they made sure that ours was big enough for you
too. We hope you like it; it's next to Utti's."

I didn't know what to say. But I did know not to say "What is your
name dear?" Heaven forbid any of my grandchildren should think I
didn't recognize them.

Gitlam saved me by stroking his chin as if he weren't sure and then
asking them, "Now which of you is Chava and which is Ahava?"

The girls giggled and one of them replied, "Grandfather, you know
very well that neither of us is Chava or Ahava."

"Then which of you is Anna and which is Hannah?"

Now both girls were laughing too hard to speak, which caused
me to join them. When I'd caught my breath, I remembered them as
Tamara and Talia, Sagar's twins.

"So are we going to be living with you?" Surely they wouldn't have
Gitlam and me living by ourselves in our old tent. A young man, whom
I recognized as my now grown-up youngest brother, Piruwi, answered,
"Anki's family lives with us, but they only have two children and he's
out with the army right now, so there's room for more."

"I hope it's stone rather than brick," I whispered to Gitlam. Most
of our boys had married girls from the nearby Simeonite tribe, which
meant their ancestors had likely been slaves making bricks for the

Egyptians. If I were them I'd rather not be constantly confronted by those unpleasant memories.

"There are advantages to both," Gitlam replied, squeezing my hand. "What I hope is that there's a private place for the two of us to sleep together."

As we walked closer to the village, I could now discern that it was not merely an area of randomly placed stone dwellings but a rectangle of buildings surrounding a protected field where vegetables were growing. Groves of olive trees grew on the terraces on both sides of the rectangle. Every so often there were breaks in the outer walls where a person could walk from outside the rectangle to its center. One break led into an empty enclosure that, from the large amount of goat pellets on the ground, had to be where the herds spent their nights.

A larger break in the perimeter was the entrance to what Gitlam and I immediately recognized as a wainwright's workshop. Only the outer walls were stone; the interior partitions were brick. All around were partially built wagon boxes and wheels as well as shelves holding tools and various lengths of planed wood. We smiled at each other and nodded. Of course some of Grandfather's descendants would have carried on his occupation. And the curtained entries on either side likely led to their homes.

Sure enough, there was Sagar standing in one of them. As much as he resembled Eshkar, with his curly hair and bronze skin, I had no doubt that he was Gitlam's son.

Sagar gave each one of us a long hug before saying, "I'm sorry, but I heard that Grandmother Asenet and Grandfather Maratti died just after the Israelites took Jericho. I expect that the rain and cold were too hard for them at their age." He sighed before adding, "It is quite an honor that Joshua allowed them to be buried at Hebron in the Cave of Machpelah. I would have liked to attend."

I took Gitlam's hand as tears filled my eyes. I felt almost relieved that Maratti and Mother had died within a short time of each other.

THE MIDWIVES' ESCAPE 269

But it must have been a heavy blow for Sagar and those other descendants who hadn't been able to say goodbye to them, especially to my mother.

"Would you like to tour the village now?" Sagar asked. "Or would you prefer to get settled first?"

Gitlam's chin quivered as he tried to hide his grief. Maratti had been like a father to him. "I think we'd like to get settled first," he said, more to me than to Sagar. "We can visit the village later."

I didn't say anything, but I wanted to go see Eshkar's grave before seeing the village.

Sagar sighed with relief when I nodded. Then he motioned us to follow him. In front of us was the house's main room, which was divided by two rows of stone pillars that supported a second floor. "It looks like these places are built from both stone and brick," Gitlam whispered.

I inspected the fabric hanging in the doorway. "With doorways covered with what remains of our tents," I pointed out.

One long room formed by the pillars was paved with stones, with an empty manger standing in the middle. The area apparently served as stables for oxen that were now out in the fields. At one end there was storage for ceramic jars of beer and large amphora of olive oil; above those were shelves of empty pottery, some beautifully decorated. I wondered which of my many daughters and granddaughters were responsible for the lovely designs. Or maybe it was Sagar's Simeonite wife, Dinah.

The main room, which was open to the sky, seemed to have many uses, most performed by women. Certainly it was an area for food preparation, as it contained tools and cooking equipment, including sets of grinding stones, and the hearth, oven, and cistern. At the rear of the main room were two storage rooms, one containing tall jars of water and the other holding dishes, bowls, and cooking pots.

On the other side of the main room, opposite the stables, were two smaller windowless rooms—windowless because they shared a wall

270 SHIFRA

with the house adjacent to it. Both were storage rooms, one for food-stuffs, especially grains; and as if to demonstrate this, when I looked into the grain room a sand cat ran out, a mouse clenched between its teeth. The other room held a variety of sleeping mats and bedding, some of which appeared to have been used recently. This room would have been stifling in the summer but warm and cozy when the weather was cold. It occurred to me that this room might be where impure women sequestered themselves following childbirth or when they had their menses. In my recollection, the majority of women in a house-hold usually had their menses at the same time, in which case this room would get pleasantly crowded.

The two side rooms on the main floor had roofs reached by lad-ders. This was where the family slept on all but the coldest nights. The back room, which housed looms, weaving materials, and a large bed, was roofed as well, providing shade for the weavers and space under their watchful eyes for children to nap and play. There would also be privacy for couples who wanted it. Gitlam and I eyed the ladders with apprehension and shook our heads.

We would be spending our nights on the ground floor.

There was a roof over the second-floor rooms at the back of the house also, but this area seemed to be used for drying washed clothes and grain stalks. The view of the lake and its oasis was impressive, as was the water channel that descended from farther up the hill to cis-terns in the village's walled open-air, center area. In the middle was a large circular flat surface on elevated ground that was smooth, clean, and hard.

"This is the village's threshing floor," Sagar informed us. "All our families here take turns using it, starting in early spring when barley is harvested. And from what I saw when I was in the fields last week, that should be anytime now. Once the barley is done, we'll have a rest until the wheat harvest after Pesach."

THE MIDWIVES' ESCAPE

Sagar was right. The barley was ripe the following week. Immediately the reapers set to work, and as Gitlam and I watched, fascinated, the men wielded flint sickles to cut down the stalks while the women collected the sheaves, bound them into manageable bundles, and stacked them in the fields. Once a certain number of sheaves was ready, they were loaded onto a cart—likely built by our wainwrights—and brought to the threshing floor. Here, the objective was to separate the grains from the stalks, collect the grains, and bring them back to the house.

First, workers opened the sheaves and spread the stalks across the threshing floor. Next, older children walked a pair of oxen pulling a heavy wooden sledge, studded underneath with jagged flints, in circles over the grain. This tore the barley ears from the stalks and loosened the grain itself from the husks. This process served to cut up the straw and crush the husks around the grains, which the children then placed in broad, flat winnowing baskets and tossed in the air with great enthusiasm.

Ideally, the husks were blown away by the wind, letting the short torn straw land nearby to be used for kindling, to feed animals, and in weaving baskets. The heavier grain would fall at the winnowers' feet, where women efficiently collected it using sieves of various sizes. Lastly, the women and girls brought the grain to the house where it was stored in the large granary bins.

Watching all the workers, I gave thanks to Elohim for having given us manna. I still enjoyed caring for our goats. When I was young, I milked them twice a day, fed them straw and spoiled vegetables, and after rain brought up weeds along the streets, herded them outside to eat. When I was older, Mother let me assist when the pregnant goats gave birth. Once she saw that I was ready, I became her midwife apprentice.

Now I was too old to herd goats or deliver babies, although I could advise younger midwives what to do during difficult births. Gitlam was old too. His hands shook when he tried to plane or whittle wood. Our grandsons could all sling farther than him, but at least he could teach the younger ones how to do it. I could no longer see well enough to thread a needle or weave. I didn't even have strength enough to grind wheat into flour or cut up olives and dates. I was ashamed of my hands, dotted by so many dark spots from the sun. It seemed that every time I looked down, there were new pools of blood under the surface of my ever-thinning skin. Yet I couldn't recall my hands bumping into anything.

But I still knew what to say when children asked, "Grandmother, tell me a story?"

I told tales of the Egyptian plagues, crossing the Sea of Reeds, Elohim's speaking to us at Sinai, Elohim's cloud moving over the Tabernacle, Aaron's sons dying because they offered strange fire to Elohim, my friend Haggith eloping with the Moabite prince, Gitlam's fighting the Amalekites with his first sling—which he still had—Moses's Nubian wife taking their daughters back to teach Torah to the Cushites, Maratti's defeating Og the giant, and Joshua leading us in the battle of Jericho.

The boys liked battle stories; the girls didn't. The girls liked romantic stories; the boys didn't. But they all, except for the youngest, liked scary stories. So for at least the hundredth time, I recounted my memories of the ten plagues—which all the children were too young to have experienced.

I began by asking, "Which plague do you think was the least terrible?"

They argued briefly, comparing frogs and locusts, before deciding that while both might be annoying, a person could at least eat locusts. I pointed out that locusts would devour every crop growing in Egypt long before people could eat them. The children then decided that lice and flies were both irritating, but boils were painful. Having water turn into blood was disgusting, but it was only for seven days. But they couldn't decide what was worse—murrain, which only affected cattle and sheep, or fiery hail, which smote everything outdoors.

Their biggest argument was about how bad three days of darkness were. It wasn't as though the darkness could hurt anyone, some of

THE MIDWIVES' ESCAPE

273

the children posited, especially if it only lasted three days. But others reminded them that nobody knew how long the darkness would last until it was lifted, which had to have been frightening. To my surprise, there was disagreement about how terrible the slaying of the firstborns was.

"People would just die in their sleep," one boy said. "It wouldn't be painful, and I would get all my brother's things."

"It would be sorrowful for the families of the dead," a girl challenged him.

"I wouldn't mind if my older brother died," a younger boy said. "Then I wouldn't have to endure how he teases and torments me."

I couldn't discipline him for saying something so mean. Not since I had been relieved to wake up and learn that my older brother had not only died but had already been buried while I slept that night.

A woman's authoritative voice interrupted our discussion. "Only the Egyptians suffered these plagues." I turned around to see Serach bat Asher in the doorway. "None of the Hebrews had frogs, lice, or flies in our homes or locusts in our fields. Our water didn't change into blood, our cattle didn't get sick, and we didn't get boils. No fiery hail fell on us, and the inside of our homes stayed light while the Egyptians' were dark."

She didn't need to remind us that none of the Hebrew firstborns died. She concluded, "I was there, and I saw it."

None of the children disputed her or questioned her. They sat there in awed silence until I announced that story time was over; it was bedtime. Then they walked over to Serach and let her give each one a hug and a blessing as they left.

When it was just the two of us, I thanked her and asked where she was staying.

Serach looked at me sadly and took my hand before saying, "I'm merely passing through. I wanted to see you one last time in this world."

It was only a few days later, when I suddenly felt too weak to stand, that I realized I was the one leaving this world, not her.

AUTHOR'S NOTE

WRITING A HISTORICAL NOVEL based on parts of the Bible, especially those parts that are well known, is a challenging and controversial project. Many people believe the Bible is holy writ, although others deem its contents legends or myths, and more than a few people consider the Bible to be no more than historical fiction. Biblical scholars are debating whether the Exodus of Israelites from Egypt actually happened, and if it did, is the Bible's description accurate?

It's easy to doubt the Bible's accuracy when, according to Exodus 12:40–41, the Israelites lived in Egypt for 430 years. Yet according to Exodus 1:5, only seventy persons of Jacob's issue came to Egypt, one of whom was Levi, the great-grandfather of Aaron, Moses, and Miriam. But Levi was also their grandfather, since his daughter Joheved was their mother. Now it would seem impossible for only two generations of Levites to span 430 years unless miracles are involved, yet there is no mention of miraculously long lifespans and fertility.

Based on the lack of evidence of the millions of people whom the Bible says were wandering in the Sinai desert for forty years, Rabbi David Wolpe asserts that the biblical Exodus is a fiction. Two million people—603,550 males and their families, as the Torah describes—should have left some remnants that we would find. But few think that this number is historical anyway, not when the total population of Egypt at that time was about two million people.

However, there is no archaeological evidence against the historical occurrence of an exodus if a smaller group had left Egypt. And sure

AUTHOR'S NOTE

enough, according to Richard Elliott Friedman, bestselling author of *Who Wrote the Bible?* and *The Exodus: How It Happened and Why It Matters*, evidence indicates that this smaller group of Semitic people consisted of Levites, who were members of the group associated with Moses, the Exodus, and the Sinai events depicted in the Bible. In the Torah, Moses is identified as a Levite. Also, in all of Israel only Levites had Egyptian names: Moses, Phinehas, Hophni, and Hur are all Egyptian names.

Friedman's book on the Exodus is fascinating, well-written, and less than three hundred pages. I encourage those who want details on his theory to read this book.

Another challenge for me was how much of the Biblical account to include and how much to leave out. The Book of Numbers includes many battles the Israelites fought against the Canaanites; however, to me, one clash was pretty much the same as another. So I limited myself to describing in detail only the most important: the battles against Amalek, who attacked the Israelites twice; against Og, the giant king of Bashar; in Kamon, where the town surrendered; and most famously, the capture of Jericho.

On the subject of Jericho, I feel obliged to discuss how the Exodus story is filled with miracles. According to the *Oxford English Dictionary*, a miracle is "a surprising and welcome event not explicable by natural or scientific laws and is therefore considered to be the work of a divine agency."

I admit to being a skeptic when it comes to miracles. Some people would consider it a miracle that GOD communicated with Moses out of a burning bush that was not consumed, but others might think it was some sort of delusion or hallucination.

And while many Israelites might consider Pharaoh's daughter pulling baby Moses from the Nile to raise in the royal household miraculous, this action is easily explicable as natural. Unlikely perhaps, but not a miracle.

AUTHOR'S NOTE
277

What about the plagues? Several microorganisms could have turned the Nile red so it appeared to be bloody. Frogs, lice or gnats, and flies live in the area, and natural causes could have increased any of their populations over their usual levels. Many diseases that affect animals can also infect humans. Hailstorms and locusts are natural phenomena that destroy crops. And darkness for three days could have been caused by sandstorms. However, it is impossible to conceive of any natural occurrence that would kill only firstborn males. Thus, the tenth plague should be considered miraculous.

Next, how did the Hebrews cross the Sea of Reeds, if not by a miracle? True, the pillar of fire that kept the Egyptian army at bay all night couldn't have been natural, but what happened in the morning likely was. Think about how tides are affected by the moon and sun. When the sun, moon, and Earth are in alignment (at the time of the new or full moon), the solar tide has an additive effect on the lunar tide, creating ultra-high high tides, and ultra-low low tides. During the vernal and autumnal equinoxes (about March 21 and September 23, respectively, in the northern hemisphere), the sun is positioned directly above the equator, causing even higher high tides and lower low tides.

Consider when Hebrews observed the first Passover—when the full moon coincided with the vernal equinox, which would have produced the highest high tides and the lowest low tides. In a narrow, low-lying wetland, such as the Sea of Reeds, people could walk on crushed reeds during low tide, but the high tide would be over fifteen feet deep.

So the crossing was not a miracle. Neither were the various timely earthquakes.

What about all the people who left Egypt, not only Israelites, hearing GOD proclaim the Ten Commandments at Mount Sinai? A mass hallucination or a miracle? Certainly, there's no natural explanation for the manna that appeared each morning, exactly enough for each person, or the fire that issued from the Tabernacle and killed Aaron's sons

AUTHOR'S NOTE

Nadav and Avihu when they offered alien fire. And of course, there's Balaam's talking donkey.

I refuse to take sides. In writing *The Midwives' Escape*, I accept the world as the Bible describes it, even if I don't believe it. To those who object that I made things up or left things out, you're right. After all, I wrote a historical *novel*, which the dictionary defines as a "work of fiction."

ACKNOWLEDGMENTS

KUDOS TO MY DAUGHTER, Emily, a voracious reader and writer of fan fiction, who spent hours critiquing my early drafts and never hesitated to lambast any scenes that didn't measure up to her exacting standards. She recommended the podcast *Writing Excuses*, which offers advice on how even seasoned authors can improve their writing and introduced me to the "save the cat" scene, where characters are shown doing something that makes readers root for them (such as saving a cat) so readers will instantly be more invested in those characters. Upon learning that rare endangered sand kittens had been born at an Israeli safari park, I couldn't resist having my characters rescue a pair of them from hyenas.

Thanks to my publicist, Rachel Gul of Over the River Public Relations, who created a great press kit for getting the word out to trade publications and Jewish media.

To all the friends and fans who continuously encouraged me by asking—via Goodreads, Facebook, and personal emails—when my next novel was coming out, your long wait is over.

Finally, I offer my love and gratitude to Dave, my husband of over fifty years. When I can't think of a certain word for a specific situation in a scene, he stops what he's doing to provide exactly the one I need. He doesn't complain about my late nights working on book business, is always ready with a silly pun or dad joke when I need cheering up, and—last but not least—provided the twenty-eight illustrations in this book.

ABOUT THE AUTHOR

MAGGIE ANTON is an award-winning author of historical fiction as well as a Talmud scholar with expertise in Jewish women's history. She was born Margaret Antonofsky in Los Angeles, California, where she still resides. In 1992 she joined a women's Talmud class taught by Rachel Adler. There, to her surprise, she fell in love with Talmud, a passion that has continued unabated for thirty years. Intrigued that the great Jewish scholar Rashi had no sons, only daughters, she started researching the family and their community.

Thus the award-winning trilogy Rashi's Daughters was born, to be followed by National Jewish Book Award finalist *Rav Hisda's Daughter: Apprentice* and its sequel, *Enchantress*. Then Anton switched to nonfiction, winning the Gold Benjamin Franklin Award in the religion category for *Fifty Shades of Talmud: What the First Rabbis Had to Say about You-Know-What*, a lighthearted in-depth tour of sexuality within the Talmud. Her most recent work, *The Choice: A Novel of Love, Faith, and the Talmud*, is a wholly transformative novel that takes characters inspired by Chaim Potok and ages them into young adults in 1950s Brooklyn.

Since 2005, Anton has lectured about the research behind her books at hundreds of venues throughout North America, Europe, and Israel. She still studies women and Talmud, albeit mostly online. Her favorite Talmud learning sites are *Daf Shevui* and *Mishna Yomit*, provided daily via email by the Conservative Yeshiva in Jerusalem at https://www.conservativeyeshiva.org/learn/.

ABOUT THE AUTHOR

You can follow Anton's blog and contact her at her website, www
.maggieanton.com. You can also find her on Facebook and Goodreads.
And if you liked this book, please give it a nice review at all the usual
websites.

Preview of
SERACH'S STORY
CHAPTER ONE

I WAS SAD TO SEE Shifra die—not so sad as Gitlam or their children felt in their bereavements, but I was sad nonetheless. At least Gitlam didn't even live for the entire thirty days of mourning before joining her. I, on the other hand, have outlived almost everyone I've ever known. I don't know why Elohim chose me for the "honor" of being a living witness to His miracles and wonders, but it has made me leery of establishing any close relationships.

I had no idea that I would be the one to help Moses fulfill the oath sworn to Joseph to carry his bones out of Egypt. When the Israelites were ready to leave Egypt, they were occupied taking booty, so Moses was the one concerned with Joseph's bones. When he learned that I was the only person of that generation still alive, he came to me and asked, "Do you know where Joseph is buried?"

Of course I knew. Joseph's entire family was at his burial. I told Moses, "The Egyptians made a metal coffin for him and sank it in the Nile so that its waters would be blessed." I walked with Moses to the place and showed him.

Moses then stood on the bank and shouted: "Joseph, Joseph, it has come time for the oath that Elohim swore to our father, Abraham, to redeem his children. Do not delay our redemption. If you show yourself, it will be well, and if not, then we are free from your oath and we will leave you here to go forth from Egypt." Joseph's coffin immediately rose to the surface and Moses took it. The coffin traveled in the Tabernacle until Jericho fell, after which Joshua had it reburied in Shechem in the portion of the Promised Land given to Manasseh, Joseph's son.

After Shifra died, I couldn't stay in Kadesh Barnea. Too many people who knew me from earlier times would notice and become suspicious of my longevity. Besides, my work there was done. Hebrews who'd been slaves in Egypt for generations were now capable of living as a people, a society. After more than thirty-five years in Kadesh, they'd learned self-sufficiency. They made their own beer, wine, and olive oil to drink and trade. They raised sheep and goats for wool to weave and milk to make cheese. They restarted the Amalekite copper mines, and with tin from Nubia, they specialized in crafting bronze jewelry, weapons, and kitchenware. From the Ishmaelites, they learned the all-important process of turning wheat and barley seeds into bread and cakes.

Once the twelve Israelite tribes had settled in their allotted lands, I moved north. I first thought I'd live in Tyre, in the land of Asher. But people from my own tribe would be the most likely to recognize me. So I opted to travel via the eastern route past Moab and avoid lands where the Israelites had settled. To my surprise the Arabah Road was crowded with people, mostly Hebrews, coming from the north, where there was a famine. Many were families, including one from Bethlehem consisting of a middle-aged father, his wife, and two young sons who befriended me.

The talkative mother, Naomi, bemoaned the famine in Judah that had forced them to move to Moab for food. "Just when we were settled in the Promised Land, the rains stopped. Look how thin my husband and I have become, trying to save as much food as possible for our little boys—who should be growing much faster."

The two boys did look undersized, but before I could commiserate, Naomi turned to me. "How is it that you, such an elderly woman, are traveling alone? Don't you have any companions? Aren't you afraid?" Her brows were furrowed with concern.

"I travel this road regularly," I replied. "I know people in Moab." I was thinking of Haggith and her daughter, Ruth, but I had no intention of saying any more than was necessary. For all I knew, Haggith could have remarried—or even died.

Naomi asked no more questions. She introduced her husband, Elimelech, and her young sons, Mahlon and Chilion, while I, feigning more exhaustion than I felt, nodded but didn't give my name. They trudged on quietly as Naomi described the stunted crops and poor harvests. Finally Moab's red rocks came into view, and the entire family was struck dumb by the awesome sight.

It wasn't long until Moabite guards intercepted us. "I am the queen mother Haggith's aunt," I whispered to the leader in a confidential tone. "Please escort me to her quarters." Then I pointed to Elimelech's small group and addressed the leader again, this time in an authoritative voice, "And have your men direct this family to where other refugees are staying."

To my relief, Haggith, along with her toddler, Ruth, were staying in the same rooms that they had been before, along with their maid-servants. Haggith joyfully embraced me while Ruth hid behind her mother's skirts. "What brings you to visit us?"

I explained about the Hebrew family I'd met on the road.

"Bring us some refreshments," Haggith told her servants. Then she turned to me and spoke in Hebrew. "We've had plenty of rain here in Moab. The Hebrews, and others, are welcome to set up tents and grow crops on our lands as long as they pay us one-fifth of their harvests."

Something in her tone made me think she missed her own people. "Would you like to meet this family?" I asked. "The boys could use a good meal."

Haggith nodded. "The mother and boys are welcome to spend the Sabbath with us, but quarters in this part of the palace are for women and young children only. I don't dare have a strange man come to my rooms."

Six years passed swiftly. Naomi's husband, Elimelech, died the first year, and she was left with her two sons, Mahlon and Chilion. Ruth became prettier every year, while Naomi's boys grew tall and sturdy. However, Haggith looked increasingly haggard. One Shabbat, after Naomi asked me whether anything was wrong with her, I could no longer keep silent.

"For the last two years, Nikkal, Asherah's high priestess, has been visiting Haggith every few months, ostensibly to check on her health. But we suspect that Nikkal is interested in recruiting Ruth as an acolyte in service to the goddess. She keeps mentioning Asherah as Elohim's consort."

Naomi gulped. "But Ruth is a Hebrew girl. We don't pray to goddesses."

I sighed. "As long as Haggith remains in good health, she controls Ruth's future. But a girl as beautiful as Ruth would draw many, especially men, to venerate Asherah. I suspect that is Nikkal's true goal."

"Ruth is too young to be a temple prostitute," Naomi wailed.

"But she's not too young to start learning about the responsibilities and duties of Asherah's priestesses," I replied. "Most Moabite girls would be honored to be chosen."

"Can you do anything to prevent this?"

"Haggith is worried about it too, but she's already thought of a solution. She suggests that Mahlon marry her."

"What! They are far too young."

"They are not too young to become betrothed," I said. "That will keep Nikkal at bay."

Two years later, Haggith was bedridden when Mahlon became betrothed to Ruth and his brother, Chilion, became betrothed Ruth's friend, Orpah. A happy year went by until a pestilence struck Moab, resulting in the deaths of thousands—including Haggith, Mahlon, and Chilion. Thus Naomi was left without her two sons and her husband. I was eager to leave Moab, not because I was worried about the pestilence affecting me but because it seemed a good time for me to begin a new life elsewhere.

Thus when Naomi heard that there was bread in Israel, she became determined to leave Moab and return home to Bethlehem. So Naomi said to her two daughters-in-law, "Go, return each of you to your mother's house. There you may find rest, each of you in the house of a husband." Then she kissed them farewell.

But they began to cry and told her, "No, we will return with you to your people."

Then Naomi said, "Turn back, my daughters. Why will you go with me? Are there more sons in my womb, that they may be your husbands? Turn back, go your way, for I am too old to have a husband. Even if I should have a new husband tonight, and then bear sons, would you wait for them until they were grown to remarry?"

They cried even more, and Orpah kissed Naomi farewell. But Ruth clung to her.

So Naomi said, "See, your sister-in-law has returned to her people and her gods. Go follow her."

But Ruth replied, "Intreat me not to leave you, nor to prevent me from following after you. For wherever you go, I will go; wherever you lodge, I will lodge; your people shall be my people, and your god my god. Where you die, I will die, and there I will be buried."

When Naomi saw that Ruth was determined, she stopped arguing with her. So we went on until we came to Bethlehem at the beginning of the barley harvest. Thankfully Elimelech's old house was uninhabited. While we inspected it, Naomi's neighbors and friends ran out to meet her.

SERACH'S STORY

Naomi began to weep as they embraced her. "My lot has been bitter. I went out full and have come home again empty, for the Almighty has brought misfortune upon me."

"You are not empty," I admonished her, and looked at Ruth. "You have your widowed daughter-in-law here with you." I suddenly had a premonition. "Are there no remaining members of your husband's family who can help you?"

Naomi thought for only a moment before her face lit up. "There is a kinsman of my husband's, Boaz, who was a man of substance."

The woman embracing Naomi abruptly let her go and smiled. "Boaz is still wealthy, and . . . recently widowed."

Ruth, Naomi, and I exchanged significant looks but said nothing.

We laid out our bedding and made ourselves at home in the house. In the morning, Ruth told Naomi, "I would like to go to the fields and glean among the ears of grain behind someone who may show me kindness."

"Yes, daughter, go," Naomi replied. "I will clean things up here."

So she went, I along with her, and we gleaned in the field after the reapers; and, as luck would have it, it was a piece of land belonging to Boaz.

Presently, Boaz himself arrived, a handsome, full-bearded man. He stopped to address the reapers. "The Almighty be with you." And we answered him, "The Almighty bless you."

Boaz noticed Ruth and paused to stare at her. When she met his eyes and blushed, he asked, "Whose girl is this?"

I beckoned Ruth to join me. "She is a Moabite who came back home with me and Naomi. I am Serach, and her name is Ruth." I hoped Boaz would notice her Hebrew name.

Ruth said, "Please, let me continue to glean and gather among the sheaves after the reapers."

I added, "She has been on her feet since she came this morning. She has hardly rested at all."

SERACH'S STORY

Boaz turned to Ruth. "Listen to me, daughter. Do not glean in another field. Do not go elsewhere, but stay here close to my maidservants. Keep your eyes on the field they are reaping, and follow them. I have ordered my workers not to harass you. When you are thirsty, go to the jars and drink some water that my workers have drawn."

I was pleased to hear Boaz address Ruth as a kinswoman. Then, to my surprise, she bowed herself to the ground and asked, "Why are you so kind as to single me out when I am a foreigner?"

Boaz helped her up and smiled. "I have been told of all that you did for your mother-in-law after the death of your husband, how you left your mother and the land of your birth to come to a people you had not known before. May you receive a full reward from the god of Israel, under whose wings you have sought refuge."

Ruth blushed again and replied, "You are most kind, my lord, to comfort me and to speak gently to your maidservant—though I am not so much as one of your maidservants."

At mealtime Boaz singled Ruth out again. "Come sit here and partake of the meal." He offered her roasted grain and said, "Dip this in the vinegar." So we sat down beside the reapers, ate our fill, and had some left over.

When we got up to glean again, Boaz commanded his young men, saying, "Let her glean among the sheaves, without interference. Make sure that some stalks fall before her for her to glean, and do not harass her."

So Ruth and I gleaned in the field until evening, and when we beat out what we had gleaned, it was an ephah of barley. We carried it into town so Naomi could see what we had gleaned.

Surprised at the large amount, Naomi asked her, "Where did you glean today? Where did you work? Blessed be he who took such generous notice of you!"

Ruth told her, "The name of the man I worked for today is Boaz."

SERACH'S STORY

Naomi raised her hands to her cheeks and exclaimed, "Blessed be the Almighty, who has not failed to show kindness to the living and to the dead. For," Naomi explained to Ruth, "this man is related to us; he is one of our redeeming kinsmen."

I knew what "redeeming kinsmen" meant, so I added, "It is best, Ruth, that you go out with his maidservants, and not be accosted in some other field."

Ruth nodded. "He told me to stay close by his workers until all the harvest is finished."

So Ruth gleaned with Boaz's girls until both the barley harvest and the wheat harvest were finished. Then she stayed at home with Naomi and me.

One day, Naomi said to her, "Daughter, I must seek a home for you, where you may be happy. Now there is our kinsman Boaz, whose girls you were close to. He will be winnowing barley on the threshing floor tonight."

"What do you want Ruth to do?" I asked, my anticipation growing.

"She should bathe, anoint herself, dress up, and go down to the threshing floor," Naomi began. "But not disclose herself to Boaz until he has finished eating and drinking. Then, when he lies down, she should go next to him, uncover his feet, and lie down. He will tell her what to do."

I admit I was too filled with excitement to sleep well that night. Naomi's daring plan was a gamble that might end in success or disaster for Ruth. The next morning I overslept and was awakened by Ruth talking to Naomi.

"I went down to the threshing floor and did just as you instructed me. I watched as Boaz ate and drank and, humming a cheerful tune, lay down beside the pile of grain."

I couldn't restrain my curiosity. "Then what happened?"

"When I heard him snoring, I stealthily walked over to him, uncovered his feet, and lay down."

"What happened next?" Naomi asked eagerly.

"If you stop interrupting me with questions, you'll find out sooner." Ruth giggled and waited briefly while Naomi and I remained silent. "In the middle of the night, Boaz gave a start and sat up—there I was, a woman, lying at his feet! 'Who are you?' he demanded. First I replied that I was his handmaid Ruth. When I saw him relax and smile, I said, 'Spread your robe over your handmaid, for you are a redeeming kinsman.'"

Naomi was straining to keep her mouth closed, and Ruth embraced her happily. "He exclaimed, 'Be blessed of Shaddai, daughter! Your latest deed of loyalty, to have sought out a kinsman of your deceased husband, is greater than the first, in that you have not turned to younger men, whether poor or rich.'"

Naomi and I both cried tears of joy as Ruth continued. "Then he told me to have no fear, that he was willing to do on my behalf whatever I asked. But while it was true that he was a redeeming kinsman, there was another, closer redeemer. I almost cried with despair, until Boaz asked me to stay for the night. Then he told me that, in the morning, if the other man would act as a redeemer, let him redeem. But if the man did not want to act as redeemer, then he, Boaz, would do so himself!"

Naomi embraced Ruth. "Hallelujah!"

"He told me to lie down until morning. So I lay at his feet until dawn and rose before there was enough light for one person to distinguish another, so nobody would know that a woman had stayed the night on Boaz's threshing floor."

Ruth was smiling and blushing furiously; I had no doubt that she and Boaz had not merely slept during that long night. "He gave me these six measures of barley, saying, 'Do not go back to Naomi empty-handed.'"

SERACH'S STORY

291

Then Naomi said, "Stay here, daughter, until we learn how the matter turns out. For I am confident Boaz will not rest but will settle the matter today."

I stood up and put on my headscarf. "I will walk down to the city gate and see what happens. The other redeemer would recognize you, Naomi, but I am a stranger here."

When I got to the gate, Boaz was already sitting there. As the redeemer whom Boaz had mentioned passed by, Boaz called out, "Come over and sit down here, Mister!" So the man came over and sat down. Next Boaz approached ten town elders and said, "Be seated here." When they sat down, Boaz addressed the redeemer. "Naomi, now returned from the country of Moab, must sell the piece of land that belonged to our kinsman Elimelech. I thought I should disclose the matter to you and say: Acquire it in the presence of those seated here. If you are willing to redeem it, redeem! But if you will not redeem, tell me, that I may know. For there is no one to redeem but you, and I come after you."

"I am willing to redeem it," he replied.

I gasped in dismay. Then Boaz told him, "When you acquire the property from Naomi and from Ruth the Moabite, you must also acquire the wife of the deceased, so as to perpetuate the name of the deceased upon his estate."

As Boaz must have expected, the other redeemer frowned. "Then I cannot redeem it for myself, lest I impair my own estate by expending capital for property that will go to the son legally regarded as Mahlon's." He looked at Boaz and shook his head. "You must take over my right of redemption, for I am unable to exercise it."

Thankfully my headscarf covered all of my delighted face except my eyes.

In Israel, to validate any transaction concerning redemption or exchange, one party would take off a sandal and hand it to the other. So

292   SERACH'S STORY

when the redeemer said to Boaz, "Acquire for yourself," he drew off his sandal, and I held my breath.

I sighed in relief as Boaz stood, took the sandal, and addressed the elders along with the rest of the people, "You are witnesses today that I am acquiring from Naomi all that belonged to Elimelech and all that belonged to Chilion and Mahlon. I am thus acquiring Ruth the Moabite, Mahlon's widow, as my wife, so as to perpetuate his name upon his estate, that Mahlon's name may not disappear from among his kinsmen and from the gate of his hometown. You are witnesses today."

The people at the gate and the elders answered, "We are witnesses. May the Almighty make the woman who is coming into your house like Rachel and Leah, both of whom built up the house of Israel!" Then the men approached Boaz and embraced him while offering their congratulations.

So Boaz married Ruth, and though they were both widowed, the wedding was as extravagant as a prince's. Less than one year later she bore a son they named Obed. The local women celebrated Naomi's good fortune, saying, "Blessed be Shaddai, who has not withheld a redeemer from you today! May the name of Obed be perpetuated in Israel! He will renew your life and sustain your old age; for he is born of your daughter-in-law, who loves you and is better to you than seven sons."

I stayed one month to celebrate Obed's firstborn-son ceremony. By that time too many people knew me as Ruth's mother's aunt and were curious about our Hebrew ancestry. Using the excuse that I must return to my family's home, I packed my things and joined a caravan traveling north.

I had decided to move into the smallest tribe's territory, that of Dan. Instead of hot desert sand surrounding me, here there were flowering vines and trees that provided cooling shade. Here multiple springs merged into four rivers that eventually became the River Jordan. Here I never thirsted for water.